"I'm proud to stand up and say, 'My name is Charlaine, and I'm a Chocoholic!'"
—#1 *New York Times* bestselling author Charlaine Harris

Praise for the Chocoholic Mysteries

The Chocolate Castle Clue

"This book is a real winner. . . . [Carl] is a truly gifted mystery writer. One warning though: If you like chocolate at all, have a stash ready for when you read this book! Otherwise, you'll have to put this page-turner down long enough to run to the store when the chocolate cravings hit!" —MyShelf.com

"An entertaining whodunit." —The Mystery Gazette

"It has everything a cozy should: cute mysteries, fun themes, likable characters, and an interesting setting. If you are a chocoholic or a fan of cozies, then you might want to try *The Chocolate Castle Clue*. It's a fun way to spend a few hours!"
—Booking Mama

The Chocolate Pirate Plot

"[A] fun caper that's as fresh as a truffle just carefully placed in the chocolate case by the hairnet ladies." —AnnArbor.com

"Cozy as cozy gets, *The Chocolate Pirate Plot* is the tenth book in this gentle, entertaining series. Longtime readers will not be disappointed. JoAnna Carl has filled her story with an entertaining plot sprinkled thoroughly with chocolate trivia. This is the perfect book to snuggle with to forget about any unpleasant winter weather while getting to know some of your favorite characters a bit better. Fireplace and hot chocolate are optional but recommended." —Fresh Fiction

The Chocolate Cupid Killings

"Deliciously cozy. *The Chocolate Cupid Killings* is richly entertaining and has no calories."
—Elaine Viets, author of the Dead-End Job mysteries

"A chocolate-drenched page-turner! JoAnna Carl satisfies your sweet tooth along with your craving for a tasty whodunit." —Cleo Coyle, author of the Coffeehouse mysteries

continued . . .

"A deft mix of truffles and trouble. Chocoholics—this book is for you!" —Laura Childs, author of the Tea Shop mysteries

"Anyone who loves chocolate—and who doesn't?—will love this delicious, fast-paced addition to the Chocoholic Mystery series. It has more twists and turns than a chocolate-covered pretzel, but this treat won't add any pounds, so you can indulge without guilt!"
—Leslie Meier, author of *English Tea Murder*

"A sweet mystery of how helping others can at times come back and bite you in the backside. JoAnna Carl definitely knows how to pen a sweet read."
—The Romance Readers Connection

The Chocolate Snowman Murders

"Dollops of chocolate lore add to the cozy fun."
—*Publishers Weekly*

The Chocolate Jewel Case

"[A] fun, very readable book, with likable characters that are knowable whether you've read all seven novels in the series or whether this is your first." —Suite 101

The Chocolate Bridal Bash

"Entertaining and stylish. . . . Reading this on an empty stomach is hazardous to the waistline because the chocolate descriptions are . . . sensuously enticing. Lee is very likable without being too sweet." —*Midwest Book Review*

"Everything about JoAnna Carl's books are delicious treats, from the characters to the snippets of chocolate trivia. . . . All [are] fantastic characters who have come to feel like good friends. *The Chocolate Bridal Bash* stands alone, but once you've read it, you'll be craving the other books in this series." —Roundtable Reviews

The Chocolate Mouse Trap

"A fine tale." —*Midwest Book Review*

"I've been a huge fan of the Chocoholic Mystery series from the start. I adore the mix of romance, mystery, and trivia . . . satisfying." —Roundtable Reviews

The Chocolate Puppy Puzzle

"The pacing is perfect for the small-town setting, and the various secondary characters add variety and interest. Readers may find themselves craving chocolate, yearning to make their own. . . . An interesting mystery, fun characters, and, of course, chocolate make this a fun read for fans of mysteries and chocolates alike." —The Romance Readers Connection

The Chocolate Frog Frame-Up

"A JoAnna Carl mystery will be a winner. The trivia and vivid descriptions of the luscious confections are enough to make you hunger for more!" —Roundtable Reviews

"A fast-paced, light read, full of chocolate facts and delectable treats. Lee is an endearing heroine. . . . Readers will enjoy the time they spend with Lee and Joe in Warner Pier and will look forward to returning for more murder dipped in chocolate." —The Mystery Reader

The Chocolate Bear Burglary

"Descriptions of exotic chocolate will have you running out to buy gourmet sweets . . . a delectable treat." —The Best Reviews

The Chocolate Cat Caper

"A mouthwatering debut and a delicious new series! Feisty young heroine Lee McKinney is a delight in this chocolate treat. A real page-turner, and I got chocolate on every one! I can't wait for the next." —Tamar Myers, author of *Batter Off Dead*

"One will gain weight just from reading [this] . . . delicious . . . the beginning of what looks like a terrific new cozy series." —*Midwest Book Review*

Also by JoAnna Carl

The Chocolate Castle Clue

A Chocoholic Mystery

JoAnna Carl

AN OBSIDIAN MYSTERY

OBSIDIAN
Published by New American Library, a division of
Penguin Group (USA) Inc., 375 Hudson Street,
New York, New York 10014, USA
Penguin Group (Canada), 90 Eglinton Avenue East, Suite 700, Toronto,
Ontario M4P 2Y3, Canada (a division of Pearson Penguin Canada Inc.)
Penguin Books Ltd., 80 Strand, London WC2R 0RL, England
Penguin Ireland, 25 St. Stephen's Green, Dublin 2,
Ireland (a division of Penguin Books Ltd.)
Penguin Group (Australia), 250 Camberwell Road, Camberwell, Victoria 3124,
Australia (a division of Pearson Australia Group Pty. Ltd.)
Penguin Books India Pvt. Ltd., 11 Community Centre, Panchsheel Park,
New Delhi - 110 017, India
Penguin Group (NZ), 67 Apollo Drive, Rosedale, Auckland 0632,
New Zealand (a division of Pearson New Zealand Ltd.)
Penguin Books (South Africa) (Pty.) Ltd., 24 Sturdee Avenue,
Rosebank, Johannesburg 2196, South Africa

Penguin Books Ltd., Registered Offices:
80 Strand, London WC2R 0RL, England

Published by Obsidian, an imprint of New American Library, a division of
Penguin Group (USA) Inc. Previously published in an Obsidian hardcover
edition.

First Obsidian Mass Market Printing, October 2012
10   9   8   7   6   5   4   3   2   1

PUBLISHER'S NOTE
This is a work of fiction. Names, characters, places, and incidents either are the
product of the author's imagination or are used fictitiously, and any resem-
blance to actual persons, living or dead, business establishments, events, or
locales is entirely coincidental.

The publisher does not have any control over and does not assume any responsibility for author or third-party Web sites or their content.

For Dave,
with thanks for bouncing those ideas back
when I throw them at him

Chapter 1

I didn't set out to solve one of the biggest mysteries in Warner Pier's history. All I intended to do was clean out the garage.

And I wasn't happy about it. It was too pretty of a day to be cleaning out a garage. It was one of those glorious fall days with mellow light everywhere, a pale blue sky, soft air I wanted to wallow around in, and Michigan's trees all wearing muted shades of yellow, orange, brown, rust, burgundy, and green.

I would definitely have preferred to be taking a boat ride out into Lake Michigan, hiking through the local nature reserve, eating an ice-cream cone in the Dock Street Park, or even sitting at my desk in the office of TenHuis Chocolade. But no, I'd put the garage storeroom off as long as I could. The time was here. I had to sort through it that afternoon.

Luckily, I had help. Dolly Jolly, chief assistant to the chief chocolatier for TenHuis Chocolade, was up to her vivid red hair in dirt and debris as the two of us investigated boxes and filing cabinets full of . . . well . . .

stuff, and tried to fill up the bed of my husband's pickup truck. Filling the bed of that truck was one of our goals, and it was already looking as if we'd fill it twice.

My husband, Joe Woodyard, drove a pickup because he owned a boat shop, so he had to be prepared to haul boats. He restored antique wooden power boats. That was half his workweek. During the other half he was a lawyer, practicing poverty law with a nonprofit agency thirty miles up the road, in Holland. The reasons for his split personality—professionally—are too complicated to go into, but I admire both his personas.

The garage storeroom Dolly and I were clearing out was across the alley, behind the TenHuis Chocolade factory, offices, and shop on Fifth Street in Warner Pier, Michigan. My aunt and uncle, Phil and Nettie Ten-Huis, founded the company ("Luxury Chocolates in the Dutch Tradition") thirty-five years ago. Uncle Phil died in a car wreck five years ago, so Aunt Nettie was now sole owner of the company. I'm Lee McKinney Woodyard, their Texas niece, and I've been business manager for three and a half years.

TenHuis Chocolade had rented the garage and storeroom across the alley for twenty years. Uncle Phil, and occasionally Aunt Nettie, had used it to store obsolete equipment and old business records. More recently we'd crammed the contents of the garage side into the storeroom side so that Dolly Jolly could use the remaining half for her Jeep SUV. She lived in an apartment above TenHuis Chocolade, so a space down the stairs and just across the alley had been handy for her.

Aunt Nettie owned the TenHuis Chocolade building, but the storage space we were working on was in a building that faced the next street over. Now that building had changed hands, and the new owner wanted his space back. We had to vacate, and we couldn't take all our stuff out until we'd sorted, tossed, and packed. I was prepared to rent a storage unit for the things we wouldn't be able to get rid of, and Dolly would have to park on the street until another downtown garage space opened up. Garage spaces in Warner Pier's business district were scarce.

That Friday Dolly had moved her Jeep onto Fifth Street, so we had a fair amount of room for the sorting, tossing, and packing. After Labor Day there was always plenty of on-street parking in a resort town like Warner Pier.

We'd begun the day by piling up some pieces of old equipment for the dump and sending others to the secondhand restaurant-supply dealer. Aunt Nettie had declared all of it useless, "unless it goes to some museum."

Next we'd packed up plastic buckets, plastic bins, and plastic lids from containers that had originally held fondant and other chocolate-making supplies. This was typical of Uncle Phil's pack-rat tendencies: saving bins, buckets, and plastic lids for twenty years just in case anyone ever wanted them. No one ever had, and no one ever would. These we put into giant garbage sacks to be taken to the recycler. Joe had carried those away at midmorning.

I had rented a heavy-duty shredder, and after the plastic was gone, Dolly and I started on the papers.

Aunt Nettie was taking the day off, but she came by for a few minutes. She was descended from west Michigan's Dutch pioneers—her maiden name was Vanderheide—and all she needed was a cap with starched wings and some wooden clogs to look as if she'd just stepped off a canal boat in Amsterdam.

"You two make me feel guilty," she said, patting her

gray and blond hair. "You're working so hard, and I'm spending the week visiting with old friends."

"You'll work hard all week, since you're the main hostess," I said. "And you've worked hard to get ready for this reunion."

"I just hope all the girls have fun."

Aunt Nettie referred to her high school pals as "the girls" even though they were all in their sixties. It was the first time the group of six friends had all been together in more than forty years.

Their reunion was part of a larger one. Five years of Warner Pier High School graduating classes were to gather a week later. A banquet, a picnic, tours, a boat excursion out into Lake Michigan—all sorts of activities were planned.

Aunt Nettie had even ordered special molds so she could make Warner Pier High School mementos out of chocolate. Tiny models of the old high school (torn down thirty-five years ago), little diplomas, and miniature mortarboards had all been embellished with the graduation class years and were ready to be handed out to the old grads.

She had also created more historic molds, including a tiny version of the *Warner B*, the boat that brought one of the first groups of settlers to the area; the old Root Beer Barrel, a drive-in popular in Aunt Nettie's youth; and the first school, a one-room structure torn down a hundred years ago. But the most spectacular chocolate piece was a model of the Castle Ballroom, a landmark in Warner Pier from the early twentieth century through the 1970s. Aunt Nettie had made a three-dimensional replica two feet high, plus smaller two-dimensional versions.

And Aunt Nettie and her five friends were the stars of the reunion. They had all worked together as waitresses at the Castle Ballroom and had also been a prize-winning vocal group at their high school. They were to perform again at the reunion banquet. Their private weeklong reunion was partly for fun, but it also gave them an opportunity to rehearse. They had to learn to sing together again.

Now Aunt Nettie gestured around the storage room. "This place is awful!"

"Is that your fault?"

"Actually, I think I'm pretty good about throwing things away. Apparently I even threw all my high school souvenirs away."

"Oh, Aunt Nettie! I'm sorry."

"It can't be helped now. I have no idea when they disappeared." She shrugged. "But Phil—well, he wanted to hang on to everything. Even those useless old buckets."

We both smiled. One reason everything in the storage area was so dusty was that almost everything in it had been there since before Uncle Phil died.

"Uncle Phil was a wonderful person," I said. "I'm sorry we have to get rid of his treasures."

"Phil's treasures are now officially declared trash!" Aunt Nettie's vehemence made Dolly and me laugh. "If I get a break from the girls, I'll come back and help you."

Dolly's voice boomed out. She can't speak at a normal decibel level; every sentence is a shout. "We don't want to be here until your reunion is over! We want to get through! So don't worry about coming back!"

We shooed Aunt Nettie on her way and kept digging. I looked at things and tried to be ruthless, and Dolly operated the shredder. Tax records older than seven years, correspondence about orders for chocolates shipped back in 1990, bills paid long ago—all turned into strips of scrap paper. The garbage bags began to pile up.

At one o'clock Joe came back with his pickup, and the three of us filled its bed again. Joe, Dolly, and I then ate lunch in Dolly's tidy apartment—she provided homemade pimiento cheese for sandwiches, and Joe picked up a carton of coleslaw. We finished the meal off with some chocolates from the TenHuis reject bin— Italian cherry ("amarena cherry in syrup and white chocolate cream, encased in dark chocolate") and Bailey's Irish cream ("classic cream liqueur interior in a dark chocolate square"). They tasted wonderful, even though all of them had been embellished with the wrong designs on top.

After lunch Joe left, and I was finally ready for the three oldest filing cabinets.

I sighed. "Dolly, I don't know what's in those babies, but you've worked like a dog all morning. Plus, you fed Joe and me lunch. Why don't you quit now?"

Dolly answered in her usual shout. "I don't mind, Lee! I hate to leave you out here all alone!"

"Downtown Warner Pier isn't exactly the wilderness, Dolly. And there are still people in the shop, just across the alley."

"I know. But I'll stay!"

I hated to admit it, but I appreciated her company. After all, Aunt Nettie and I had once made a very unpleasant discovery in that garage. And although we were in the middle of downtown, Warner Pier is a village of only twenty-five hundred, and we were a couple of weeks past the end of the tourist season, so it was pretty lonely in our alley.

The three filing cabinets were themselves oldies but goodies. I knew Aunt Nettie and Uncle Phil had started

TenHuis Chocolade with secondhand office equipment, so these cabinets were already old when they had bought them. They were heavy even without the pounds and pounds of paper filling them. And they were sturdy. Today's filing cabinets simply didn't compare with these suckers. If their drawers had been locked—and luckily it seemed none of them were—it would have taken brute force to open them since we hadn't seen any keys for them.

I pulled out the top drawer of the first filing cabinet and resolutely started going through files. "More trash." I muttered the words as I found a file folder full of brochures on food-service equipment for sale thirty years earlier.

"Hand it over!" Dolly boomed. She stuffed the brochures in the shredder, and I emptied the rest of the drawer. I didn't even try to save the used file folders. They went into the trash.

The next drawer held employment files. I shuffled through them. They reached back to the first people Aunt Nettie and Uncle Phil had hired, during the third year they'd been in business. Before that they had done all the work themselves.

The earliest file, I saw, was one for Hazel TerHoot, who had been Aunt Nettie's chief helper for more than twenty-five years. She had retired two years previously, and Dolly had replaced her. Today Hazel was one of the high school chums Aunt Nettie was entertaining.

The employment files ended ten years ago. I assumed the reason for their sudden halt was that Uncle Phil put such files on the computer about that time.

I didn't have the nerve to toss out the old employment files, although I saw no use for them. I put them in a storage box. They'd go to the new rental unit.

I kept at it. One whole filing cabinet was full of correspondence. Three big drawers. I sighed. Honestly, Uncle Phil, I thought, who cares about a letter asking you to join the West Michigan Business Association in 1984? Bless your heart; you were a great guy, but what a pack rat! All the old letters went into the shredder.

There were drawers of bills. And drawers of tax records—not just the completed forms. Oh no! Uncle Phil had kept the supporting documentation as well. I began to fear the shredder would break down.

I slogged on. And on. And on. And finally—finally—I came to the bottom drawer of the third filing cabinet.

"Yahoo!" I stood up to stretch. I waved my arms in the air. "Dolly! I'm down to the last drawer!"

"Whoopee!" Dolly did a little dance. This was quite a sight, since she's even taller than I am—I'm five eleven and a half, but Dolly's six foot one—and is built more like an oak tree than a willow.

"I'll get the push broom and start sweeping!" Dolly shouted. She went across to the shop.

After I'd stretched until my back felt a bit more like a back is supposed to feel, I pulled my folding chair in front of the final filing cabinet. I leaned over and pulled on the bottom drawer.

The darn thing wouldn't open.

"Don't tell me," I said. "I finally came to a locked drawer."

I jiggled. I tugged. I put my foot on the drawer above it and pulled the handle. It didn't budge.

By then Dolly was back with the broom. She jiggled, tugged, and pulled on the drawer.

"Careful!" I said. "We don't want to yank the handle off."

"Why not? You said these cabinets were going to the dump!"

"I guess you're right. We might as well pry it open. If we had something to pry with."

"I'll get my tool kit!"

"Tool kit?"

Dolly nodded. "When I left home my father gathered up some old tools for me! I think there's a pry bar in the collection!"

She went across the alley to her apartment and came back with a wooden toolbox—the open, homemade kind with a handle on top, like the ones carpenters are likely to carry. She plunked it onto a small workbench that was against the back wall on the garage side of the area. She flipped on the light over the bench—a mechanic's work light that clamped onto a nail in the wall. The glaring light revealed the contents of the toolbox. And in the bottom of it was a strong-looking black crowbar about two feet long. Dolly waved it triumphantly.

"That ought to open anything in this garage," I said.

Dolly inserted the narrow end behind the top of the locked drawer and pressed on it. The lock broke, and the drawer popped open about an inch.

"Aha!" I said. "You've done it. Now, I wonder what in the world Uncle Phil thought was worth locking up."

I pulled the drawer out. The first thing on top was a trophy. It was lying on its side.

I picked it up. It had a heavy black base and was at least two feet tall. On its top was a model of a castle.

"What in the world?" Dolly's voice boomed. "I can understand displaying a trophy, or I can see throwing it away! But locking it up seems kind of odd!"

I read the plaque. The top line was in small letters:

FIRST PLACE, followed by the year. The next lines were in larger letters: TALENT SHOW. The final lines were very large: CASTLE BALLROOM.

"Oh, ye gods!" I said. "This is the trophy Aunt Nettie and her friends won the last night the Castle Ballroom was in business."

I looked at Dolly. "But why did Uncle Phil lock it up?"

Chapter 2

Dolly spoke in her usual shout. "Is this the group that's having a reunion this weekend?"

"Yes. They're having a sort of slumber party at Aunt Nettie's tonight. Several of them are staying with her all week."

I pulled out the first item under the trophy. It was a scrapbook. On the first page was a picture of six pretty young girls, dressed in the styles of forty-plus years ago. They were standing in that traditional angled pose—right shoulders toward the camera—that photographers use to get heads close together in a group shot. The caption under the photo read, THE PIER-O-ETTES. In smaller letters were the words PHOTO BY SHEPPARD STONE.

A young Aunt Nettie, with hair as fair as the gray-blond mixture she had today, was in the middle. I was surprised to realize that I recognized only one of the others. I knew two of the old Pier-O-Ettes very well, but Hazel TerHoot was the only one I could pick out of the forty-five-year-old photo.

Under the scrapbook was a framed certificate recognizing the Pier-O-Ettes for winning some high school competition.

"Until all this came up I never knew that Nettie sang!" Dolly yelled.

"I gather that this group won lots of high school contests," I said. "Plus, they sang at community events."

"I guess they never recorded or anything!"

"Not professionally. They broke up after their senior year."

I lifted out more items. "Look. Here's a box of souvenirs—programs and pins and notes and such." I picked up a ribbon. It was attached to a cluster of what must have once been flowers. "Even an old corsage."

I looked at Dolly. "This must be the stuff Aunt Nettie said was lost."

Dolly nodded solemnly. "She'd like to have this!"

"I'll take it over to her house after we're through."

I taped a new storage box together and wrote "Nettie's Memorabilia" on the outside. The pictures and other items fit in easily, but the trophy was too large. I went across the alley to the TenHuis kitchen and got a plastic garbage sack and several dish towels. I wrapped the trophy in the towels and put it into the sack. Then I stashed all the items in my van, which was parked in my reserved spot in the alley.

Dolly and I finished sweeping the garage. Joe and I would come by later to pick up the boxes that were to go into the storage unit and to cart the empty filing cabinets away. Even empty, the cabinets were heavy, but I assured Dolly that Joe and I could load them into his truck.

I thanked Dolly for all her work and told her I'd close up the garage and the shop. Dolly ceremoniously presented me with the garage door's remote opener as a sign that she no longer was going to park there.

"Here!" she shouted. "Add this to your string of fish!"

We both laughed, and I pulled the paraphernalia she was referring to from the side pocket of my purse. It was a short ring of chain—actual chain—with gadgets attached to it by key rings. It held a miniature flashlight, a small Swiss Army knife, a zippered coin purse the size of a credit card, extra car and house keys, and a container of pepper spray. My friend Lindy Herrera had given it to me for Christmas. She called it the "no-harm charm bracelet," because all the "charms" were related to personal safety.

Of course, no one could actually wear the thing on an arm. It was too bulky. Joe had joked that its main use for personal safety would be as a weapon.

"Hit an attacker with that collection," he had said, "and you'd be likely to take his nose off."

I didn't use it for my regular car keys, of course. I kept those hooked to a ring that hung on the outside of my purse. But I'd used the knife and the flashlight of the "no-harm charm bracelet" a few times, and it was nice to know I had extra keys and a folded-up ten-dollar bill stashed away in my purse.

So I lugged it around, and now I held it up for inspection. "I can't add the garage door remote," I said. "It doesn't have a ring on it to attach."

I punched the remote then, and the garage door went down. But the light on the actual opener, the gadget overhead, didn't go on.

"Dolly," I said, "why didn't you tell me the door opener's light is out?"

"I always use the central overhead light instead of

that one!" she yelled. "I just never got around to putting a new bulb in it!"

"Well, we're not going to bother now," I said. "We'll turn the garage over to the owners with a dud bulb."

Dolly and I were finally through with our chore.

Dolly went up to her apartment, and I closed the door for the final time and went into the shop. It was nearly five o'clock, so the twenty-five women who were making chocolate were about to quit working. I checked to see that there were no immediate problems, then headed for the restroom. Its mirror confirmed that I looked as if I'd spent the day cleaning a dirty storeroom.

I wanted to drop the high school souvenirs by Aunt Nettie's, and I was sure she'd introduce me to her old friends. It was going to take a little work to make myself presentable.

Luckily, I had some emergency makeup in my purse. After ten minutes spent cleaning up, I looked a bit more human. I took off my dirty sweatshirt and substituted a plaid wool shirt of Joe's I found in the office closet. Heaven knows why it was there, but it almost made my jeans and tee look like a deliberately casual outfit.

I decided my grooming update would give me enough confidence to spend ten minutes with Aunt Nettie's old school pals, and ten minutes was all I intended to spend. I was eager to get home and take a shower. That evening, I decided, Joe and I were going out for dinner.

Aunt Nettie and her husband, Hogan—she had remarried a year and a half earlier—lived in a pleasant white house built in the 1940s. They had remodeled it extensively the previous year. It was in Warner Pier proper, in contrast to the house where Joe and I live.

We're out on Lake Shore Drive, the road that skirts Lake Michigan. Every town on the Great Lakes has either a Lake Shore Drive or a Lakeshore Drive.

When I pulled up at Aunt Nettie's, I saw two cars parked in her drive. Neither of them belonged to Aunt Nettie's husband, Hogan Jones. Hogan, who is Warner Pier's police chief, had conveniently arranged to be away teaching a two-week workshop when the high school reunion came up. I had told him I found the timing highly suspicious, but he just grinned.

"I sure wouldn't want Nettie talking to my high school friends," he'd said. "I wasn't in law enforcement when I was sixteen. More like law breaking."

I got the box of souvenirs and the trophy out of the van and went to the front door. Before I could touch the bell, the door swung open, and all the confidence I'd tried to paint on with makeup and to add along with Joe's wool shirt disappeared at the sight of the petite woman who faced me.

She was no more than five feet tall, and she probably weighed less than a hundred pounds. Her silvery hair was cut crisply, and her clothes were perfect. No jeans and plaid shirt for her. She wore perfectly tailored wool slacks and a sweater, both in winter white. Toes of brown boots peeked out from under her slacks, and her only jewelry was an intricately carved green jade necklace.

"I hope they're gift wrapped," she said.

It was Margo Street. *The* Margo Street. I'd been eager to meet her, but I hadn't expected to be struck speechless when I did.

The Margo Street Aunt Nettie had gone to high school with was the same Margo Street who had been written up in *Fortune* magazine. The one who founded Sweetwater Investments. The one I had done a research paper on in college. The one I had admired as one of the nation's top women in business.

The one who was glaring at me and making me feel that I must look like the ragged end of a misspent life.

My stomach flipped over, and I nearly dropped the box.

"Hi," I said. "I'm Nettie's noose."

Ms. Street lifted one eyebrow.

"Niece!" I yelped the word. "Nettie Jones is my aunt."

"Then you're not from the frame shop?"

"No. I work for Aunt Nettie at TenHuis Chocolade."

"I see. You'd better come in."

I slunk in, still embarrassed over my slip of the tongue and surprised by her ungracious welcome. "Were you expecting someone else?"

"I requested a delivery. Perhaps I'd better call about it." Ms. Street gestured toward the back of the house. "The others are out on the porch."

Ms. Street—I certainly wasn't bold enough even to think of her as Margo—disappeared into the bedroom hall, and I went through the dining room and toward the porch, wondering how this woman managed to look so young. There had been a fine network of wrinkles on her cheeks, so I didn't think she'd "had work done," as they say. But I would have guessed her age at late forties, if I hadn't known that she'd graduated from high school the same year Aunt Nettie had. And Aunt Nettie was sixty-three.

Did having money make you look young?

As I entered the dining room, the kitchen door popped open, and Hazel TerHoot came through with a handful of silverware.

"Hi, Lee. I didn't know Nettie invited *you*." Her tone implied that I was not only uninvited, but also unwanted.

I didn't take offense. That was Hazel. She completely lacked tact, but after working with her for a couple of years, I knew she didn't really mean to be rude. Things just came out that way.

"I'm not here for the reunion dinner. I just brought something by for Aunt Nettie. Is she out on the porch?"

"Oh, yes. With the rest of the gang."

Somehow Hazel made the word "gang" sound as if she thought her former classmates were planning to write graffiti all over Warner Pier or start a fight with a rival sextet. I didn't understand, so I asked about it.

"Are things not going well?"

"Well enough. It's just that—we've all grown in different directions. You know. It always happens that way. Life."

"Aunt Nettie seemed to be looking forward to seeing everyone, Hazel. I thought you were, too."

"Maybe I'm just not in the mood."

I motioned with my box. "Hazel, if I had a hand free, I'd give you a big ol' Texas hug!"

Hazel smiled and waved her handful of silverware. "I'll collect one later, Lee. If you get close now, I might puncture you with a fork."

"It's nice of you to help Aunt Nettie out."

Hazel shrugged. "Nettie was my boss for a lot of years. I'm used to helping her out."

I gave what I hoped was an encouraging smile and headed on toward the porch. Hazel's comment had surprised me. She had always appeared to be a happy housewife with few ambitions for a career, content with a job that paid her a reasonable wage and kept her in close contact with an old friend. But Aunt Nettie owned a successful business, and Hazel had merely worked for hourly wages. I wondered whether it rankled.

Aunt Nettie's porch is comfortable and attractive, furnished with a collection of wicker pieces that include a couch and two large chairs with striped cushions. The porch was connected to the dining room by French doors. When I drew near them, I was greeted by a gale of laughter. Its fruity, rich tone told me Ruby Westfield was there.

Ruby might be the most interesting person in Warner Pier, or so I thought, and I paused to observe her for thirty seconds before I went out onto the porch.

Ruby probably held the Warner Pier record for marriages and divorces. She'd made it to the altar at least six times, and she had four children, each with a different father. And she'd done all this marrying and divorcing and reproducing in a town of twenty-five hundred people.

Amazing.

What was even more amazing was that each of Ruby's husbands was an upstanding, responsible citizen. Ruby wasn't one of those women who picked guys up in bars and rushed them to the altar after a few drinks. She also wasn't one of the types who had public fights and kept the "domestic incident" statistics high. And she definitely wasn't one of the sirens who went after married men. Each of Ruby's husbands had been single, solvent, and sober when he fell for her. Each was also intelligent and gainfully employed. All the exes still lived in Warner Pier, and I knew several of them. One was an electrician, one owned a hardware store, one was street superintendent for the city, and one was a retired teacher. Two others I didn't know much about.

None of the ones I knew ever had anything bad to say about Ruby. Even after the splits, all the men in her life liked her. Apparently Ruby simply had "it," whatever "it" is.

The other remarkable thing about Ruby's marital history was that she wasn't particularly attractive.

If an actress were cast for a role like Ruby in a movie, the producers would select some sexy, ultra-good-looking gal. But Ruby was very ordinary looking, at least to me. She was plump and comfortable, with frankly gray hair and a happy smile. Plain. But the latest word around town was that the city's most eligible older guy—a doctor who recently retired here—had been calling on Ruby. None of us thought it unlikely.

Joe agrees that Ruby is plain, but he says she broadcasts pheromones. I guess that's as good an explanation as any.

As for gainful employment, Ruby was an expert seamstress—so expert that she limited her clientele to brides and beauty queens. She created only gorgeous, elaborate, sequin-encrusted gowns for special occasions. She farmed the simpler bridesmaids' dresses out to several other women. And not even the mothers of the brides argued with Ruby, or so I'd heard. If Ruby said a bustle would make the bride look fat, by golly, the bride did not wear a bustle. Her word was law, and brides came from as far away as Lansing or Grand Rapids for a Ruby original.

Ruby and Aunt Nettie were sitting in the big wicker chairs, facing the French doors. The matching couch was in front of the doors, with its back to the dining room.

"Hi, Lee!" Ruby said. She had a voice as comfortable as her figure. "We're telling dirty jokes!"

Aunt Nettie laughed. "Just like high school!"

"Only now we understand them!" Ruby laughed again. "Nettie, remember how rotten we were to your brother?"

Aunt Nettie rolled her eyes. "Over the dirty jokes? We were awful!"

Ruby laughed. "Kids are so mean! Poor Ed. We probably gave him a complex."

"What did you do to the poor guy?" I said.

Ruby had laughed until she was crying. She dabbed her eyes with a Kleenex. "Well, Ed was three years younger than we were, you know. The summer he was fourteen, he began to ask Nettie and me to tell him some dirty jokes."

"Of course, we weren't about to," Aunt Nettie said. "You can tell your girlfriends dirty jokes, but not your younger brother!"

Ruby went on. "But we didn't just tell him no. We told him he was too young—or maybe too dumb—to understand the jokes."

I couldn't help grinning. "That *was* mean!"

"Oh, we got meaner. Finally we told him a long story. I don't remember all of it, but it ended with the sentence, 'And the light was red!' Then we laughed uproariously."

"Of course, the story wasn't dirty," Aunt Nettie said. "It wasn't anything. It was just nonsense. But after the buildup we'd given Ed—telling him he wouldn't understand a dirty joke if we told him one—he didn't dare admit he didn't get it."

"I'll bet he puzzled over that story for years!" Ruby was still laughing. "Poor Ed."

By then I was laughing, too. "You *were* rotten kids."

"Oh, we were," Ruby said. "Remember the time we caught the gym teacher and the principal's secretary over by VanHorn's farm?"

"What!" I pretended to be shocked. "You were court-busting? I thought only Texas kids did that."

"Court-busting? Is that what you called it in Texas? We did it, too, though we didn't have a name for it. But actually, that time we were with guys, and they were looking for deer, not necking couples."

"And the guys swore us to secrecy," Aunt Nettie said. "The gym teacher was assistant track coach, and they didn't want to get him in trouble."

"If y'all are reminiscing," I said, "I've brought something to add to the mix."

I walked around the couch and put the box marked NETTIE'S MEMORABILIA down on the coffee table. Then I pulled the trophy from the garbage sack, still wrapped in kitchen towels. Aunt Nettie and Ruby looked at me expectantly. I unwrapped the trophy and held it over my head proudly.

"Ta-da! Look what I found in one of the old filing cabinets."

Aunt Nettie and Ruby got almost identical expressions. Their mouths formed big Os, and their eyes got wide.

And behind me, someone screamed.

Chapter 3

I must have looked like a king-sized lemur. When a long, tall woman throws up her long, tall arms, leaps into the air kicking her long, tall legs, turns around in midleap, and lands facing the opposite direction—well, a lemur would have done it a lot more gracefully.

But that scream might have been the most startling sound I'd ever heard. I had had no idea there was anybody behind me until the shriek from hell cut loose. Aunt Nettie was lucky I didn't swarm up her rubber plant and wind up hanging from the canvas blind.

After I landed, facing the couch instead of the chairs, the excitement continued. Aunt Nettie and Ruby both jumped up and rushed to the couch.

On it sat a tiny woman with curly golden blond ringlets and a complexion of peach and ivory, so delicate it might have been painted on like an antique china doll's pink cheeks. Piercing cries were coming from her. She was shaking her hands as if they were on fire and she was trying to throw them off the ends of her arms.

Aunt Nettie and Ruby both began to—well, pet her. One sat down on each side of her, and they each began to stroke her back and make cooing sounds, as if she were a real baby, not a grown woman who looked and acted like one.

I stood there with my mouth gaped open and my heart racing, still clutching the giant trophy.

The next second Margo Street ran onto the porch. After the brusque greeting I'd received from Ms. Street at the door, I thought she might slap the screaming woman, or at least yell at her. But she didn't.

Aunt Nettie immediately yielded her seat on the couch to Ms. Street, and the famous business leader sat beside the doll-like woman and continued the stroking and gentle talk. The tiny woman with the blond curls turned to her and received an embrace. The screams faded into sobs.

"It's all right, Kathy." Margo Street spoke in a coaxing voice. "You're fine."

I belatedly remembered that two of the sextet members were sisters—Margo and Kathy Street.

My college research on Margo Street hadn't revealed that she had a sister who wasn't quite normal. But from the reaction of Ruby, Aunt Nettie, and Margo, I gathered that this was the case. At least none of them had seemed surprised by her strange outburst.

Next Hazel appeared with a glass of water. She poked it at Margo without comment. Margo took it with a nod of thanks and offered it to her sister. Hazel turned and went back toward the kitchen. She didn't look as sympathetic as the others did.

At that moment I realized that the trophy had disappeared, right out of my hands. I looked for it, but it was nowhere in sight. Instead, Aunt Nettie was standing beside me, outwardly placid.

"Lee, let's take that box into the living room and see what else is in there," she said.

I obediently picked up the box I'd dropped on the coffee table and followed her. As soon as we were out of earshot, I spoke. "What brought all that on?"

"Kathy's problem?"

"Yes. Did I do something?"

"Not on purpose."

"I didn't even know she was behind me until she started screaming."

"She was lying down on the couch. I'm sorry she startled you."

"Why all the yelling?"

"I'm not sure."

"Did the trophy upset her? Did she think I was going to hit her with it?"

"Oh, no." Aunt Nettie's face formed a smile. "Hi, Ruby. Is Kathy better?"

"Yes, she's fine. She was just startled." Ruby turned to me. "She sure threw a hissy fit, didn't she? If I'd been you, Lee, I would have wet my pants. Some excitement."

Excitement? I would have called it hysteria. But I didn't. "I hadn't seen her lying there on the couch," I said. "I didn't mean to do anything to upset her."

"You were fine. Is that the box of memorabilia?"

"Yes, I found it in an old filing cabinet. Uncle Phil must have put it there."

"What I don't understand," Aunt Nettie said, "is why Phil didn't tell me he'd put all those things out in the storeroom. I thought they had been thrown out."

She and Ruby began to look through the items in the box, taking them out and arranging them on the coffee table, lining up pictures, programs, and newspaper clippings.

"Where's the trophy?" Ruby's voice was elaborately casual.

"It's safely put away," Aunt Nettie said. Her voice was sunny and cheerful. "I was sure I threw it out thirty years ago."

Hmmm. Apparently only the trophy was seen as a threatening object by Kathy Street. The rest of the souvenirs were evidently okay. Stranger and stranger.

It was time for me to get out of there. I stood up. "Aunt Nettie, I'd better be on my way."

She made the usual hostess noises. Don't run off, you've barely come, have a glass of iced tea, blah-blah-blah. But I assured her that I wanted to get home and take a shower.

"Joe doesn't know it yet," I said, "but he's taking me out to dinner. Someplace nice."

Ruby and I said good-bye, and Aunt Nettie walked me to the front door. Just as we arrived there, the doorbell rang.

"Oh, good," Aunt Nettie said. She smiled happily and opened the door. "Julie!"

Suddenly I was surrounded by six women, and four of them were squealing the name of the newcomer. "Julie!" "Jules!" "Juliet!" "Julie!" It was a pile-on.

I couldn't get out the door, so I stepped back and observed. Everyone—even Hazel—seemed thrilled to see the woman who was greeting all her old friends as she inched through the door. This had to be Julie Hensley, the final member of the sextet.

I could hardly see her for the crowd, but what I did see wasn't particularly unusual. She was an ordinary height and size, with hair that shade of ash blond that's designed to hide gray without looking extreme. No flaming red for Julie Hensley. No, her hair was a shade of blond that looked career friendly.

The only odd thing about her was her outfit. She wore a black pants suit and a white shirt with a narrow ribbon tied into a bow under the collar of the shirt. It looked almost like a uniform. Then I remembered that Julie Hensley owned a successful limousine service. Aunt Nettie had told me that her husband had founded it, but Julie had run it solo since he died ten years ago.

Despite being in the age-group and coming from the small-town culture that might have pushed them toward housewife-hood, all of the Pier-O-Ettes had had careers. All except Kathy Street. Somehow I couldn't picture her being successful in the working world.

In fact, Kathy hadn't joined the women who were hugging Julie Hensley and squealing excitedly at her. Kathy had come in from the porch and was standing apart from the excitement, her hands clutched as if in supplication. She was smiling timidly as she waited her turn for a greeting.

Finally the group parted, almost as if the women were forming a reception line, and a clear aisle opened between Julie and Kathy. Kathy smiled timidly, and Julie took three running steps and threw her arms around the baby-doll woman.

Was it my imagination, or did the entire group breathe a sigh of relief? Had they been nervous about how Kathy and Julie would greet each other?

"Kathy!" Julie's voice was low and throaty. "It's been so long."

"Oh, Julie!" It was the first time I'd heard Kathy speak, not scream, and her voice amazed me. It was incredibly melodious and rich.

"It's so wonderful to see you," Kathy said. "You're as pretty as ever."

"I was never as pretty as you," Julie said. "I don't think you've changed at all."

They hugged again. "Can you forgive me?" Kathy said.

"All that old stuff is forgotten, sweetie."

After saying that, Julie stepped back and looked deeply into Kathy's eyes. For the first time I got a good look at Julie's face. She had deep dimples in each cheek, and her expression was pure kindness.

I should have been touched, I guess. But my nature has a real streak of cynicism. I found myself wondering how such a seemingly sweet person kept a gang of limo drivers in line.

Kathy was still talking. "I was afraid to come back to Warner Pier, Julie. I was scared you were still angry with me."

Julie didn't answer her directly. She simply put her arm around Kathy's shoulders and left it there. Then she reached in the pocket of her black jacket and pulled out something small and round. She waved it in the air.

She spoke clearly. "Pier-O-Ettes! Ready!"

I saw that the object was a pitch pipe. Julie blew into it.

Like magic, all six women came to attention. Then they turned around—did pirouettes—in unison. They all smiled—even Kathy—and they hummed to get the right pitch. Then Julie gave the downbeat with the hand that held the pitch pipe, and they broke into "Pennies from Heaven."

It was great! I stood there enthralled while they sang the whole song. The front door was clear now, but they'd have had to shove me out the door to make me leave. I saw why the Pier-O-Ettes had won so many honors. They were terrific—even forty-five years after their heyday.

And Kathy—Kathy was the lead. Her singing voice

was just as lovely as her speaking voice. She sounded like real maple syrup pouring onto pancakes. Incredibly smooth and sweet.

The performance was astonishing.

After the final note I applauded madly. I even whistled and stomped my feet. I tried to become a one-woman standing ovation.

This entertained the six singers greatly. Aunt Nettie and Ruby each gave me a big hug, and even Hazel seemed pleased by my reaction. Kathy, Julie, and Margo smiled broadly.

"Lee knows singing," Aunt Nettie announced. "She's done some herself."

"Not close harmony like that," I said. "Y'all are wonderful. Was that your signature tune?"

They assured me it was. "We're supposed to sing it at the reunion banquet next month," Aunt Nettie said.

I looked at my watch. "And now I've got to get out of here. Call me if you need chocolate! I deliver."

Aunt Nettie assured the group she had an ample supply of chocolates already in the house, gesturing to a dish piled high with them on the coffee table. The other Pier-O-Ettes oohed and aahed, and both Ruby and Julie took chocolate versions of their old high school and popped them into their mouths. Then the five of them moved back toward the screened-in porch. Aunt Nettie came outside with me.

Parked at the curb was a long white limo. "I see Julie brought transportation," I said.

Aunt Nettie smiled. "She said she'd check a limo out for the week. If we decide to go anywhere, it'll be more fun to travel together."

"It looks as if the six of you are scheduled for a great week. Except for—well, what's the deal with Kathy Street?"

"Kathy was always rather"—Aunt Nettie paused—"fragile."

"Was it the trophy that upset her?"

Aunt Nettie nodded. "Yes. Lee, I'll tell you about it later."

"It's none of my affair."

"Oh, I don't mind *you* knowing about it. But Margo doesn't like us to talk about it." She offered me a hug. "Thanks for bringing the box of stuff by."

"If there's anything you need, let me know."

When I turned back toward my van, I realized that a man was walking up Aunt Nettie's front walk. He was tall and broad, and he had silvery hair, but dark eyes and eyebrows. A square black bag, closed with a zipper, hung from his shoulder. He was quite a striking older gent.

"Nettie? Nettie Vanderheide?" His voice was deep, and I'd have expected it to be firm and commanding, but the words sounded cautious.

"That was my name a long time ago." Aunt Nettie sounded cautious, too. "Do I know you?"

The man stopped about six feet away. "I hope so," he said. "I'm Sheppard Stone."

I'd never heard Aunt Nettie mention anyone named Sheppard Stone. I checked her reaction.

Her face had turned as gray as her hair.

Chapter 4

I reached for Aunt Nettie, afraid she was going to faint. She did grab my hand and hold on tight, but she didn't fall over.

"Shep." Her voice was remarkably calm. "Where did you come from?"

"From Kentucky." The newcomer smiled, and he had a great smile. "When I left Warner Pier I went back to my roots, and I've been there ever since."

"And I never left Warner Pier."

"Your name is Jones now? I thought everybody in Warner Pier had a name beginning with 'Van.' Do I know Mr. Jones?"

"No, Hogan only came to Warner Pier seven years ago. But he's my second husband. I married Phil Ten-Huis when I was twenty. He died five years ago."

"I don't think I knew him either."

"Probably not. Though Phil did come to the Castle sometimes." She waved the hand that held mine. "This is Phil's niece, Lee Woodyard. She's the nearest thing I have to a child. Did you marry, Shep?"

"Oh, sure. Twice. No kids. But I'm single now." He gave that charming smile again. "Are you going to ask me in?"

Aunt Nettie glanced over her shoulder nervously. "Actually, Shep, this isn't the best time. How long will you be in town?"

"I don't know yet. How long will everyone be here?"

"Everyone?"

I realized that Aunt Nettie didn't want to add Shep Stone to the mix of old high school chums who were already in her house. And I thought Shep was beginning to realize that, too.

"Are all the Pier-O-Ettes here?"

Aunt Nettie nodded unenthusiastically.

"It would be great to see them."

"Well, Shep—it might not be wise."

Now the guy was definitely frowning. "Why not, Nettie? Are they mad at me?"

"It's Kathy, Shep." Aunt Nettie sighed. "She's just as wacky as ever."

"Oh. I see. And she's mad at me?"

"I honestly don't know. But she's already had one hysterical fit. Let me talk to Margo and see if I can figure it out. Then we can get together later. Where are you staying?"

Shep said he was at the Holland Holiday Inn. His smile was gone. He turned and walked a few steps down the walk, then whirled and came back.

"Nettie," he said angrily. "If you all didn't want to see me, why did you write and invite me to come?"

Aunt Nettie had invited this guy? I didn't think so. Not from her reaction. I waited to see how she'd answer him.

Aunt Nettie took her hand out of mine, stepped forward, and put that hand on Shep Stone's arm.

"I didn't invite you!" She sounded anguished. "Not that it isn't good to see you—but, Shep, I didn't even know where you were living! How could I write and invite you?"

She and the tall man stared at each other.

Finally Stone spoke. "Then who the hell did? I sure wouldn't have showed up without an invite." He turned around abruptly and walked away.

Aunt Nettie followed him. "Shep, let me talk to the rest of the group. Maybe somebody knows something about it. Do you have a cell phone?"

Stone recited the number. Aunt Nettie was still so rattled that going back into the house for paper and pencil seemed to be beyond her. Luckily I had a notebook and pen in my purse, so I wrote the number down at the bottom of a grocery list. Then I copied it onto a fresh page and ripped it out. Aunt Nettie put my note in her pocket, and I hoped that she'd be able to find it later.

Shep Stone left. I stood and watched him drive away—he had a nice-looking black SUV—then turned to Aunt Nettie. "Now, what was that all about?"

"I don't know, Lee! I certainly didn't invite Shep to the reunion."

"Who is he?"

"Back when we used to sing at the Castle, Shep worked there." She shook her head. "We were all so young then!"

"You're not over the hill yet. What did Shep do?"

"I don't know, really. I never understood just what happened."

"I meant his job. Was he a bartender? A waiter?"

"Oh! He checked IDs, kept things in order. Anything Mr. Rice wanted done."

"So Shep was a bouncer. And who was Mr. Rice?"

Aunt Nettie seemed to come back from a faraway

place. She didn't answer my question. "Oh, Lee! You need to go home."

"Joe won't go to pieces if I'm a little late. Who was Mr. Rice?"

"He owned the Castle. Listen, this is a long story, and we really can't go into it now. You go home, and we'll talk later."

She gave me a loving little push. I argued a bit more, but she kept urging me to leave. Finally I left, telling her to call me if she needed anything. Such as help.

Why did I have the feeling she might need help?

As I drove off, Aunt Nettie was still out on her front lawn. Julie Hensley had joined her, and they were conferring seriously. I felt a little less worried at the thought that she was apparently willing to confide in at least one of the Pier-O-Ettes.

When I got home, Joe greeted me with that smile that seemed to mean he was really glad to see me. It made me feel a lot better.

"Where've you been?" he said. "I went down the alley and saw that you and Dolly had closed up the storage room."

"Oh, I had quite an experience," I said. "For one thing, I got to hear the Pier-O-Ettes sing."

That got Joe's attention; he had to hear the whole story. We got a couple of Labatts from the refrigerator and went out onto our own screened porch, and I told all. By the end of the story, life seemed to have improved—except for one thing. I was still just as mystified by the events at Aunt Nettie's as I had been when I left there.

Why had Uncle Phil hidden—yes, that was the right word for it, I decided—Aunt Nettie's high school souvenirs?

Why had Kathy Street gone nuts at the sight of the trophy?

How did Aunt Nettie and the other Pier-O-Ettes know the rest of the souvenirs wouldn't upset her?

What was wrong with Kathy, anyway? She could sing like an angel. But why did she act so odd? Why did all her old friends protect her? All except Hazel.

How did Shep Stone fit into the picture? He must be in his late sixties, but he was still a handsome man. He must have been a heartbreaker at twenty-two or twenty-three. Had one—or more—of the Pier-O-Ettes been in love with him?

Who had written and asked him to come to the reunion? Why had that person used Aunt Nettie's name?

I laid all the questions out for Joe. He didn't have any answers. "I could ask my mom," he said. "She might know something."

Joe's mom, like Aunt Nettie, has lived in Warner Pier all her life. She owns the town's only insurance agency, and she's married to the mayor, Mike Herrera. If anybody knows where the bodies are buried, it's Mercy Woodyard, but she's careful not to tell everything she knows. That's a valuable quality in an insurance agent. Also in a mother-in-law.

I thought about Joe's offer seriously. Should I ask Mercy if she knew anything about the Pier-O-Ettes and their days at the Castle Ballroom?

"No," I said finally. "Your mom is nearly ten years younger than Aunt Nettie, so she might not know anything. Plus, I think I'd be overstepping Aunt Nettie's confidence. I'd better stay out of it. But believe me, once this reunion is over, I've got some questions for Aunt Nettie."

By then my idea of going to dinner "someplace nice" had faded. Joe pointed out that I wouldn't have to get dressed up to go to the Dock Street Pizza Place. Truth is, I was so tired that I was easy to convince. A pizza, another beer, and I could hit the shower with nothing planned for afterward but climbing into my pajamas. Unless Joe came up with a better idea.

The Dock Street Pizza Place is a Warner Pier legend. It's not fancy. The ambiance consists of red-checkered tablecloths, a beer and soft drink cooler, and a pickup counter. It simply has great pizza and salad and pretty good spaghetti and meatballs.

No Warner Pier restaurant is crowded after the tourists have gone home in the fall, so Joe and I were able to snag our favorite booth, the one at the back. We were even able to sit together on one side—the side facing the door—without feeling like teenagers on a date.

We had just ordered a large pepperoni with mushrooms when the door opened and a woman came in. I tried not to stare, but she was definitely worth a second look.

My first thought was that she looked like a tiny gnome grandma. She was so bent and so thin, her bones almost poked through her skin, and she looked as if those bones must be made of twigs. Her face was a mass of wrinkles, and her white hair was wispy. She even carried a cane made of cedar. Actually, it was a gnarled staff about four feet high, something I would have expected to see in the movie version of a Tolkien book.

As soon as she was inside the door, she stopped and looked around the restaurant. The lighting isn't particularly dark in the Dock Street, so I could see her plainly. Her head was turning slowly, and her black eyes scanned around like searchlights. When her eyes reached our booth, her head stopped moving. And she began to walk toward us.

As she approached I remembered that I had seen her before. The last time I'd been in the Warner Pier Public Library, she'd been using one of the library computers.

Joe was looking toward me, not toward the door. I nudged him discreetly. "Joe, who's that woman who just came in?"

He looked. "Good night! It's Mrs. Rice."

"Who?"

The old woman might look frail, but she was walking at a normal pace. By then she was standing beside our booth, and it was too late for Joe to answer my question.

He slid out of the booth and stood up. "Hello, Mrs. Rice. It's been a long time."

"Is this your wife?"

Her remark hadn't sounded friendly, and Joe turned to face her, placing his body between the newcomer and me. "Yes, Mrs. Rice. This is my wife, Lee. Lee, I used to mow Mrs. Rice's lawn when I was in junior high."

Mrs. Rice's hard, black eyes drilled in on me. "You're Nettie Vanderheide's niece."

"Yes."

"She was one of those little Pier-O-Ette bitches."

I'm sure I gasped. Then I spoke. "I beg your pardon, Mrs. Rice. I can't sit still . . ."

Actually, I couldn't do anything but sit still. That's one effect of sitting in a booth. You can't jump to your feet. I did start sliding along on the wooden seat, moving toward the end of the booth. From there I would be able to get up.

But Joe kept me from doing that. He stood at the end of the booth like a door, blocking my exit. And he put a hand behind his back, palm toward me, giving me a clear signal that said, "Stay where you are!"

When he spoke, he used his calm, lawyer voice. "Mrs. Rice, I don't know what problem you have with Mrs. Jones, but she's always been kind and wonderful to Lee and me. I suggest you move along now."

"Kind and wonderful!" The old woman spit the words out.

"Yes," Joe said. "Kind and wonderful."

I was leaning forward, still ready to jump to my feet and take on this old—well, witch. But Joe was still blocking me in. The only way I could get out would have been to slide under the table and crawl out at the end. Not very dignified.

And even as mad as I was, I understood that wouldn't be a good idea. Yelling at an old woman— who was obviously crazy—in a public place wouldn't make me look good. Besides, she was the one with the big stick.

I sat back in my place, seething, and let Joe do his soothing act. He's the professional negotiator, after all.

He managed to get her headed away from our booth. He even walked along with her for a few steps. His voice was gentle. "Did you come in for dinner, Mrs. Rice?"

"No. I saw that truck of yours in the parking lot, and I came in to give your wife a message for Nettie."

She turned around and came back to the booth. She seemed ready for another confrontation.

But Joe again stopped her. "What was the message?"

She leaned over the table and looked closely at me. "You tell that aunt of yours and all those slutty Pier-O-Ettes that this time they're going to get their come-up-er-ance. This time justice is going to be done."

She shook her stick one more time, turned around, and walked toward the door.

Chocolate Chat

Chocolate Places: Indianapolis

I was introduced to Elizabeth Garber, owner of the Best Chocolate in Town, in Indianapolis, by Jim Huang, bookseller and mystery expert. "You've got to meet Elizabeth," Jim said. "She makes great chocolate, and she's a mystery fan."

In that first meeting, Elizabeth gave me facts on chocolate that became key to *The Chocolate Jewel Case*, and she's still a real pal. I can call Elizabeth and ask anything about chocolate. She knows the answer, and she's nice about sharing it.

Elizabeth says that she's a self-taught chocolatier. She began working with chocolate while in college, looking for a way to earn extra money. This experience led her to establish her own chocolate factory and shop after graduation. Today her delicious handmade chocolates are sold in around fifty outlets, mostly in the Indianapolis area, and in her own shop.

Elizabeth's Web page is bestchocolateintown.com.

But watch out! The truffles and other goodies on that Web page may have you drooling all over the keyboard.

Chapter 5

I watched Mrs. Rice go out the door. So did everyone else in the restaurant. She was definitely the most unusual person who had been in all night.

The Dock Street's owner, H. G. Brown—universally known as "Brownie"—came out of the kitchen and walked toward us. Brownie is bald and has the kind of paunch an expert pizza maker should have. He gestured toward the door, now closed behind Mrs. Rice. "Sorry, folks. Every town has a nutcase or two. I'm sorry I didn't get out in time to head her off."

Joe was sliding back into the booth. "No problem, Brownie. Mrs. Rice lived around the corner when I was a kid. I used to mow her lawn. I've known her my whole life."

"I haven't!" I said. "Who is she? And why does she have it in for Aunt Nettie?"

Brownie and Joe both ignored my questions. "I try to keep her out," Brownie said, "but she comes around. For the obvious reason."

Joe nodded, but I was completely mystified. "What

obvious reason?" I said. "I've never seen her in the Dock Street before."

Brownie spoke again, still aiming his remarks at Joe. "I've had to tell her not to come here. But sometimes she wanders in anyway." He went back to the kitchen.

"Who was that woman?" I said.

Joe took a drink of his beer before he spoke. "Lee, you've lived in Warner Pier what—four years? I figured you would have run into all the local characters by now."

"I've seen her in the library, but I don't know who she is. Mrs. Rice? Was that her name?"

"Verna Rice. Does that ring a bell?"

"No." I spoke firmly, but then a bell did seem to give a tiny ting, way in the back of my mind. "Wait. Did Aunt Nettie refer to the owner of the Castle Ballroom as a 'Mr. Rice'?"

"You got it. Dan Rice was the owner of the Castle Ballroom. He was found shot to death in his office more than forty years ago. Mrs. Rice is his widow. She never got over the tragedy."

"Oh. Well, I'm sorry for her, Joe, but she can't simply bad-mouth people the way she did Aunt Nettie. What does she have against the Pier-O-Ettes?"

"I have no answer for that question." Joe grinned. "Mrs. Rice has made public scenes so often that her relatives tried to commit her for treatment, but the psychiatrists say she's just cranky, not crazy. So, unlike most of us Warner Pier–ites, she's been certified as sane."

That made me smile, and I began to feel less annoyed. "I've been told that Warner Pier is too small to have a village idiot, so we all have to take turns. Nice to know I'm not competing with Mrs. Rice for the honor."

Our salads came then, and for the next ten minutes we concentrated on salad greens, tomatoes, purple onions, and Italian dressing. The pizza was on the table before I brought up Mrs. Rice again, and then the reference was indirect. "Joe, ever since I came to Warner Pier as a sixteen-year-old kid, I've heard of the Castle Ballroom. But I've never really known much about it."

"It was demolished ten or fifteen years before I was born, but I've heard about it all my life, too," Joe said. "It must have been really something. It was built in the early twentieth century, and in those days it was one of the few stone buildings in Warner Pier."

"I guess that was the big lumbering era."

"It was the tail end of it. Anyway, excursion boats from Chicago used to bring people over to go to the Castle, just the way people came over to visit the Pavilion, up at Saugatuck. Later—in the thirties and forties—the big bands played there."

"Benny Goodman?"

"Yes, and Glenn Miller. My grandparents went to hear him at the Castle before they were married. My grandmother never forgot it."

"I never knew it was that . . . well . . . special."

"It was. You'll have to go over to the library and look at the pictures. The Castle was enormous—a block long and a block wide. It had a stone tower at each corner, and a deck along the river. Electric lights were strung along the roof and along the deck and outlined the towers."

"It must have looked beautiful reflected in the water."

"The summer people used to come in their boats and tie up for the evening. And an evening at the Castle was elegant."

"What did they have for attractions after the big-band era ended?"

"That's when the story gets a little vague. Mom tells me the sixties weren't kind to Warner Pier in general. Apparently a druggie crowd moved in."

"That must have been a shock. So many of the cottages around here are owned by families who've been coming to Warner Pier for generations—some of them for a hundred years."

"Exactly. Warner Pier has always been a family resort. Even now there's hardly any nightlife."

"True. The wildest entertainment is the piano bar at the yacht club or the deejay on weekends at the Dockster."

"Yeah, and as the former city attorney, I can testify that the city fathers like it that way."

"Today they do."

"They did back then, too. I've read the files. You can't believe the city ordinances they tried to pass in those days—all aimed at keeping the 'hippie element' out. Or at least the Supreme Court wouldn't have believed the ordinances they tried to pass. Freedom of speech wasn't a major concern for the city council back then."

"How did this affect the Castle?"

"The unconstitutional city ordinances probably didn't bother it, but the era itself nearly killed it. Rice tried to keep the Castle respectable. But it was a losing battle. Big ballrooms just weren't popular, and the place had closed up by the time the disco era arrived. I think the talent show that the Pier-O-Ettes were involved in was a last-ditch effort to attract so-called family entertainment. Then Rice was found shot to death."

"Was it suicide?"

"Nobody knows. Rice was shot in the heart at short range. The wound could have been self-inflicted. Or he could have been shot by some attacker. Or a stretch of the imagination would allow for an accident."

"What was the law enforcement ruling?"

"They didn't really know. The insurance company claimed it was suicide, but that was to their advantage."

"Rice must have had a newish policy."

"Right. He was way under the two-year limit. If it was suicide, the insurance didn't have to pay off. Of course, Mrs. Rice tried to prove it was an accident."

"Double indemnity?"

"Right again. If it was an accident, she got a double benefit."

"So nobody wanted it to be murder?"

Joe laughed. "Nope. That didn't benefit anybody financially. Plus, Mrs. Rice swore her husband was such a wonderful man that no one could possibly want to shoot him." Joe raised his eyebrows quizzically. "But Mrs. Rice is still today trying to prove it was an accident."

"After forty-five years! I guess you have to admire her tenacity."

"I don't know. There comes a time to let go of the past. Mrs. Rice inherited the place, but she didn't try to keep it open. Finally the banks foreclosed, the property was sold at auction, and the building was demolished. If she proved her case today, the whole thing would go to legal fees.

"Today Mrs. Rice is almost a recluse. Now and then she emerges, just to put on some sort of scene."

"Why does she haunt the Dock Street, Joe? Why did Brownie say Mrs. Rice came in 'for the obvious reason'?"

"The Dock Street Pizza Place sits on the site of the Castle."

"Ye gods!"

Joe called Brownie back, and the two of them explained where the Castle had stood. Actually, Brownie said, the building's site occupied an area that today is on both sides of the street, plus the street itself.

"The street went around it then. Or rather it ended on one end and took up again on the other," Brownie said. "I've seen maps. Anyway, once the Castle was gone, the city nabbed a right-of-way through the property and extended Dock Street—the way it should have been in the first place."

"Brownie," Joe said, "you have to remember that when the Castle was built—when? 1900?—this was the edge of town. Dock Street dead-ended into the Castle."

"I'd forgotten that." Brownie scratched his paunch. "Today's layout is much better. The city took the land for the park along the river and ran the street itself through the area in a logical pattern. Then Mrs. Rice sold the lots on this side of Dock Street."

"The bank sold them," Joe said. "She refused. The bank had to foreclose. At least I heard that someplace."

"I guess she fought everything all the way," Brownie said.

Joe nodded. "As far as Mrs. Rice is concerned, Dan was a victim of a tragic accident. She still wants to prove that."

I shook my head. "She's sad."

"Sure." Brownie nodded. "It's a sad case. But she's not coming in here and making scenes with my customers."

He nodded firmly as he went back to his kitchen.

Joe and I finished our dinner. We'd just put the left-over pizza into a to-go box when my cell phone rang.

I looked at it. I didn't recognize the number, and I almost didn't answer. Finally I punched the proper button and gave an unenthusiastic hello.

An excited voice answered me. "Lee? This is Aunt Nettie!"

I instantly knew something bad had happened. It wasn't ESP. It was my familiarity with Aunt Nettie's voice. She sounded upset.

"What's wrong?" I said.

"We've had a wreck!"

"Who?"

"All of us. Julie took us for a ride in her beautiful limo and—"

"Is anybody hurt?"

"No! No, we're all fine. Just shaken up. Is Joe with you?"

"Sure." I spoke to Joe. "The Pier-O-Ettes have had a wreck." Then I punched the button that put the cell phone on speaker. "Now Joe can hear."

Joe leaned close. "Nettie, where are you?"

"We're at Fifth and Peach, just down from the shop."

"We'll be right there."

"No!" She sounded panicky. "I mean, that's not why I called you."

"Then, why?"

"I want you to ask the patrolman not to tell Hogan about this! I don't want his workshop to be interrupted."

Joe shook his head. "I'll be right there," he said. "Then we'll see." The two of us ran for the door.

Joe spent more than a year as Warner Pier's city attorney. It's only a part-time job, since the city doesn't have that many legal affairs. But Warner Pier's city hall houses the police station as well as other city offices, so just by proximity Joe got acquainted with the entire Warner Pier Police Department—the chief, the secretary, and all three patrolmen. Of course, he also got acquainted with Chief Hogan Jones by marrying his wife's niece—me. Joe has a new job now, but he still knows all the guys on the force and is an in-law to the chief. So he was a good person for Aunt Nettie to ask to intercede with the investigating officer.

As we got into Joe's truck, he spoke. "Nettie's going to have to understand that Hogan's patrolmen have to tell their boss his wife was in a car wreck. It would be a firing offense not to."

"Surely she'll see that," I said.

We drove the three blocks to TenHuis Chocolade and parked in front of the building. I could see the big white limo sitting catty-corner in the intersection. But it was the only car there.

"Did they just run into a streetlamp or something?" I said. "It doesn't look as if another car was involved. It's hard to believe a professional driver like Julie Hensley would do that."

"Maybe they'd had a few glasses of Michigan wine," Joe said. "Though that's hard to believe, too, if they had dinner at Nettie's house. She doesn't usually serve drinks before and wine with."

We walked up to the corner. The Pier-O-Ettes were standing in a clump. Aunt Nettie, looking anxious, was near Julie. Julie held a handful of papers. She apparently knew what the investigating officer would ask to see and was ready for him. Ruby Westfield was chattering away, speaking to Hazel, who was clutching her jacket around her, looking annoyed and ignoring Ruby. Kathy Street, naturally, was crying—softly, this time— and Margo Street had her arm around her sister.

Joe and I went straight to Aunt Nettie, and she greeted us effusively. She and Julie Hensley listened as Joe quietly explained that the patrolman who investigated the accident would be forced to tell Hogan about it.

"If you don't want Hogan to come home," he said, "your best bet is to call him yourself, explain just what happened, and assure him you have the situation under control."

"I'll do that, of course," Aunt Nettie said. "He's presenting the opening session of the workshop tomorrow, and he's involved all week. He's worked hard on it, and I don't want him to drop it."

"If no one's hurt, I don't think he'll feel that he has to," Joe said. "You've already called the cops?"

Julie Hensley nodded. "We called. The dispatcher said there was only one patrol car on duty, and he was tied up for fifteen or twenty minutes. So we're waiting."

Joe grinned. "Welcome to small-town America."

Mrs. Hensley gave a derisive snort. "Small-town America indeed! I can't believe this happened in my old hometown. It was a hit-and-run!"

"Hit-and-run?" Joe sounded incredulous.

"Yes! We were driving slowly past Nettie's shop—all taking a good look at it—and this car came up behind us. I'll swear it deliberately rammed us! It wasn't going too fast, or someone would have had whiplash. Then the car backed up, swung out to the left, and passed us. After it got around us, it speeded up, turned left at the corner, and disappeared."

"Did you get its license number?"

Mrs. Hensley shook her head. "No, but the car was unmistakable. It was a bright red Buick, a real antique. I'd guess it was at least forty years old!"

Joe looked at Aunt Nettie, and she nodded miserably. "Yes, Joe," she said. "It was Verna Rice in her old red Buick."

Chapter 6

I was still taking that in when the sound of a siren cut loose. The patrolman had apparently waited until he was within a block of the accident to turn it on, because it immediately was so loud that it drowned out all conversation.

Joe and I stepped aside, and I thought about all this.

Verna Rice had deliberately collided with Julie Hensley's fancy limo? Why on earth would she do that?

It had a sort of twisted logic. If Mrs. Rice was angry with the Pier-O-Ettes, then saw them driving by in a limo, maybe the impulse to hit them simply hit her. Whammo.

It would have been a stupid thing to do, but Verna Rice didn't seem to operate on the rules of common sense.

But how would she have known the six old friends were in the limo? I looked it over carefully. The windows of the passenger section were heavily tinted. Mrs. Rice couldn't have seen inside it. But she could have seen the driver. I quickly asked Aunt Nettie if Julie had been alone in the driver's seat.

Aunt Nettie shook her head. "I was sitting up front with her," she said.

So Mrs. Rice might have seen Aunt Nettie.

Jerry Cherry, the Warner Pier patrolman, took down the information from Julie Hensley and assured her he would talk to Mrs. Rice immediately.

"I don't want her arrested or anything," Mrs. Hensley said. "I knew her—more than forty years ago. I guess she has some sort of grudge against us—the six of us. But I swear I never deliberately did anything to harm her."

The others chimed in, all denying any ill feeling toward Mrs. Rice. They sounded a little defensive.

Mrs. Hensley went on. "But she can't just hit somebody with her car. This is going to cost something for repairs. And someone could have been hurt."

"Frankly," Jerry said, "for a long time the chief's been wanting to find a reason to take her license away. We'll see what he says. And I'll go by her house tonight and take her car—as evidence."

The limo was still drivable, so we all parted. The Pier-O-Ettes went back to Aunt Nettie's, and Joe and I went home. I finally got that shower I'd been wanting since four o'clock. At about nine p.m. Jerry Cherry called to say Verna Rice hadn't gone home yet, and he was going to put off looking for her car until morning. By that time I was ready for bed, and Joe was already in it—wearing his pajamas and propped up so he could read some papers he'd brought home from the office.

I didn't care about big, old, red Buicks. I crawled over to Joe's side of the king-sized bed and snuggled against him. He let go of his papers and hugged me.

"In bed at nine o'clock," I said. "Are we turning into an old married couple?"

"I think we are," Joe said. "Wonderful, isn't it?"

Before I could agree, the phone rang again. It's on my side of the bed. I stayed on Joe's side, with his arms around me, until it rang for the third time. Then he released his hug. "Guess we'd better see if the Pier-O-Ettes have had another wreck."

I crawled across the bed and answered the phone.

"Hello." My voice was not very friendly.

"Mrs. Woodyard?" The voice sounded like wood cracking. "I would appreciate it if you could allow me to speak to Mr. Woodyard."

Hmmm. A formal request. I decided I could be formal, too. "May I tell him who is calling?"

"Mrs. Dan Rice."

I nearly fell out of the bed, of course. Then I answered. "Just one moment."

I put my hand over the talking part of the receiver.

"Are you 'in' for Mrs. Dan Rice?"

"You're kidding, I hope."

"Nope." I shoved the receiver toward him, with my hand still covering the lower part of it.

Joe groaned. Then he took the phone. He held it the same way I had.

"If she's started bugging people at bedtime, the judge may have to take another look at her sanity," he said.

He put the receiver to his ear. "What is it, Mrs. Rice?"

He listened, then spoke. "Mrs. Rice, I have an office. You can call me there."

He listened again. "Have you been arrested?"

I could hear the angry squawk—"Certainly not!"— Joe's question brought. Words that were not so loud followed.

"A client who's in jail is usually the only reason I come out this late, Mrs. Rice."

Another pause to listen. "Just what is the emergency?"

Pause.

"Yes, my agency represents indigent clients, but we have certain rules and policies. . . ."

Pause.

"Just what sort of new evidence?"

Pause.

"Forty-five years? Mrs. Rice, if this evidence has waited that long, surely you can wait until morning."

Pause.

"No, I don't come to clients' houses this late."

Pause.

"Then where are you?"

Joe listened only a few more seconds before he spoke. "No! No! You can't come here! Mrs. Rice!"

He sat there with the receiver in his hand, looking annoyed. "She's coming over."

"Call her back."

He tried, but the phone went unanswered. Joe sighed deeply, punched the telephone's OFF button, then swung the covers back. "I'll get some clothes on. You don't have to get up."

"Joe, I don't care what the judge said—that woman is crazy. It's dangerous to let her in the house."

"Surely I can handle an eighty-five-year-old woman."

"Not if she has a gun."

"I doubt she's armed. But I'll be cautious." He gave me a kiss and picked up the jeans he'd draped over the bedroom chair.

I got out of bed. "I'm wide-awake. I'll put something on. I can't cope with Mrs. Rice in a flannel nightgown." Joe protested, but I got dressed.

If I needed clothes, it was because Michigan's fall nights are crisp, but Michigan natives such as Joe don't think they should turn the furnace on until mid-October. I found some sweatpants and a sweatshirt, then added socks and tennis shoes.

When I went into the living room, Joe had turned on the outdoor lights. He was sitting in his easy chair wearing jeans, tennis shoes, and a University of Michigan sweatshirt. "This is ridiculous," he said.

"Does she even know where we live?"

"She asked if we didn't live in the 'old TenHuis' house."

"Darn! I was hoping she'd get lost on the way over and give up on the whole project."

"No such luck. She should be here any minute."

We sat and waited. And waited. And waited.

After twenty minutes, Joe spoke. "I hope she changed her mind."

"What was this 'new evidence' she said she had?"

"She wouldn't tell me. If she's talking about Dan Rice's death—well, the idea of evidence turning up after forty-five years is pretty flaky."

Then he frowned. "You know, Lee, I got the feeling she had somebody there with her."

"Any idea who?"

"None. Maybe we should go back to bed."

"That would guarantee that she shows up."

Thirty seconds later we heard a siren for the second time that night. It came closer and closer, until it almost sounded as if it was in our yard. Then it died away, sounding as if someone had strangled it.

We both walked swiftly into the bedroom, where the windows face Lake Shore Drive, and looked out. The heavy foliage of summer was thinning out as the season changed to fall. We could see glimpses of flashing lights through the trees. Not close. Maybe a quarter of a mile up the road.

"It just can't be her," I said.

"There's not a lot of traffic in this area this time of night," Joe said. "Who else would be coming this way?"

I immediately named a neighbor. "Duncan Delany. His wife told me he's working until nine o'clock every night now."

"I'd better go see what's happened."

"I'm going, too."

We each grabbed a flashlight and a jacket. We walked down our lane to Lake Shore Drive, then turned toward the lights. Our neighbors were also beginning to stir. In the fall, after the summer cottages are closed and the summer people go home, our area is pretty lonely. Only a few families, such as Duncan and Jane Delany, live along the lake in the winter. The school bus picked up the Delany kids, but I think their house was the only stop it made for a mile.

The siren had attracted a few people, and the lights of a few houses were visible through the trees. I did notice a vehicle was nosed into the driveway of Garnet and Dick Garrett's house, which was directly across the road from us. This surprised me, since I knew they weren't likely to be down on a weekend during football season. They're big Michigan State fans.

I took another look at the vehicle in their driveway, aiming my flashlight at its rear end. It was a small truck in some dark color. I decided it must be someone who had stopped to see the accident. Some jerk always shows up to get in the way. The figures on the license plate—7214—caught my attention because I'm a number person, but I didn't notice the letters. I made a mental note to check it out later, since I was sure the Garretts weren't there.

As we got closer to the sirens, Duncan Delany popped up beside us. "Someone hit the big oak tree," he said. "I was the first person on the scene."

His SUV was parked on the shoulder, headed south. "You weren't hurt?" I said.

"Oh, no! I wasn't involved at all. I just stopped and called 9-1-1."

Joe spoke. "Anybody in the car?"

"An old woman. She seemed—well, I told the operator to send an ambulance, but I think it's too late."

I clutched Joe's arm. "Wait here," he said. He walked around the police car.

I moved closer to the scene but stayed behind the patrol car. Now there was enough light to see the wrecked car.

It was red.

It was a big old Buick.

"Darn!" I said.

"What's the matter?" Duncan said.

"I think I know who it is," I said. When Duncan asked me more questions, all I said was, "Maybe I'm wrong."

There were more sirens as the state police and an ambulance showed up. To prove the remoteness of our neighborhood, only one or two cars had been halted by the police cars blocking the road.

It was between five and ten minutes before Joe came back. "It's her," he said. "Or, as Mrs. Rice would have said, it is she. I told the officer she had been headed for our house."

The red car looked as if it had plowed into the big tree head-on. The radiator grill was deeply caved in, but the body of the car didn't look as if it had been damaged.

"I guess she was thrown into the windshield," I said.

Joe leaned close to my ear. "The whole thing looks kind of funny to me."

We stood around until the officers said they didn't need us, then walked home. As soon as we were in the house, I quizzed Joe about why he thought the accident looked funny.

"It seemed to me that the blood was in the wrong place," he said. "I expected to see that Mrs. Rice had been thrown into the windshield, the way you did."

"Which would mean blood on her face."

"Right. But all the blood I saw seemed to be on her shoulder and the back of her head." He made an impatient gesture. "But I'm no expert on car accidents. And I didn't get a good look. I'll leave it to the state police."

We decided not to call Aunt Nettie with the news of Mrs. Rice's death. We went to bed, but now neither of us was feeling very romantic. I fell asleep, and Joe read his papers for a long time. Or at least he propped himself up on several pillows and held the papers in his lap. Every time I roused enough to look at him, he was still awake, but sometimes he didn't seem to be reading.

I think I was able to sleep because sleeping meant I didn't have to think about telling Aunt Nettie and the Pier-O-Ettes about Mrs. Rice's accident.

If it was an accident.

I rolled over and punched my pillow. Golly! Where did that thought come from?

I did finally fall soundly asleep, and I was barely out of bed at eight a.m., when the phone rang. I caught it on the bedside phone and heard Joe pick up in the kitchen at almost the same moment. He spoke before I did.

"Joe?" The voice belonged to Aunt Nettie. "I'm afraid I'm going to need a good lawyer."

"What's happened?"

"It's Verna Rice. Apparently she was ranting all over town last night, mad at the Pier-O-Ettes. And now Jerry Cherry came by to say she was found dead in her car at about ten o'clock."

"Yeah, it happened just down from our house. We walked over to see the wreck. But what does this have to do with you?"

"Oh, Joe! She was at the Superette, at the Dock Street, maybe a couple of other places, and she threatened all of us, all the Pier-O-Ettes. And now Jerry says they've called in the state police! He says we'll all have to make statements."

Chapter 7

Aunt Nettie rarely loses her cool, and she didn't then. She was excited, but she talked calmly as she told us that Jerry Cherry, who's worked for the Warner Pier PD longer than any of Hogan's other officers, had come to her house at seven thirty to tell her about Mrs. Rice. He'd asked the Pier-O-Ettes to stick around so they'd be handy if the investigating officer had questions.

"We were all together—sort of—from the time of the accident until Jerry came by this morning," she said. She gave a laugh. "So we all have alibis. Sort of."

"I doubt you'll need them, any more than you'll need a lawyer," Joe said. "But I'm afraid it wasn't natural causes."

He paused, and I wondered if he was considering telling Aunt Nettie that Mrs. Rice's death had looked suspicious to him. But he went on without describing what we'd seen the night before.

"Since she was found in a car, and the car had run into a tree, Nettie, the state police would have to be called in."

"Then it's a traffic death?"

"The medical examiner will have to rule on the cause of death."

"Of course. I just hope Hogan doesn't have to come home."

Joe sounded puzzled. "Why are you so determined that Hogan not be involved in this? After all, he is the police chief. He can't ignore Warner Pier events even if he's out of town."

Now Aunt Nettie began to sound less calm, even a bit dithery. "Oh, he's worked so hard on his presentation for this workshop. I just . . . I just don't want it to be ruined."

We all three hung up, and I went into the kitchen, thinking about the state police. The Michigan State Police not only patrol the state's highways; they're also the agency charged with helping small towns—like Warner Pier—investigate serious crimes.

Joe was still standing by the telephone. He looked puzzled.

"Good morning," I said. "Do you know any way to find out what's going on?"

"Probably Mike knows." Mike Herrera is Joe's stepfather and is mayor of Warner Pier. The city police usually tell him what's happening on the crime front. "For that matter, Jerry would probably tell me."

"Let's let it go until after breakfast," I said.

I fixed bacon and eggs, since it was Saturday, but halfway through the meal I realized Joe and I were wolfing our food. I was feeling more and more urgency about the situation with Mrs. Rice's death. I wanted to get breakfast over and go to Aunt Nettie's house. I might find out something more there.

I suspected Joe was also feeling as if he should find out more, and my suspicions were confirmed when he poured his second cup of coffee into a plastic mug that fits the pickup's cup holder.

"I guess I'll try to find out what's going on with Mrs. Rice's death," he said.

I didn't argue. And I didn't take more than twenty minutes to stick the dishes in the dishwasher and get my clothes on. And that included makeup. I wasn't facing Margo Street without makeup.

I arrived at Aunt Nettie's house at nine thirty, remarkably early considering that I hadn't gotten out of bed until eight o'clock. Lots of cars were there. At the curb were Julie's limo, with its crushed bumper, and the Cadillac with an Illinois license tag I assumed that Margo and Kathy Street had arrived in. In the drive were two cars with Michigan plates—a small Chevy I'd seen Hazel in dozens of times and a big blue minivan that Ruby must use for delivering bridal gowns and transporting her extensive family.

And there was one more car. Parked across the end of the driveway, blocking Ruby and Hazel, was an antique Corvette.

I parked my minivan in front of the house next door, then sat and stared at the Corvette. Hmmm.

My dad owns a garage in Prairie Creek, Texas, and as a child I hung out there enough to acquire an interest in cars. When I saw that Vette, I had to swallow quickly to keep from drooling.

I didn't think it was one of the earliest models. It was old enough to be classified as an antique, but it was no pioneer. What it was, was gorgeous.

It was white. Not creamy or pearly, but that bright picket-fence white of a Corvette that still has its original paint job. The top was down, and I could see the tan leather interior clearly. Every bit of its chrome—the luggage rack on the flat lid of the trunk, the trim around the dials and gauges on the dashboard, the spindly spokes of the steering wheel, and even the Stingray logo on the side—every shiny bit of chrome caught the sun and sparkled like a diamond necklace ought to sparkle. And this car would probably cost as much as twenty carats of diamonds would.

What on earth was it doing parked in the drive of a homey frame house in Warner Pier, Michigan?

If it had been summertime, I wouldn't have wondered so much. Lots of our "summer people" might park a car like this one in front of their multimillion-dollar "cottages." I just wondered what it was doing at Aunt Nettie's house.

I got out of my plain vanilla minivan—useful for delivering chocolate, but not very exciting—and started down the sidewalk. As I passed the Corvette, pretending not to stare at it, I saw the decal that identified the dealer who had sold the car to its owner. And there, in bright red letters, was a well-known phrase: GOOD-TIME CHARLIE. HOLLAND'S FUNNIEST USED CAR DEALER.

I laughed. Any reference to Good-Time Charlie is good for a laugh in southwest Michigan. Charlie Mc-Coy is a major advertiser on the evening news, and he does his own ads. So we all see the tubby bald guy nearly every day, begging us to buy used cars. He uses a loud, harsh voice and dumb puns to make his message memorable. Or I guess that's why he uses them. He's a buffoon, but at least he's distinctive.

But who did Aunt Nettie know who would be driving a Good-Time Charlie car? And not just any car—a fancy antique Corvette. I was still wondering about that as I rang the doorbell.

I heard a deep, raspy voice call out, "I'll get it!" Then the door was opened by—ta-da!—Good-Time Charlie himself.

I stepped backward and nearly fell off the porch.

I had not expected Aunt Nettie's door to be answered by a local television celebrity, though I belatedly remembered that she had once told me she had known the super salesman in her younger days.

"Watch out, little lady!" Charlie's voice boomed as raucously in person as it did on the ads.

"Hello." I didn't know if I should be amazed or annoyed. Where did Charlie get off answering my aunt's front door? And how could he call a woman at least five inches taller than he was "little lady"?

I tried to go for dignity. "I'm Mrs. Jones' niece. May I come in?"

I wasn't aware that I had offered to shake hands, but somehow he had hold of one of mine and was shaking it as if he were a puppy and my hand was his favorite toy. I almost expected him to chew on it.

"Lee Woodyard, right? I'm really glad to meet you. Nettie's been telling us all about how you saved her business!"

"She's being kind. If her chocolates hadn't been sublime, there wouldn't have been any business to save."

"That's not what she says! Come on in!"

I followed him into the living room, wondering who had appointed him host. Aunt Nettie was seated on the couch, with a coffee carafe on the coffee table in front of her. Shep Stone was sitting beside her. He nodded to me. He looked rather uncomfortable.

"Hi, Lee," Aunt Nettie said. "Shep and Charlie came by. They both worked at the Castle Ballroom in the old days. We all were waitresses there, and we hung around a lot in the days when we were singing."

Shep and Charlie had done more than come by. They apparently had joined the party.

Why? Their arrival mystified me.

"I'll get more coffee!" Charlie snatched the carafe from in front of Aunt Nettie and headed toward the kitchen.

Shep Stone watched him go, shaking his head. "I guess that even forty-five years ago we should have figured out that Charlie would make his mark as a used-car salesman."

"That's not all bad," I said. "My dad sells a few used cars, and he's a pretty nice guy. He found the van I'm driving for me—it's an oldie but goodie." I turned to Aunt Nettie. "Have you heard anything more about Mrs. Rice?"

"Not yet." Aunt Nettie smiled graciously. "Shep and Charlie brought doughnuts. Would you like one?"

"Maybe later. Joe and I had a big breakfast. Then he went out to try to find out more about your earlier question."

Aunt Nettie seemed to be stuck for a reply to that, and I realized I was extremely curious about just why Charlie and Shep were there. Of course, I'd learned the day before that Shep Stone had worked at the Castle Ballroom at the time the Pier-O-Ettes sang there. But where did Charlie McCoy fit in? Apparently he had worked there, too. But even if they'd known the Pier-O-Ettes in the remote past, why would the two of them horn in on the reunion? Had they gone to Warner Pier High School?

I got ready to ask as soon as I got an opportunity. Reverting to my past life, I called up the social skills I learned back when I was the wife of a successful Dallas real estate developer. I smiled at Shep Stone. "What do you do, Mr. Stone?"

"I'm retired now. But I spent most of my career as a photographer." He held up a camera he had stashed in his lap. "I've been trying to get a few pictures today."

"Oh? You're an artist? Or did you do commercial work?"

"Commercial, mainly. I've worked for newspapers and done some magazine work."

Aunt Nettie leaned forward. "Shep, I always suspected that Dan Rice hired you at the old Castle because he wanted someone to talk photography with."

Charlie rushed back in then, but Shep kept talking. "Dan was a pretty good amateur," he said. "I was always surprised at the stuff he could get just standing on the deck at the Castle. And he had a good Leica."

It's weird how men react. Charlie's head whipped toward Shep. The two men exchanged a stare. Then Charlie dropped his gaze. He seemed to try to become the center of attention. He had a dish towel draped over his arm, in a parody of a waiter, and he held the coffee carafe in one hand and a mug in the other.

"It's a new brew," he said. "But remember—drinking too much coffee can cause a latte problems."

I rolled my eyes, and Shep groaned. "Charlie, you're worse than ever."

"I've made a career of puns," Charlie said. "They've paid off for me big-time. But I know puns are the lowest form of wit, and I can prove it."

"How?" I said.

"I never eat buns," he said. "Because buns are the lowest form of wheat."

All three of us groaned. In fact, Aunt Nettie looked so pained that I decided I'd better turn my social skills on Charlie, just to keep him from talking to her.

"Mr. McCoy—"

"Charlie! Everybody calls me Charlie!"

"Charlie. And you worked at the Castle Ballroom?"

"Oh, yes! Bouncer for two summers." Charlie began to talk to me while Aunt Nettie concentrated on Shep.

"So, you handle Nettie's finances," he said.

"Among other things. In a small business everybody does everything. Yesterday Aunt Nettie's chief assistant and I cleaned out the garage."

"Custodial duties, too?" Charlie laughed, and I explained that we had to give up use of the storage area across the alley from our back door. "I found a whole drawer of Aunt Nettie's high school souvenirs," I said.

Then I tried to turn the conversation to Charlie. "How did you come to work at the Castle Ballroom?"

He had worked at the ballroom while he was in college, Charlie said. He'd been quite a bit older than the Pier-O-Ettes, in his mid-twenties, since he'd already done a tour in Vietnam. "Of course, mentally I'm just a kid."

Charlie was originally from Detroit, but he said he had been rather at loose ends at that time in his life.

"I was a wild one then," he said proudly. "Shep— now, he had a deceptively mild exterior. But I liked to party."

"That's not too unusual for guys that age."

"True. But I'm afraid all the girls' mothers told them to stay away from me."

"A warning from a mother tends to make guys even more attractive."

"Not in my case!" He turned away. "Hey, Nettie! Do you remember the night I bought the sparkling grape juice and told you girls it was champagne?"

"Oh, yes, I remember." Aunt Nettie's voice didn't sound amused.

Charlie laughed. "If Shep hadn't been such a gentleman, I might have gotten all six of you drunk."

"Hush, Charlie," Aunt Nettie said. "Lee isn't interested in all those old pranks."

Actually, I was quite interested in them. Taking a look at my rather prim Aunt Nettie as a high schooler—a girl so innocent she couldn't tell sparkling grape juice from champagne—was quite interesting.

But Aunt Nettie didn't look amused. "Lee," she said, "would you do me a favor? Run back to my bedroom and bring me my white sweater. It's in the closet."

"Sure." Was I being headed off? I couldn't imagine that Aunt Nettie had actually taken part in anything improper, even when she was seventeen.

But at that moment she certainly had a better idea than I did about what was going on with the Pier-O-Ettes and their gentlemen callers, Shep and Charlie. If she wanted to change the subject, I would follow her lead.

So I obediently went down the hall to the master bedroom. I wasn't too surprised to find the door closed, since Aunt Nettie probably wouldn't have yet had time to neaten it up.

I expected the room to be empty, but as a precaution I knocked. No one responded, so I opened the door and went in. I went to the closet and pushed back the louvered door.

And I found myself face-to-face with Kathy Street.

Chapter 8

I gave a huge gasp.

All I could think was that I must not startle Kathy. I certainly didn't want her to shriek the way she had the day before. So I'm sure that my face showed all the surprise I felt, but I managed not to yelp out loud, and I hoped Kathy would keep quiet, too.

When I did speak, I tried to keep my voice calm. "You caught me by surprise, Ms. Street. Are you avoiding Charlie and Shep?"

She nodded timidly.

"They seem pretty harmless. But there's no reason you can't wait in here until they're gone."

Kathy Street spoke in a whisper. "Charlie?"

"Good-Time Charlie, the car salesman? Yes, he's here. Is he the one you don't want to see?"

"I don't want to see either of them."

"That's up to you." I gave what I hoped was a bright and cheerful smile. "Aunt Nettie sent me to get her white sweater. It's someplace in that closet. If you could sit on the bed for a minute, I'll find it."

"Close the door. Please." Her voice was barely audible.

"Sure." I closed the bedroom door, and Kathy Street came out of the closet and obediently sat on the edge of the bed. She hadn't dressed yet. She wore a cotton housecoat printed with little pink flowers. House slippers were on her feet.

I began to search through the closet. I hummed as I did this, probably because I was nervous, but I don't know what made me pick an old folk song to hum.

I had just found the white sweater when Kathy Street began to sing along with my humming.

"Black is the color of my true love's hair," she sang.

She sang so quietly it would have been hard for anyone outside the room to hear her. And she sang without any—well, commotion. She just opened her mouth and this beautiful sound poured out. There was nothing fancy about it; no vibrato, no embellishments. The sound was pure and simple and lovely. It was as if I'd been walking through a meadow, and a passing shepherdess suddenly began to sing to her sheep.

Clutching the sweater, I sank onto a padded stool in front of Aunt Nettie's dressing table, and I listened until Kathy Street came to the end of the song.

When she finished, I leaned forward. "That was wonderful! Thank you for showing me how lovely that song can be."

She smiled shyly. "I've always liked it."

"I can tell that you do."

"Nettie said you used to sing."

"Not like you do! You have a wonderful voice." I stood up, ready to return to the living room.

But before I could say good-bye, the bedroom door swung open. Kathy Street gave a little "Oh!" that sounded afraid, and her sister came into the room.

"There you are, Kathy! I've been looking all over for you."

"Nettie's niece says it's all right for me to be in here."

Margo Street sent me a flash of anger, but only a flash. She didn't have any time for me. Her concentration was on Kathy.

"Shep Stone and Charlie McCoy have dropped by. You'll have to come out and speak to them."

"No. Please."

"Yes, Kathy. It will look odd if you don't."

"No, Margo. No." Kathy's lower lip pouted. She ducked her head and looked up at her sister like a three-year-old.

Margo sighed. "I really think that you should make an effort, Kathy. You don't have to carry on a conversation. Just say hello."

"Please don't make me."

I wanted to leave, but Margo Street was standing in the bedroom doorway, and I couldn't get to it without asking her to move. And she was ignoring me.

But Kathy wasn't ignoring me. She pointed at me. "She said I didn't have to talk to them."

Margo turned her full attention on me, shining a spotlight of anger in my direction.

"Oh, really? Lee—isn't that your name? When did you become my sister's adviser?"

"I think you're misunderstanding the situation, Ms. Street."

"Oh? Just what am I misunderstanding?"

I took a deep breath. "When I found your sister here in Aunt Nettie's bedroom, I assured her that Aunt Nettie wouldn't mind her being here. And I'm sure that is blue. I mean, true!"

Darn! She'd made me nervous, and I'd gotten my

tongue tangled. I tried to pretend it hadn't happened, and I plunged on.

"Kathy said she didn't want to see Shep and Charlie. Of course, since she's a grown woman, that's her pergola. Her prerogative! That's all I told her."

Margo Street's voice was like ice. "But not seeing them would be most unwise."

"You may be right. But as a general rule, if grown-up people don't want to associate with some particular person, we don't have to."

"But avoiding them may make her look foolish."

"I don't know about that." I clutched the white sweater. "And now I should take Aunt Nettie her sweater."

For a moment I thought I was going to have to shove Margo Street out of the way, but when I walked toward her, she moved aside and let me out the door.

I went out feeling relieved to escape—I didn't want to be caught up in a quarrel between the two sisters—but I also felt mystified. I didn't understand the Street sisters' relationship at all.

Was Kathy mentally deficient in some way? Or just nervous? Or—maybe—spoiled?

The day before, she had shrieked at the sight of the trophy won by the Pier-O-Ettes forty-odd years ago. Why?

Yesterday Aunt Nettie had refused to allow Shep Stone to enter her house, using Kathy as her reason. Why?

Now Kathy was hiding—actually hiding in a closet—to avoid Shep and Charlie. Why?

And her sister Margo was insisting that she come out and see Charlie and Shep. Why?

I stopped in the hall and took several deep breaths. Margo Street had closed the bedroom door behind me, but it hadn't caught just right, and I could hear her voice.

"Come, Kathy, you'd better get some clothes on."

"I don't want to, Margo!"

"You'll feel better if you do, Kathy. You don't want to call attention to yourself by being the only Pier-O-Ette who doesn't talk to Shep and Charlie."

"Are you sure that I should?"

"Yes, sweetie. Come on, and we'll find your clothes. You can wear your pretty blue outfit."

I dashed on down the hall before they caught me eavesdropping. But the situation was mystifying.

I went back into the living room and handed Aunt Nettie her sweater, resolving to find an excuse to get her alone and try to get some answers to my questions.

The chair I'd been sitting in earlier was now occupied by Ruby Westfield, and Ruby was giving Shep her full concentration. The pheromones, or whatever her attraction was, were broadcasting like mad, and they were aimed at him.

I found that interesting. Some people in Warner Pier believed Ruby was a gold digger, but if she had been interested in money, I would have expected her to go for Charlie rather than Shep. After all, Charlie was a successful used-car dealer, and Shep was a retired photographer. Shep, of course, was much more attractive than Charlie. And I knew very little about the financial side of photography. Shep might well be loaded.

As Ruby talked, Shep raised his camera and snapped several pictures of her. I found another chair, sat quietly, and listened while Ruby gave Shep the treatment. It was easy for me to do this; when Ruby was around, no other woman got any masculine attention.

However, it was soon obvious that, while Ruby might be concentrating on Shep, Charlie was determined not to be ignored. The two men were vying for her attention.

Charlie was trotting out his ghastly puns. "You heard about the guy from Indiana who applied for a job in a grocery store," he said. "But he didn't get it. The manager said, 'Baggers can't be Hoosiers.'"

I rolled my eyes, but Ruby smiled. "You always had a lot of jokes, Charlie. Shep was always more serious. Quiet. We all thought he was mysterious."

"I just didn't have anything to say," Shep said. "As the old saying goes, it's better to shut up and let people think you're stupid than to speak up and remove all doubt."

"We were all stupid back then," Ruby said. "Remember how we teased poor Mr. Rice? We probably nearly ruined his marriage."

"His marriage wasn't much anyway," Shep said. "Mrs. Rice was a real pain, and he knew it."

"Yeah," Charlie said. "Dan would have loosened the Castle up, made it more attractive to the younger crowd. At least he could have hired rock musicians. It was Verna Rice who kept harping on 'family-oriented' entertainment. I always thought she was the reason the place went under."

"She was the most unpopular teacher at WPHS," Ruby said. "I had her for typing and for bookkeeping."

Charlie's eyes narrowed. "Were you girls responsible for the hang-up phone calls that Verna Rice complained about?"

Ruby and Aunt Nettie looked at each other. Both smiled, and Aunt Nettie spoke. "What phone calls?" Her voice was unbelievably innocent.

"We were pretty rotten kids," Ruby said. "I wonder if the calls started after graduation."

Shep grinned. "I gather that Verna Rice has been

known as the biggest oddball in Warner Pier for years. But there was nothing new about that. She was already peculiar forty-five years ago. And believe me, Dan Rice knew it. They were definitely not the happiest couple I ever knew."

I found that interesting. According to Joe, Mrs. Rice had spent more than forty years devoted to her husband's memory and working to prove he didn't kill himself. Yet Aunt Nettie, Ruby, and Shep all felt that her marriage hadn't been happy. Had Mrs. Rice been acting out of love for her husband? Or out of guilt?

Ruby again became the center of the conversation, and I seized the moment to speak to Aunt Nettie. "I think there's a problem in the kitchen. May I take you away for a moment?"

She nodded—she may have looked slightly relieved—and the two of us left the room.

She spoke as soon as we were out of the room. "What's wrong in the kitchen?"

"Nothing that I know of. I lied. I just wanted to talk to you. Where can we go?"

"The kitchen ought to be empty." She led the way in that direction.

But the kitchen wasn't empty. Hazel was there. She was cleaning the stove top, industriously scrubbing it down with spray cleaner.

"Hazel!" Aunt Nettie sounded annoyed. "What are you doing?"

Hazel jumped guiltily. "Just neatening up a little."

"I tried to plan meals that didn't need any work."

I saw a tray on the kitchen counter. It held a half dozen cinnamon rolls but had obviously held more of them earlier. Beside it were two pitchers, one filled with orange juice and the other with tomato. A thirty-cup coffeepot—I recognized it from the TenHuis Chocolade break room—was plugged in and giving off a nice aroma. Paper plates, coffee mugs, and juice glasses completed the picture of a serve-yourself continental breakfast.

Hazel had the grace to look embarrassed. Aunt Nettie just looked annoyed.

"Hazel, I thought people could put their own dishes in the dishwasher. I'd hoped no one would have to hang around in the kitchen."

"I know, Nettie. It's just that—well, it gives me something to do."

"How about talking to the others? You're a guest, not the hired girl."

"It's just— Oh, I never fit in with this bunch. Not when we were kids. Not now. I was the tall, gawky one."

I put my arm around Hazel's shoulder. Hazel is around five-eight, and I tower over her by several inches. "Should I take that personally?"

"Oh, Lee, you can carry off your—stature. But when it came to the Pier-O-Ettes, they were all short. All but me. I was the one the director was always telling to stand in the middle. Just look at that picture of us all at sixteen. There are five cute little girls and an ugly giant."

"Hazel!" Aunt Nettie sounded horrified. "I never knew you felt that way."

Hazel hung her head. "And after high school— everyone else had a successful career. Julie has her own company. You do, too. Even Ruby has a business. She's been tremendously successful at what she does. And, of course, Margo—she's rich and famous. I was only a cook."

"Only a cook! There's nothing 'only' about what you did! TenHuis Chocolade would not be what it is without you, Hazel. I had hoped that I'd told you how much I appreciated everything you did, how the whole company relied on you."

"You did tell me, Nettie! You did!"

Aunt Nettie and Hazel fell on each other's necks, both sniffling.

I edged out of the kitchen. I still had a lot of questions about Mrs. Rice and about the personal dynamics of the Pier-O-Ettes. But right at that moment, Hazel's crisis was more important to Aunt Nettie than my questions were.

I wandered back to the living room. Margo and Kathy hadn't appeared yet, and Ruby was still the target of the masculine attention. But Julie Hensley had come in. She was rearranging the mantelpiece.

I stopped, wondering if Aunt Nettie was going to be annoyed with Julie for changing her décor. Then I saw what Julie was doing. She was arranging a series of small paintings, each of them showing a group of young girls.

I stepped close. They were paintings of the Pier-O-Ettes as they had appeared in the group photo I'd found in the old filing cabinet. But the pose was different. The picture I'd found had shown the young singers in a formal, rather stilted pose. This showed them in an informal snapshot. All of them were laughing and clowning for the camera. They were wearing their Pier-O-Ette dresses.

The pictures were perfectly delightful. And I realized that each one was an original watercolor.

"These are wonderful," I said to Julie.

"Shep took the original picture," she said. We both looked at Shep, and he tried to look modest. "He's a great photographer."

"He certainly is. And turning the photograph into watercolors was a fabulous idea!"

"Margo had them done by an artist here in Warner Pier," she said. "Aren't they great souvenirs? I ran out and got some plate stands so we could display them together this weekend."

As we stood there, oohing and aahing, the doorbell rang.

Charlie yelled, "I'll get it," but I waved him aside, gesturing as firmly as I knew how, and went to the door myself. But when I opened it, I wished that I'd let him answer.

Standing on the porch was a tall, lanky guy with thin, colorless hair combed flat against his head. His eyes were an icy blue. He extended a hand, but it wasn't for a handshake. In his hand was a badge.

"Hugh Jackson," he said. His voice was as cold as his eyes. "Michigan State Police."

Between the icy eyes and the chilling voice, I felt as if he had thrown cold water over me.

"Come in," I said. "My aunt said you were cooling. I mean, coming! Mrs. Jones said you were coming for their staterooms. I mean, statements!"

Jackson didn't laugh. He didn't frown. He didn't react at all to my idiotic remarks. He might not be "cooling," but he was a cool customer, I decided. I stepped aside and motioned for him to come in.

I'd met several of the state police detectives before, but Jackson was strange to me. Quite strange.

I called Aunt Nettie from the kitchen and introduced her to Jackson.

She smiled. "What's the news on Mrs. Rice?" she said.

"It looks as if someone hit Mrs. Rice in the head."

"Oh dear!" Aunt Nettie pressed her hand over her mouth. "Not murder!"

"We don't know yet. Since you and your friends

were among the last people to see her, I'm going to have to ask each of you for a statement."

"A statement?"

"Yes. About the accident when Mrs. Rice apparently ran into Mrs. Hensley's limo. And about your activities later."

"I'm sure all of us will be glad to talk to you, Lieutenant."

"Ooooh!" A squeal sounded behind me. It wasn't as piercing as the shriek I'd heard the day before, but I still jumped. When I whirled around, I saw that it was—who else?—Kathy Street.

"Oh, goodness!" she said. "It's hard to believe Mrs. Rice is finally dead. I wanted her to die long ago, but she wouldn't do it. And now someone has killed her."

I automatically looked for Margo, but she was nowhere in sight. Someone had to shut Kathy up, so I moved to her side. "It's all right, Kathy. We don't know who harmed Mrs. Rice, but all the Pier-O-Ettes were together at the time she was killed."

Kathy nodded solemnly. "Oh, yes. We were all together. At the football game."

Chocolate Chat

Chocolate Places: Oklahoma

If you're driving between Oklahoma City and Dallas on I-35, be sure to stop at Bedré Fine Chocolate. It's in Pauls Valley, Oklahoma, exit 70, and it may be the only chocolate company in the world owned by an American Indian tribe.

Bedré is part of the Chickasaw Nation's economic development program. American Indian economic development is associated with gaming, and the Chickasaws do own casinos. But the tribe is a national leader in diversified activities. It acquired Bedré in 2000. Between forty and one hundred people are employed at the showplace plant, depending on the time of year.

The Bedré plant and its retail outlet are well worth a stop. The kitchens are state-of-the-art, with giant vats to melt chocolate and a cooling tunnel five times as long as Aunt Nettie would need at TenHuis Chocolade. The chocolate-making operation is open to public view, and special tours can be arranged.

The plant supplies retailers all across the country. They specialize in chocolate-covered chips and pretzels and candy bars, with lots of other goodies available. And, yes, they offer Oklahoma souvenirs, including chocolate cowboy hats and boots.

Their Web site is bedrechocolates.com.

Chapter 9

Kathy's remark was provocative. Anybody who's ever been to a small-town football game will understand why. A small-town football game is total chaos. There's confused milling around, tackling, signaling, throwing things, yelling, and screaming—and that's just in the stands.

Being at the football game is no alibi at all, unless you're on the team.

I'm joking, sort of. In Warner Pier, just as in my Texas hometown of Prairie Creek, lots of people go to the Friday night high school football game. After all, we all know someone who attends Warner Pier High School. We're likely to know someone who plays on the football team, or marches with the band, or performs with the flag corps—or even someone who sells concessions for some high school club—and we want to see them strut their stuff.

The bleachers at the WPHS stadium hold about five hundred people, and on nearly any Friday night in the fall every seat will be filled. Between three hundred

and four hundred of those people will be from Warner
Pier, with the rest of the spectators supporting the visiting team. Besides the people lining the bleachers,
there are the ones walking around talking. Some people never sit down. They may never even look at the
field.

Joe and I rarely go. I'm tired on Friday nights, and
we both like to catch *Washington Week*. But Aunt Nettie
and Hogan usually are there. Hogan says the police
chief has to know what's going on in his community,
and on Friday nights in the fall, that means football.

But I wouldn't have expected the Pier-O-Ettes to
take in the WPHS football game forty-five years after
they graduated.

I touched Aunt Nettie's arm. "Why did y'all go to
the football game?"

"Ruby's grandson is the quarterback. She's very
proud of him. We just saw part of the second half."

"Did you all stay together?"

"Well, we found seats together. But, you know,
there's always a lot of milling around."

So probably, I thought, none of them could swear
where the others were for the whole game. At least
they were all in one car, Julie's limousine. Even if they
couldn't provide alibis for one another, none of them
had any way to get out to our Lake Shore Drive neighborhood, several miles away, where Mrs. Rice had
been found.

But within a second I knew that argument wouldn't
cut any ice. The stadium was only two blocks from
Aunt Nettie's house. In fact, it's hard to find a place to
park in her block on game nights. Any of the Pier-O-
Ettes could have left the stadium, walked to Aunt Nettie's, picked up her own car, and driven off to meet
Mrs. Rice. It would have taken only a minute to hit her

on the head, and only ten or so to bring the car back to Aunt Nettie's. That late in the game, parking would not have been a problem. Any Pier-O-Ette could have walked two blocks back to the stadium, shown a ticket stub, and reentered the game.

As a matter of fact, the ticket takers usually leave their posts after the half, and the box office closes then, too, so the Pier-O-Ettes probably hadn't even bought tickets.

As I was thinking about all of this, Jackson was asking Aunt Nettie if she had a private room where he could take statements from each of her guests. The only one to raise an objection was Good-Time Charlie McCoy.

"But I wasn't even in Warner Pier last night," he said.

Jackson looked at him coolly. "Then we won't need a statement from you," he said.

He allowed Charlie and Shep to leave. Charlie seemed relieved. Shep, a little more chivalrous, offered to stick around for moral support. But Aunt Nettie and the other Pier-O-Ettes made it clear they didn't require moral support, and Shep followed Charlie out the door. In a moment I heard the motor of the Corvette revving.

Aunt Nettie offered to give the first statement. I guess the police chief's wife has to set a good example.

That meant I still wasn't able to ask her the questions I wanted to ask. Maybe I could ask Hazel some of them.

Hazel had settled on the couch, finally becoming part of the group, just the way Aunt Nettie had urged her to. I was terribly tempted to ask her to go into the kitchen and talk to me, but I didn't. Instead, I picked up the carafe from the coffee table and took it into the kitchen.

Hazel immediately followed me.

Okay, I admit I'd figured she would.

As soon as we were in there, I turned to her. Since any of the group could have come in at any moment, I kept my voice low.

"Hazel, what is the deal with Kathy Street?"

Hazel dodged my gaze. "Deal?"

"Is she disabled? Mentally ill? Why do she and Margo have such an odd relationship?"

"They've always been that way."

"But why?"

"It's their mother's fault, I guess. Kathy . . . Well, I guess you'd say she's in the lower reaches of normal, mentally. She had some kind of brain damage at birth. Kathy and Margo are twins, you know. Not identical, obviously, but twins. Anyway, their mom always made Margo be responsible for her."

"And, of course, Margo is naturally dominant," I said. "It's an odd situation."

Hazel shrugged. "Margo told us Kathy has been diagnosed with something called dependent personality disorder. I guess it's none of my business."

"Why did the trophy frighten Kathy?"

"The trophy?"

"Yes, Hazel. Yesterday I innocently pulled out the trophy y'all won at the Castle Ballroom, and Kathy went—well, I guess the technical term for it is 'bananas.'"

"I don't know why the trophy upset her."

"How about Shep? And Charlie? What does she have against them?"

Hazel looked surprised. "I didn't know she had anything against them. None of us really wanted to see them, but Kathy came out to talk to them like the rest of us."

I decided not to describe the arm-twisting Margo had used to get Kathy into the living room.

Hazel had filled the carafe from the big coffeepot, and she was turning toward the door, obviously heading back to the living room. But I had one more question.

"Hazel, yesterday when Kathy greeted Julie, she asked if Julie had forgiven her."

"Um." Hazel kept walking.

"What was that all about? Why did Julie need to forgive Kathy?"

Hazel turned toward me. Her mouth was like a vise—straight and firm—and she gave me a look that made me feel as if I were being pinched by a vise.

"Let's not bring that up again," she said. "He's been dead more than forty years."

Hazel left the kitchen with a tread so determined it would have taken a bulldozer to stop her. She left me feeling completely blank.

What in the world had she been talking about? At least I knew Kathy and Julie's problem had involved a "he." Probably a boyfriend, since both were teenagers the last time they'd seen each other.

Had they been romantic rivals? It was an odd idea. Kathy was so childlike that the idea of her having a boyfriend was hard to picture. But that was definitely what Hazel's answer had implied.

I wondered who "he" had been. Someone who'd been dead for forty years. That described Dan Rice. But it described a lot of other people as well, of course.

Dan Rice. Hmmm. Was he the reason Mrs. Rice had hated the Pier-O-Ettes? Had she been jealous? Had Dan Rice been one of those men who chase young girls? Hmmm, again.

I left the kitchen. Aunt Nettie was just coming in

from the screened-in porch, where Jackson had set up shop for his interviews. I followed her into the living room.

"Who's next?" Aunt Nettie said cheerfully.

Ruby stood up. "I'll go. Does he just want to know about what we were doing during the time we were at the football game?"

"He wants to know about the whole evening," Aunt Nettie said. "But especially the football game."

"That's easy," Ruby said. "I was right with you."

Aunt Nettie looked slightly surprised, but she didn't say anything.

She sat down, and I knelt beside her. "I guess I'm just in the way," I said. "I'll run along."

"No!" Aunt Nettie's answer was quick. Then she spoke softly. "Stay for a while, Lee. I may need some help."

So I sat on the floor next to Aunt Nettie's chair and listened. Some of the Pier-O-Ettes' conversations were funny and some weren't. Like any six different women, they'd had different experiences since they'd graduated from high school.

Margo brushed off comments about marriage, but the reason she was single seemed pretty obvious to me—Kathy. As long as she felt responsible for giving her sister a home, it was hard to let a man into her life.

"I always concentrated on getting ahead in the company," Margo said. "And it paid off."

Did it ever. I'd read that Margo was among the fifty most highly paid women in American business.

"Kathy has always worked, too," Margo said. "She's a nursery school music teacher."

Everyone made encouraging noises at Kathy. "How wonderful." "That must be really rewarding." "Now we know how you've kept your voice."

Kathy smiled slyly. "Sure. Singing 'Itsy Bitsy Spider' really makes you practice."

There was a moment of awkward silence, and Hazel spoke. "The only singing I've done was church choir."

"Church soloist," Aunt Nettie said.

Hazel shrugged. "It's not a big deal."

"It is to the choir director," Aunt Nettie said. "She's told me how great it is to have a really good singer to rely on."

Kathy smiled brightly. "We're both volunteers, Hazel."

Margo bit her lip.

Watching the Pier-O-Ettes was like watching a soap opera.

One by one the women went out to the screened-in porch to give their statements. One by one they came back. Nobody said much about what they had told Jackson until after he left. Then the conversation burst out.

They also celebrated by passing the chocolates.

A dish of TenHuis molded pastilles—flat pieces of chocolate—had been sitting on the coffee table all morning, and I hadn't seen anybody touch one. As soon as Jackson left, Ruby gave a loud, "Whew!" and reached for the dish. She grabbed a pastille with a silhouette of the old high school and wolfed it down. Julie went for a milk chocolate version of the historic boat. Hazel took a dark chocolate diploma. Kathy nibbled a tiny mortarboard, and Margo ate a replica of the pioneer school. Even Aunt Nettie went for a dark chocolate version of the old Root Beer Barrel, and I had a tiny school.

All of them reported that they had told the detective they stayed together. "Of course, I did go to the restroom," Ruby said. "But I'd come to see Craig play, so I waited until the opposing team had the ball."

Aunt Nettie looked at her lap and frowned.

"I did step around behind the bleachers to make a phone call," Julie said. "I called my assistant."

Aunt Nettie frowned again.

"I'm afraid I sat there like a lump," Hazel said.

Aunt Nettie looked a bit surprised.

"I was with Margo," Kathy said.

Aunt Nettie studied her fingernails.

Margo didn't offer any report on her activities during the game. She obviously wasn't in the habit of explaining her actions.

Aunt Nettie stood up. "I'm going to call about our lunch reservation," she said. "And, Lee, I'm going to ask you to do an errand for me. Come along, and I'll explain it."

I obediently followed her into the kitchen, expecting her to use the phone there to call the restaurant where I knew the Pier-O-Ettes were booked for lunch. But Aunt Nettie walked right by the phone and out the back door. She crossed the yard, with me trailing along, headed for a large evergreen shrub in the corner. She went around the shrub, then turned to face me.

"Lee," she said. "They're all fibbing, and I don't know what to do about it. You're going to have to help me."

Chapter 10

I nearly dropped my teeth all over the lawn.

"Fibbing? How do you know they're all fibbing?" I said.

"I was there, Lee. They did not spend the whole second half innocently sitting in the bleachers."

"What did they do?"

"They wandered. When we got there, a lot of people had already gone home, so we found seats on the fifty-yard line, about halfway up the stands. Immediately—immediately—the girls began to go in different directions."

"I'd already figured out that leaving the stadium without anybody noticing would have been the easiest thing in the world."

"Of course it would! There's always a mob in the stands when the game starts. But the numbers clear out late in the game. All the band parents begin to head for the exits after the halftime show, for example. And people go to the restrooms or to buy coffee—they keep milling around."

"Yes, but it's hard to think of the Pier-O-Ettes joining the milling throng. Mostly people move around to talk to their friends, but three members of your group are from out of town these days. They hardly know anyone to mill with."

"They still got up and walked off. I don't know where they went. I do know I did stay in the group of seats we'd picked. But I was the only one who was there the whole time. Even Ruby left, and she was the one who supposedly wanted to see the game. I was never alone—I mean, some of the girls were with me at all times, but the five of them were never with me all at once. To add to the confusion, of course, people who weren't part of our group came over to talk."

She sighed. "I just can't tell Sergeant Jackson all this."

"I doubt he's even interested. It doesn't really matter."

"It could matter, Lee. I'm relying on you to figure it out."

Her remark didn't make sense to me. "Figure it out? I doubt if anyone could ever figure it out."

"If anyone can, it's you, Lee. And I'm asking you to give it a try."

"Are you asking me to check the Pier-O-Ettes' alibis?"

"Yes. You can talk to people. Maybe someone saw one of them leaving the stadium."

"What? Aunt Nettie, I can't do that! It would take a trained corps of detectives weeks to check on where each of the Pier-O-Ettes was during the game. And even if I were able to do it logistically, Jackson wouldn't like it at all. Why can't you talk to him? If he needs to know, he'll check up himself."

She looked at me pleadingly. She had tears in her eyes. "Lee, these are my oldest friends. I can't tell the police that I don't believe their stories."

"If you think one of them killed Mrs. Rice . . ."

"No! I'm sure none of them would ever hurt any-one."

"Then why do you want their stories checked?"

"Because they've forgotten how small a town this is. Jackson is sure to find out they're not telling the truth. And that's going to make them look bad. If I knew of any   discrepancies, then I could urge that person to tell Jackson herself. That would look much better."

Aunt Nettie smiled through her tears. She seemed to think her convoluted reasoning was convincing, but it sure wasn't to me. I opened my mouth, ready to give her a firm refusal.

Then she put her hand on my arm. "Lee, please help me."

Bang. A direct hit. My life flashed before my eyes. I was sixteen and angry because my parents were get-ting a divorce. Aunt Nettie and Uncle Phil took me in for the summer. Uncle Phil taught me to balance the cash register and other elementary bookkeeping and made me feel grown-up. Aunt Nettie was ready to lis-ten anytime I wanted to talk. Then I was twenty-eight and in despair over my own divorce, and Aunt Nettie took me in again. Again she listened when I wanted to talk, and she convinced me that I was the only person who could save her livelihood. She made me feel use-ful. I owed her—if not my present happy life, then at least the more normal elements of my mental health.

I thought her desire to check the alibis of the Pier-O-Ettes was silly. But if she asked me to swim the one hun-dred miles across Lake Michigan, I'd go put on my bathing suit. I owed her.

"All right," I said. "I'll see what I can do. But if I can't find anything out quickly, I'm going to drop the whole project." I took a deep breath. "And you're the first person I need to ask a few questions."

"Cross my heart, Lee. I sat right in those bleachers. I can give you a list of the people who stopped to talk to me."

"That list would be a good thing to have. But my questions are not about the football game. For beginners, let's go back to yesterday afternoon. Why did Kathy get hysterical when I pulled out the trophy?"

"You think that the trophy brought on her hysterical fit?"

"Well, after you hid the trophy, she calmed down. So I assume *you* think it brought the whole thing on."

"I hid the trophy because Margo signaled for me to do that."

"Oh. But why was the trophy a problem?"

She stared at the tree in front of us. "I have no idea, Lee."

"Did you ask Margo about it?"

"No. We didn't discuss it."

I went on to another question. "Why wouldn't you let Shep come in the house yesterday? And why did you use Kathy's emotional state as an excuse?"

"Kathy tends to be afraid of men. I wanted Margo to prepare her."

"Now we come to the big question. What is Kathy's problem?"

"Her problem?"

"Come on, Aunt Nettie! Don't act innocent. Why is she so dependent on Margo?"

That was the only question Aunt Nettie answered the same way that Hazel had. Kathy had some sort of brain damage, a birth injury, she said. The girls' mother had always insisted that Margo help take care of her.

"You know how kids say, 'You're not the boss of

me.' Well, Margo always was the boss of Kathy. I don't know if that made Kathy dependent or it made Margo dominant."

"Probably both."

Aunt Nettie nodded unhappily. "I admit they have a warped relationship. But, Lee, Margo really does love Kathy. It's not—exploitive. Margo wants what's best for her sister."

I stood there and thought about all this.

"People sure are funny," I said finally. "I'll ask around and see what I can find out about the football game."

My answer pleased Aunt Nettie. "You can start with Maggie McNutt," she said. "The Drama Club was selling concessions last night. Maggie was right by the front gate, running the popcorn machine."

Aunt Nettie went inside then and began to gather the Pier-O-Ettes together to go out to lunch. Afterward they were to meet with the Warner Pier High School choir director to rehearse their numbers for the reunion. They politely invited me along, but I declined. I used lunch with Joe as an excuse, even though I wasn't sure I could find him.

I did one more thing before they left. I got the old friends to pose while I took a photo with my cell phone. No one demurred. I also took several snapshots while they were climbing into Julie's fancy limo. It was what I call a rock-star limo—with a horseshoe-shaped seat lining the back and the left-hand side, lots of flashing lights, and spaces for ice and bottles of refreshments. It was a playful vehicle, and the Pier-O-Ettes were enjoying it.

They'd driven off before I realized I'd forgotten to ask Aunt Nettie one of my key questions: Why did

Kathy ask Julie to forgive her? I'd have to find another opportunity to ask that one.

As soon as they were out of sight, I went to TenHuis Chocolade, called Joe's cell phone, and arranged to meet him for lunch in an hour. I raided the throwaway bin in the back room, helping myself to a mystery chocolate. It turned out to have an exterior decorated to look like a crème de menthe bonbon—a dark chocolate square with white chocolate covering the top—but the interior was raspberry cream. Yummy, but we couldn't sell it.

Then I spent forty-five minutes on the computer, working on the Pier-O-Ette photos I'd taken with my cell phone. I printed up six copies of the group shot, so I could give each of them one as a souvenir. Then I printed close-ups of each of the "girls." When I got through, I had passable individual pictures of each Pier-O-Ette. That might help me in the probably fruitless effort to trace their movements.

At the proper time I walked down to the Sidewalk Café to meet Joe for lunch. The Sidewalk is just a block from my office, and it's one of the few restaurants open in Warner Pier after the Columbus Day weekend, the time when the summer tourist season is finally, definitely over.

Because of that, it wasn't too surprising to see Charlie McCoy's antique Corvette parked near the entrance. He and Shep had to eat lunch somewhere.

I pointed the sports car out to Joe, and we looked it over.

"It's a beauty," Joe said.

"Right!" A voice boomed behind us. "And you can own it for only ten times what it cost originally."

It was Good-Time Charlie, of course. He had come

out of the Sidewalk when he saw us looking at the car. I introduced him to Joe, and Charlie told us about the Corvette.

"It belonged to a little old lady who only drove it to church on Sunday."

"Sure," I said. "Pull the other one."

Charlie grinned. "Actually, it was a high school graduation gift to a girl from a well-to-do Grand Rapids family. She took it to college, but after her freshman year she got married and joined the station-wagon crowd. Somehow the Vette got stored away in her parents' garage. Nobody drove it regularly, but nobody sold it either. Last year the parents' home went on the market, and the lady in question—now well into middle age—finally sold it. I will say she had a very firm grasp of how much it was worth."

"I love it," I said. "Judging by the fact that you don't have a dealer's tag on it, you love it, too. It's your personal car, right?"

Charlie nodded. "Right. It's the car I always wanted when I was a young guy. Actually, now that I think about it, I dreamed of being a taxi driver, but I just couldn't hack it."

Joe and I gave the expected groans. I tapped the Corvette's license plate. The figures on it were 7321.

"Seven times three is twenty-one," I said.

Charlie laughed. "You noticed that."

"I'm a number person. I see patterns in numbers all the time."

"You've guessed my secret. Seven is my lucky number, and so are multiples of seven. But people rarely catch on."

"Joe can tell you I remember numbers," I said. "But sometimes I can't remember why."

"Yes," Joe said. "Early on I learned not to forget her birthday."

I ignored him. "There was some car I saw recently that had a number with a similar pattern. But that one was seven times two equals fourteen."

Charlie stared at me for a moment. "You really are a number person," he said. "Listen, Shep and I just ordered lunch. Why don't you two nice people join us?"

Before I could say no, Joe agreed. I wasn't pleased. I wanted to consult Joe about Aunt Nettie's request, and I couldn't do that in front of Charlie and Shep.

Our lunch was fine, I guess. The Sidewalk food is always good, and the ambiance is fun. The restaurant's décor is inspired by children's sidewalk games, with hopscotch diagrams painted on the floor and with roller skates, antique scooters, and jacks hanging on the walls. It's one of the three restaurants operated by Joe's stepfather, Mike Herrera. Mike wasn't there to come over and greet us, so we didn't mention the connection. We won't let Mike give us a discount.

I couldn't figure out why Joe wanted to eat lunch with Shep and Charlie. The meal was almost over before I caught on.

"I guess you guys both knew Mrs. Rice, back in the old days," Joe said. Shep and Charlie probably thought Joe was just making conversation, but the casualness of his voice told me he'd come to the point.

Joe didn't get an immediate answer. Shep and Charlie just looked at each other. Then they both laughed.

Charlie finally spoke. "Are you trying to get us to speak ill of the dead, Joe?"

"Not unless there's ill to be spoken."

Shep's voice was a growl. "There's not a lot of good. Mrs. Rice was always disagreeable. She was, oh, maybe around forty in those days, and still pretty good-looking. It must have been just recently that she began to look like a witch and act like a bitch. But she and Dan were a pair."

"They fought?"

"Oh, sure. She was determined that the Castle would continue to be 'family oriented.' Dan wanted it to make money."

"I can understand that if he was about to lose the place."

Charlie leaned forward. "It was the sex, drugs, and rock 'n' roll era, you know. Warner Pier was— Well, somebody was selling drugs on nearly every corner."

Shep glared at Charlie. "It wasn't that bad."

"Maybe not, but there was a lot of dealing. Of course, I'm not suggesting Dan could have saved the Castle by opening a drug emporium—not unless he wanted to go to jail. But the Castle was missing out on everything because Verna Rice didn't even want Dan to hire rock groups." He folded his arms. "Some people made a lot of money in Warner Pier back then. But not Verna and Dan. All they did was fight about it."

"It was kinkier than just a disagreement," Shep said. "They liked fighting."

"So they were one of these quarrelsome couples?" Joe said. "The ones who always have it in for each other?"

Shep answered. "They were sweetie-sweet to each other when anyone was around. Never a cross word. It was when the crowd left—when she went in the office and closed the door behind herself. That's when it broke loose."

"I guess you could hear them fighting."

"We couldn't miss it! They must have known that everything said in the inner office could be heard in the outer one." Shep looked at Charlie, and Charlie slowly nodded.

Shep spoke again. "Dan would put the two of us to work in the outer office, see. Counting the gate. Then he and Verna would go into the inner office and go at it. She had a mouth on her!"

"So did he," Charlie said.

"Did it ever come to blows?"

Shep and Charlie both shook their heads. "I used to think she might hit him," Charlie said. "But nobody ever hit anybody while I was there."

"What I can't get over," Shep said, "is that I hear she spent the past forty years 'devoted to his memory.' That's what Nettie called it anyway."

Joe nodded. "That pretty much sums it up. She's fought the courts and the insurance company trying to prove he didn't shoot himself on purpose. She insisted his death must be an accident."

"Of course," Charlie said, "thinking he didn't kill himself and liking him are two different things."

"Yeah," Joe said. "But she apparently refused an insurance settlement because it didn't state clearly that Dan didn't commit suicide."

"I assumed that his insurance had a suicide clause," I said. "Wasn't she just trying to get more money?"

"It may have begun that way, but eventually the legal battle became counterproductive. The lawyers were going to get everything. And she was never able to find a buyer for the Castle property. The banks foreclosed. I doubt she got a penny."

"Joe," I said, "was there any evidence that Dan Rice's death was an accident?"

"I looked up the police report. Dan Rice was shot with his own gun. Accidently or on purpose? Who knows? I suppose it's even possible that somebody else got hold of his gun and shot him. But they did test his right hand for gunpowder residue, and Rice had fired a firearm recently."

"Mrs. Rice's attitude was strange," Shep said. "But if she didn't get the insurance, and she quit her teaching job, then what did she live on all these years?"

"That's a good question," Joe said. "The state police are looking into that right now."

Shep drained the last of his beer. "I'm wondering if she wasn't the one who wrote and asked me to come here."

Chapter 11

Why would Verna Rice have wanted Shep to come back to Warner Pier for the Pier-O-Ettes' reunion? Why would she have wanted that badly enough to write him a letter and sign Aunt Nettie's name to it?

"That's hard to believe," I said. "Did the letter sound like something Aunt Nettie would have written?"

Shep shrugged. "I have no way of knowing. It had been more than forty years since I'd seen Nettie. I wouldn't recognize her handwriting or her writing style. It was a very plain little note."

"Why would Mrs. Rice have written it?" Joe said.

"Because she was nuts!"

"No, I mean why would she want you to come back?"

Shep repeated his previous opinion. "Because she was nuts!" Then he stood up. "Joe, I have no idea why she would have wanted me to come back."

Shep motioned to the waitress for the check. "Come on, Charlie. I'd appreciate a ride back to the motel. And tomorrow I'm heading back to Kentucky."

Joe, Shep, and Charlie argued over who was going

to pay for lunch, and Charlie won. Then Charlie and Shep left. But before they could get out the door, Joe followed them. He talked to Shep a moment. Shep left shaking his head.

I waved at the waitress and asked her to refill our coffee cups. I didn't want to trail out of the restaurant hard on the heels of Charlie and Shep. Besides, now I finally had a chance to talk to Joe.

I moved my chair sideways so I was facing him. "Okay, big guy," I said. "I need to talk to you about Aunt Nettie. But I'll start with an unrelated topic."

"That sounds ominous."

"First, how did you get a look at the file on Dan Rice's death? Frankly, I'm surprised such a thing still exists after forty-five years."

"I've got an in with the chief of police. Married his niece." Joe grinned. "A couple of years ago Hogan dug a copy out of some basement somewhere—he says—just because the case fascinates everybody in Warner Pier, and he wanted to know about it. I called him this morning, and he told me where I could find his copy."

"Why all the questions for Charlie and Shep? Why are *you* interested in Mrs. Rice?"

"She's the victim, Lee. And I find the idea that she might have invited Shep here—pretending to be Aunt Nettie—very interesting."

"I wonder if Shep still has the letter."

"Apparently not. That's what I followed him to ask about. He said he had it until he talked to Nettie. Then, when she denied she'd written it, he was disgusted and threw it away."

"Then there's probably no way to prove Mrs. Rice wrote to him?"

"I'm afraid not. Of course, she may not have written him. The letter may have come from a completely different person."

"Why would anybody write him? I mean, Shep seems like a nice enough guy, but why trick him into coming to a reunion?"

"That might turn out to be a very important question. I sure don't know the answer."

"What did you find out this morning? Cough up."

"I don't really know a lot more. For some reason Mrs. Rice wanted to talk to me. She started out for our house in her big red Buick, but she ran into a tree on the way. She got knocked in the head and died."

"Got knocked in the head? Or was knocked in the head? Apparently Jackson thinks somebody did it."

"I don't know exactly what the medical examiner found, of course. Last night it looked to me as if she'd been hit in the back of the head, when I would have expected the injury to be in the front. I suppose there could be some logical explanation. But since Jackson is taking statements, he must think someone hit her. He's not acting as if it was a traffic death."

I leaned closer to Joe. "Why did Mrs. Rice want to talk to you last night? And why did she want to talk to you immediately?"

"That's a real mystery, since she said she had new evidence, but she wouldn't tell me what it was. I've been trying to figure it out. Now, what were you going to tell me about Aunt Nettie?"

I outlined her request that I try to find out about where each of the Pier-O-Ettes had been during the football game.

Joe looked as amazed as I had felt when I got the original request. Then he laughed. "Why does she care where they were?"

"She claims that if Jackson discovers any of them were lying, he'll suspect them."

Joe laughed. "Nobody could possibly suspect any of those nice ladies of killing anybody."

"Ha-ha! You are so naive, Joe. I assure you that little old ladies can be just as nasty as anybody else."

"True. Think of Mrs. Rice."

"Aunt Nettie and her cohorts aren't *that* nasty. But a defense attorney I live with told me once that anybody can kill if they're pushed hard enough."

"Did I say that?"

"You sure did."

"Well, it's almost true. Anybody but Aunt Nettie could kill."

"Aunt Nettie would kill to protect me. And I'd kill to protect her. Or you."

Joe frowned as he took my hand. "I guess you're right. Because I'd kill anybody who tried to hurt you. Though I'd try to come up with an alternate plan first."

"But I agree that it's hard to picture any of the Pier-O-Ettes luring Mrs. Rice to a spot near our house to kill her."

"She may not have been lured there for that reason. She may have been lured for a different reason and the lurer then decided she needed killing."

"Such as, she tells someone, 'I've told that handsome, athletic lawyer Joe Woodyard I'm on my way to his house, and I'm going to Tell All.'"

"Right. And that someone replies, 'I'll meet you at the big oak tree and explain things.'"

"Did Jackson find anything that could have been used to hit her?"

"If something was used to hit her, Lee, it was the proverbial blunt instrument. It's hard to identify which blunt instrument in an area that contains lots of logs and rocks and tire irons and . . ." He broke off and shrugged.

"How did the killer lure Mrs. Rice out there? Mechanically, I mean. Did he phone? Wire? Send smoke signals?"

"Probably a phone call. But Jackson doesn't have her phone records yet either. He should have them this afternoon."

"That may make the whole thing plain as day."

"True. In case the killer—if there was a killer—used his or her own phone. But most people are smart enough not to do that these days."

I sighed. "Guess I'd better stop this speculation and go ask Maggie if she saw any of the Pier-O-Ettes leaving the football stadium last night."

Joe laughed. "I think that's a waste of time."

"If Aunt Nettie wants my time wasted, who am I to complain?"

I started with Aunt Nettie's suggestion and called Maggie McNutt. Luckily, I found her home. "I'm cleaning house," she said. "I'd love an excuse to stop. Come on over."

Maggie is one of my best friends. She and her husband both teach at Warner Pier High School. Ken teaches math, and Maggie heads the speech and drama department—a department that in a school as small as WPHS consists of herself and one other teacher. Maggie is one of the most popular teachers at WPHS, and it's easy to understand why. She's intelligent, talented, and cute—petite, with dark curly hair. And, or so her students whisper, Mrs. McNutt actually worked in Hollywood. This has a magic ring to her drama students, but Maggie doesn't say much about it. In fact, she's in therapy over some of the things that happened to her in Hollywood. I don't ask questions.

Ken and Maggie live in an older home in one of Warner Pier's Victorian neighborhoods. They've modernized inside but have kept the wooden porch with its gingerbread trim. As I pulled into the drive, Ken waved at me from the garage. He's a Volkswagen hobbyist, and he seemed to have a motor torn apart. I went to the front door and was greeted by Maggie with iced tea.

I took the glass and gulped a mouthful. "Ah! You're one of the few people here up north who can make real iced tea."

"You taught me how, Lee. Thanks for coming by. I was ready for a break. Now, what are you up to?"

We sat down, and I produced my file folder full of pictures, then explained why I was there.

"So Aunt Nettie wants me to find out if any of her friends left the stadium during the second half," I said.

"Gosh, Lee! We were clearing up by then, so we were kind of busy. Nettie's correct when she says we were right there by the entrance, but I certainly wasn't noticing who came and went."

"Take a look at the pictures and see if anybody looks familiar, okay?"

Maggie obediently opened the file folder. Aunt Nettie's picture was on top. "I do remember when Aunt Nettie and her group came in," she said. "The ticket office was already closed, and several of the ladies twittered around by the gate. Apparently they felt guilty about coming in without paying. But Nettie assured them it was all right."

I nodded encouragingly.

Maggie flipped to the next picture. She tapped it with her forefinger. "Yes, Ruby Westfield was in the group. I know her because she helped us with the costumes for *Cinderella*. I remember calling out to her. She waved at me. Then the whole group walked on by and went down the corridor that leads to the field."

She frowned. "I remember that tallish woman who used to work at your shop. I don't know her name."

"Hazel TerHoot."

Maggie shrugged. "I didn't know any of the others."

"Look at their pictures. Maybe you'll remember."

Maggie obediently shuffled through the photos I'd prepared.

"Now this one"—it was Julie—"I think she came back and bought popcorn. I remember telling her it wasn't too fresh, since we'd made it sometime during the first half. She said she didn't mind."

"How about these two?" I held the pictures of Margo and Kathy Street side by side. "They're sisters, and they look a lot alike."

"These pictures don't look alike."

"They're the same type—blond and unusually small. Not just short, but small-boned and delicate-looking. Though their hairdos and styles of dress are completely different."

Maggie stared at the pictures. "I have a vague memory of them being part of the group." Then she laughed. "We need Tracy!"

I laughed, too. Tracy Roderick had worked for Ten-Huis Chocolade from the time she turned sixteen until she left for college, then again the past summer. She'd also been active in the drama club Maggie sponsored. Tracy was a good enough employee, but she had one not-so-good quality. She gossiped. Maggie and I, as her supervisors at work and at school, had continually nagged her about what we considered a bad habit.

But like all good gossips, Tracy was an enthusiastic people watcher. If Tracy had been working at the concessions stand the night before, she would have been able to name every person who bought a candy bar and every person who went through the entrance gate the whole evening. But Tracy was away at college. She was no help to us.

"Yes," I said, "we could use Tracy. She's the second most gossipy person in Warner Pier. Right after Greg Glossop."

"Oh my gosh!" Maggie said. "Greg Glossop was at the football game."

"Ye gods!" I said. "He'll have a minute-by-minute list of who came and went."

Greg Gossip—I mean, Glossop—runs the pharmacy at Warner Pier's only supermarket. He really is the biggest gossip in the town, and the physical layout of his shop gives him a big advantage in collecting information. His pharmacy sits up high, so he can see the whole store. He knows who comes in and which aisles they go down. I will admit that I'd never known Greg to gossip about anyone's prescriptions, but he knows whose kids are coming to visit, who is hitting the liquor department three times a week, and who blew off her diet. You can tell a lot about people by noticing their grocery purchases, and Greg Glossop notices almost everything. And he asks nosy questions about the rest.

But I was astonished to hear that Greg had been at the football game. While Greg Glossop is definitely part of the Warner Pier scene, he doesn't usually turn up at community events. He is not usually seen at concerts, plays, recitals, or other events.

"What was Greg doing at the football game?" I said. "I don't picture him as the fond father of a football player."

Maggie frowned. "He may have been wearing his EMT jacket."

"Of course." Yes, the one community activity that drew Greg Glossop was the volunteer ambulance service. It operates pretty much like a volunteer fire department. If a Warner Pier resident or visitor breaks a leg or suffers a heart attack, Greg is likely to show up to provide first aid and get the victim to the hospital in Holland. And the EMTs always had a crew, complete with ambulance, at the football game, just in case a player got hit too hard or a spectator fainted. Besides, by performing that service, the crew got into the game free.

I finished my tea and left Maggie to her housecleaning. I headed for the Superette, hoping I could catch Greg Glossop.

As I'd hoped, Greg was in his high-up shop at the store. I spoke to him over the counter. "Hi, Greg. When you have a moment, I need to pick your brain."

"I'm pretty much caught up." He went to the end of the counter and opened the door for me. I climbed the three steps that raised his pharmacy above the rest of the store and went in.

I will say that Greg doesn't hold grudges. Aunt Nettie and I trade at the town's other pharmacy, Peach Street Drugstore, but he never seems to hold it against us. He nodded enthusiastically as I explained I was trying to trace the activities of a group of Aunt Nettie's friends at the football game. He didn't even ask the question I had no answer for: Why the heck was I interested?

No, as a person who's always curious about everybody else's business, Greg Glossop seemed to accept my curiosity as perfectly normal. He studied my sheaf of pictures as seriously as if I'd been an FBI agent trying to uncover an international spy ring.

"The Pier-O-Ettes," he said, proving that he knew what was going on around Warner Pier. "I saw the group as they came in. The EMT crew was sitting on the forty-five-yard line. So the ladies were behind us and to the left."

"Oh. If you were on the sidelines, I guess you didn't see if any of them left the stadium."

"I wasn't on the sidelines all the time. I went back out to the concessions stand." He smiled. "They always give the EMTs a free soft drink. I got a Pepsi; then I stood around out there and drank it."

I offered the pictures again. "I'm sure you knew all the locals in Aunt Nettie's group."

"Oh, sure. Ruby Westfield has traded with me forever. And Hazel TerHoot—I see her in the Superette all the time."

"Did you see any of them leave the game?"

"Hazel went over to the restroom. Ruby stood around and talked to several people."

"Did any of them leave the stadium while you were standing there?"

Greg spread the three remaining pictures out on the counter. He leaned over them, frowning.

"This one"—he tapped Julie Hensley's photo— "did. She walked out into the parking lot."

"Did she drive off?"

Greg shrugged. "I don't know, Lee. I wouldn't recognize her car."

"It was a limo. She owns a limo service, and she was driving a big white limousine."

Greg gave a whistle. "I didn't see a limo. They must have driven off while we were packing up the ambulance."

He turned back to the two remaining pictures—the Street twins, Margo and Kathy. "Now, these two—I didn't see them leave. But they did go over to the gate, and one of them made a telephone call."

He smiled. "It was a pretty interesting call."

Chapter 12

Greg Glossop had listened to Margo's call?

That was a new low, even for Greg.

I must have looked horrified, because Greg immediately began to justify himself.

"I didn't listen on purpose, Lee."

Oh sure, I thought.

"But she was standing just outside the fence, and I was inside it, minding my own business. I couldn't help hearing. I mean, she must not have minded, or she would have walked away."

I was disgusted. But was Greg any better than I was? Wasn't I there to spy on the Pier-O-Ettes?

Of course, I did have a reason. Aunt Nettie's request.

I wondered what Margo Street had had to say. What had amused and interested Greg Glossop?

I knew Greg was going to tell me unless I took some drastic action to stop him. Like telling him to shut up.

Oh heck, I thought. Maybe I need to know this.

So I didn't say shut up. I didn't say anything. I sinned by omission and let Greg tell me what he'd heard.

He leaned closer to me and lowered his voice. "I hope Nettie isn't going to give that woman any money. I think she's having trouble paying her bills."

"Margo Street?" My voice must have illustrated complete incredulity.

"This woman." He pointed to her picture again.

"She's a wealthy woman, Greg."

"That may be what everyone thinks, Lee. But I heard what she said. And she said her utilities were being cut off."

Greg was speaking smugly. He obviously believed in the truth of what he was saying.

But it was completely ridiculous. Margo Street was one of the sharpest investors in the United States. People paid big fees for her advice. The idea that she couldn't even pay her household expenses, or that she'd handed the details of her life over to someone so incompetent that her water and electric bills hadn't been paid—it was simply silly.

Of course, anything can happen in life. It was possible that Margo Street had gone from being one of the most influential businesswomen in the United States to being completely broke. The luxury sedan, the beautiful clothes, the original watercolor ordered for each of her fellow Pier-O-Ettes—they could just be leftovers from a previous life of financial success.

But I didn't believe it. No, the Margo I'd met had been too authoritative to be poor.

I had to know more. "Greg, exactly what did she say?"

He closed his eyes and made a big show of remembering. "She said she was calling to check on her utilities."

"Oh!" The light began to dawn.

"Then she said, 'I won't cough up any more.' She seemed to listen for a minute. Then she said, "What about the'—I didn't catch that word—'water'? I'm sure she said 'water.' She listened; then she said, 'Cut 'em off. I can't authorize another penny.' So it sounded to me like she was having her utilities cut off."

I beat back a desire to laugh. "Greg, utilities is a classification of stocks. Margo Street owns an investment firm. Utilities would be stocks she's investing in. She probably meant she didn't want to buy any more utilities stocks."

Greg looked crushed. "I guess I misunderstood."

I said, "It was an easy mistake to make, since you didn't know who she was." And I thought, Maybe this will be a lesson to you, bozo.

I gathered up my pictures, but Greg wasn't through talking.

"That doesn't explain the second call she made."

I mentally rolled my eyes, and I was careful not to look at Greg.

"That call was of a more personal nature," he said. "It was to someone she was planning to meet."

"Oh?" I didn't need to encourage Greg. He kept talking.

"In fact, I think she slipped away and met him right then. At least, I heard her say, 'Ten minutes.'"

Was it time for a little disbelief? I frowned at Greg. "Surely she didn't leave the football game."

"Well, I wouldn't want to say. But she sure didn't come back in that gate. And when I looked outside, she was gone."

"She and her sister?"

"The other blond woman? Small? The other one you have a picture of? No, she didn't leave."

"Where was she?"

"She was sitting on a bench. You know. One of those wooden benches right inside the gate."

"How long was she there?"

"I really can't say, Lee. I had to go back into the game." Greg looked smug. "After all, I had my own business to take care of."

I could have brained him. At the same time, I was ashamed of myself for pumping him. And I was angry with Aunt Nettie for talking me into doing her dirty work. She should have simply laid the law down to her fellow Pier-O-Ettes, told them they had to tell Jackson where they'd been during the game.

How did I get into these messes?

I repacked my file folder, thanked Greg for his information, and left.

What had I learned?

First, Julie Hensley left the stadium during the game.

Second, so did Margo Street.

Third, Margo stashed Kathy on a bench near the gate and apparently left her there. Margo kept such a close eye on Kathy's activities that I was surprised to hear that she went off and left her. Of course, it might have been for only a few minutes. Greg hadn't known how long Margo was gone.

It was strange to find myself wondering why Kathy, a sixty-three-year-old woman apparently of normal intelligence, would have been left alone at a football game.

I wondered if Hazel knew more about Kathy's actions during the game. Hazel had said that after the Pier-O-Ettes found seats in the bleachers, she left to go to the ladies' room. In fact, Greg Glossop had mentioned seeing her headed that way.

The ladies' room at the Warner Pier stadium is not too far from the concessions stand. As Hazel came out, she would have passed close to the bench where Kathy was reportedly sitting. I'd have to ask if she saw Kathy.

But Hazel was rehearsing with the other Pier-O-Ettes that afternoon. There was no way I could talk to her. Or was there? Aunt Nettie had recently decided to join the modern world and had acquired a cell phone. I hastily called her number, thinking that she might talk to Hazel. As I expected, Aunt Nettie's phone was turned off, but I left a message, asking her to call me.

Of course, I had no idea when Aunt Nettie would get around to checking her messages, but maybe she'd let me know when the rehearsal was over.

Meanwhile, I wandered back to my office. After the activities of the morning and early afternoon, I felt at a loss. What could I do that might help figure out what was going on?

The answer came from a newspaper I noticed lying on the corner of my desk. It was a copy of the latest issue of the *Warner Pier Gazette*, our local weekly. Suddenly I realized I had not yet looked at contemporary accounts of the death of Dan Rice.

I plunked myself into my chair and fired up the computer.

Modern public libraries are wonderful. Warner Pier's little library is part of a larger system that takes in maybe twenty communities in west Michigan. And the system has access to the files of around a dozen newspapers.

This means that instead of going to the newspaper office or to the library's microfilm, a researcher can read old newspapers online. I can sit at a computer—either in my office or at home—and call up newspaper stories of forty-five years ago. Or a hundred years ago. Or last year. And I can read them in the middle of the night. While wearing my pajamas. For free.

I love libraries.

I called up the *Warner Pier Gazette* files of forty-five

years ago and paged through until I found a huge headline: SHOOTING DEATH.

The words were gigantic. Underneath was the real headline: OWNER OF CASTLE SHOT TO DEATH.

Then another, smaller headline stretched clear across the page: BODY OF WARNER PIER BUSINESS LEADER FOUND IN OFFICE.

The mysterious death had happened early on a Sunday morning, not a good time for a weekly newspaper that published on Thursday. So the *Gazette* had put out a special edition on Tuesday.

The story—written in a breathless style that revealed the reporter's excitement—said that during a routine patrol at about three a.m. Sunday, the Warner Pier policeman had seen lights inside the ground-floor offices of the Castle Ballroom. Since the Castle would ordinarily be locked up tight at that time, he had investigated, approaching a door that opened into the office from the deck.

When he knocked on it, the door swung open.

That, I gathered, was the first suspicious circumstance. The door should have been locked, even if Dan Rice was there.

The patrolman called out, then went inside. There he found Dan Rice lying on the floor behind his desk, shot through the heart.

A pistol was near his right hand.

As I read the story, I realized how much emergency services had changed in the past forty-five years. The patrolman, whose name was Oscar VanWick, was apparently the only lawman in the village of Warner Pier in those days, and he seemed to function more as a night watchman than as a cop. The only help he could call on was the county sheriff's office. The volunteer EMTs west Michigan has today apparently didn't exist. An ambulance came from South Haven, but Dan Rice had been dead for some time.

Oscar VanWick called the home of Dan Rice, of course, and Verna Rice drove—in her big red Buick, I speculated—down to the Castle. She became hysterical and had to be restrained from rushing in the door of the office. Friends had taken Mrs. Rice home, and her doctor had given her a sedative, the newspaper reported.

That was the end of the story for the *Gazette*'s special edition.

I switched my reading to the Holland newspaper. I was sure that as the closest town with a daily newspaper, it would have thoroughly covered a major event like Dan Rice's death.

I was right. The *Holland Sentinel* headline stretched across the bottom of the front page: OWNER OF FAMED BALLROOM FOUND DEAD.

Their first story had much the same information as the *Gazette*'s. But during the next week, a lot of things happened.

Dan Rice was buried in the Warner Pier Cemetery. Investigators said he was killed by a single shot to his heart and that the injury could have been self-inflicted.

But the story changed in the next day's issue.

The Castle's two bouncers, Charlie McCoy and Sheppard "Shep" Stone, had been the last two employees to leave the Castle. Both had gotten off work around one a.m. Both reported that Dan Rice had said he planned to put the night's gate in the safe, then go home.

But the assistant manager of the Castle, Phin Vandercamp, said the night's money was missing.

What? Robbery?

In all the tales I'd heard about the Castle, I'd never heard that robbery was involved in its owner's end.

The Saturday night income might have been significant for the Castle Ballroom. That had been the night the big talent competition was held, the one the Pier-O-Ettes had won. It should have attracted a large number of local people, as well as summer visitors.

I was eager to know more as I went on to the next day's edition. The idea of a robbery added excitement to the whole series of events. And in the next edition I discovered a complete change in the story.

As soon as she heard that the money was reportedly missing, Mrs. Dan Rice called the newspaper, breaking her silence to make her first statement since the shooting.

"The money from Saturday night's events at the Castle Ballroom is quite safe," she said. "My husband brought it home just after closing. He then went back to the ballroom to do some paperwork. Our assistant manager, Mr. Vandercamp, was mistaken. I consider his statements extremely irresponsible."

The Warner County sheriff said she hadn't told them earlier that she had the money, and his deputies had been searching for it for several days, not knowing if it had been stolen or not. They hadn't asked Mrs. Rice about it, he said, because she had claimed to be too distraught to talk to the investigating officers.

The sheriff's statement definitely had an air of annoyance.

He certainly would have had a right to be annoyed. If law enforcement had wasted time investigating the possibility of a robbery when that wasn't a possibility—well, it would have angered a saint.

But I was interested to learn about this assistant manager Phin Vandercamp. None of the Pier-O-Ettes had ever mentioned him. Neither had Shep or Charlie.

They'd spent the morning reminiscing about former waitresses and even the janitor. But no mention of an assistant manager had come up.

Phin. It was an odd name. I wondered if his name had been Phineas. I wondered what had become of him.

I was ready for a break from reading old newspapers anyway. I walked around the office and ate a square of chocolate from the throwaway bin. I snatched one up at random, and it turned out to be a tiny replica of the old Warner Pier High School building. The design on top hadn't come out right. Then I checked the time. Yikes! Nearly five thirty. It was getting dark rapidly. I needed to think about dinner. Joe and I had eaten out for dinner the night before and for lunch that day. I ought to cook something. The thought didn't thrill me. I mentally catalogued the contents of the freezer and remembered a plastic dish containing leftover ham jambalaya. If I added a tossed salad and a can of green beans . . .

I also needed to report to Aunt Nettie. As her designated investigator, I ought to tell her the few things I'd found out. I called her home number and got the answering machine. Had the Pier-O-Ettes gone on to dinner? I told the machine I needed to come by and that I'd call back.

Then I called my patient husband, who didn't sound as patient as usual when he answered the telephone ("I've been wondering where you are"), and I promised to be home within a few minutes. He agreed to take the ham jambalaya out of the freezer, and I told him I'd bring a box of his favorite bonbons—double fudge ("layers of milk and dark chocolate fudge with dark chocolate coating").

I gave him a sweetie-sweet good-bye. "I'm so eager to see you, darling!"

Joe laughed as he hung up the phone. We get along pretty well. Usually.

I picked up eight bonbons for Joe, put on my jacket, and made sure the front door was locked.

By then it was five forty-five and only a faint light showed in the western sky I had parked in the alley behind the store, where I have a reserved space I don't use too often once the heavy tourist season for Warner Pier is past. So I now had to go out the back door and into the dark alley to get to my car—in lonely downtown Warner Pier, where every other business for several blocks around was closed and where nobody but Dolly Jolly lived. And Dolly had gone to see her cousin in Grand Rapids for the weekend. I hesitated before I opened the back door.

Then I laughed at myself. There is very little crime in Warner Pier. I wasn't afraid to walk down any street in the town or, yes, any alley in the town. Certainly not my own.

I set the burglar alarm, turned on the outside security light, and went out. I slammed the door behind myself and tested the handle to make sure it was caught. Then I walked around my van to reach the driver's side.

I always drive a minivan. They may not be cool, but they sure are handy for delivering chocolate. My dad finds me a good deal in a used van nearly every year. The current one was a light green Chevy, five years old.

As I walked around it, I did exactly what my dad had trained me to do. From the time I could drive, he lectured me: Don't ever get into a car—daytime or nighttime—without looking into the back to be absolutely certain that no bad guy is lurking there. I had done this since I had a driver's license. And never had anything or anyone unexpected been in my car.

But it was a good habit. So I glanced into the cargo area. Then I looked into the backseat.

And there was somebody crouched on the floor.

Chocolate Chat

Chocolate Places: Pennsylvania

Mort Rosenblum, author of *Chocolate: A Bittersweet Saga of Dark and Light*, calls Hershey, Pennsylvania, "as American as Old Glory."

Hershey was founded in 1903 by Milton Hershey, creator of the immortal Hershey Bar, Hershey's Kisses, and many other all-American treats. He planned the city as a company town, a place where workers in his factory could live wholesome lives while milk and butter for his chocolates were produced in the surrounding countryside. A giant chocolate factory opened in 1905, and the city's slogan became "The Sweetest Place on Earth."

Today Hershey is a city, but also a giant fun park. There's Hersheypark, with sixty-five rides and attractions, including eleven roller coasters. There are shows at theaters and outdoor arenas. There's the Hershey Bears hockey team, plus the Hershey Gardens, Dutch Wonderland for children, a special area on falconry, and ZooAmerica. Then there are two museums: Hershey's Chocolate World, which explores how chocolate is made, and the Hershey Story, which tells of Milton Hershey's life. "All-American" is an understatement. But the once-famous tours of the Hershey chocolate factory are no longer offered.

Hershey's Web site is www.hersheypa.com.

Chapter 13

It must have been disbelief that kept me from scream-ing.

It just wasn't possible that there was actually some-body in my car. For a split second I thought it was a joke. Then my nerves caught up with me, and I jumped all over and dropped my car keys.

That turned out to be a good thing. The keys rattled and clunked as they hit the pavement. "Darn!" I said.

I leaned over, used the tiny flashlight on my "no-harm charm" chain, and began to look for them. I found them almost immediately, picked them up, and pocketed them. But I didn't stand up. I kept creeping along beside the van, my head down, pretending to look for those keys.

When I got to the back of the van I split for the back door of the shop. In a hurry.

I admit that I had to punch in the numbers on the keypad twice. It's hard to look at numbers when you're keeping your back turned toward the keypad so you can see the van and make sure no one is getting out of it to come after you.

When the door clicked open, that click was the most beautiful sound I had ever heard. I jumped inside like a kangaroo. The sound of the door slamming and locking behind me was even more beautiful than the sound of it opening.

I was in our break room, standing with my back to the locked door and panting with the adrenaline rush.

I had pulled out my cell phone as I moved toward the door, and now I wanted to call 9-1-1. Actually, I wanted to stand inside that door, keeping it open a crack, and watch the van while I called the police. But that wasn't going to work. In ten seconds the fancy alarm system we had installed a few months earlier was going to sound off and blast the whole neighborhood. And if it did, the guy in the van was going to jump out and take off down the alley.

And I realized that I didn't want him to do that. I wanted him to stay where he was until the police got there.

Besides, leaving the door ajar while I called the cops seemed pretty stupid. Something like yelling, "Come on in, sex maniac."

So I made double sure the heavy steel door had locked behind me, flipped on the break room lights, and ran into the storage room to punch in the magic numbers that kept the alarm from blasting.

With that done, I was finally able to call 9-1-1. Because it was after five o'clock, when our local police department shuts down its office, I got an operator thirty miles away in the county seat. First she made sure I was in a safe place. Then she told me she'd have the Warner Pier patrolman there as quickly as possible.

"He's clear down by the south city limits," she said. "Some car slid into the ditch."

I knew that was a ten-minute drive, even if the patrolman left the other people sitting in the ditch.

"Stay on the line," the operator said.

She didn't say that I couldn't look out the back door while I waited for the patrolman.

Luckily, that door opened in, I guess to keep people from swinging it out and hitting passing trucks. So I'd have to open it only a crack to see what was going on.

I still tried to be careful. First I shoved one of the two family dining room–sized tables up against it, leaving a small amount of leeway. If the guy in my backseat ran at the door when I unlatched it, he'd have to move not only the door but also the heavy table before he could get in. Then I jammed a strong rubber doorstop in position to hold the door if anyone tried to open it more than a tiny bit. Next I turned out the kitchen light.

Finally, I opened the door about half an inch and peeked out.

The section of the alley I could see was deserted. The outdoor light was still on.

So were the van's interior lights.

I think that scared me more than anything else had. Maybe I'd been trying to convince myself that I'd just seen an old blanket or some other innocuous item in the floor of my backseat. I'd still harbored a hope that I had imagined the whole thing, that there had been nobody there.

Those interior lights told me differently. They meant that at least one of the van's doors was open, and I'd left all of them closed and locked.

And I could see which one was open. It was the back door on the driver's side, on the opposite side of the van from where I was now standing. It opened like a regular car door, instead of sliding back and forth as some van doors do, and it was completely agape.

And as I realized that, I heard footsteps. Thud-thud-thud-thud. Fast and heavy.

Someone was running down the alley, headed toward Pear Street.

I reported all this to the 9-1-1 operator, and at the same time I began to remove my barricade.

"He's getting away!" I said. I shoved the table, and it made a scraping sound.

"What's that noise?" she said.

"I'm moving the table I put in front of the door."

"Why?"

"So I can get out."

"Why?"

"Maybe I can get a look at him."

"No! No! Mrs. Woodyard, stay where you are!"

"I'm not going to run after him! I just want to get a look at him."

By then I had the door open far enough that I could slip through. I ran around the van and stared down the alley, still clutching the cell phone.

"Darn! He just turned onto Pear Street! Toward the lake."

"Get back inside!"

"I'll get in the van."

"No!" She didn't like my ideas, but I pretended not to hear. My purse was hanging on my shoulder, and my car keys were attached to its side pocket. I yanked them out. I slammed the backseat door—yes, first I looked to make sure there was no one in there or in the cargo area—and I got into the driver's seat. I started the motor, and I headed down the alley. The 9-1-1 operator was still objecting to everything I did, but I gave her a running account anyway.

"I just turned onto Pear Street."

"Go back! Wait for the patrolman!"

"Nobody's moving on the street. I'll cruise on down to Dock Street."

"No! He may be armed!"

"I can't just let him get away!"

"I have two cars on the way. The state police and the Warner Pier officer. He won't get away."

I tossed the phone into the passenger seat then, though I didn't break the connection. I drove slowly toward Dock Street, looking into every doorway.

Then I saw something move. A human figure. I picked up the phone.

"He's turned into the alley between Fourth and Fifth streets."

The operator's voice got really firm. "Don't follow him! Mrs. Woodyard! Go back to the shop!"

I turned into the entrance to the alley.

"I just want to see which way he goes."

"He may be armed. Mrs. Woodyard, go back! He may have a gun."

A gun. She could be right.

She didn't yell, because 9-1-1 operators are trained always to sound calm. But she spoke like she meant what she said. "Don't follow him!"

"Okay! Okay!" I backed out of the alley and turned toward Dock Street. I gunned the motor and sped to the end of the block. Then I drove a block down Dock Street, going as fast as I dared. I swung around that corner in a wide left turn. I pulled into the darkest parking place on the block, turned off my headlights, and sat there, wishing my van wasn't a light color. I waited to see if anyone came out of the other end of that alley.

There wasn't a single car parked on that block. Downtown Warner Pier was deserted. I waited. And waited.

After three long minutes, I knew my plan hadn't

worked. The person I'd been chasing had beaten me to the street and had gotten away. Or else he was hiding in the alley. And I wasn't going in after him.

I waited another minute—still no cops, and still no crook. Just me, alone in Warner Pier's quaint business district.

I had the phone to my ear, and the operator was telling me to go back to the shop.

"The cars are coming," she said. "Jerry Cherry was out by the interstate working that wreck, and the state police car was nearly to South Haven. But they'll be there any minute. I told them you were safe inside the building."

"I'll go back," I said.

I did. But I admit I took the long way. I flipped a U-turn and went back to Dock Street. I went left. And I came to Herrera's parking lot.

"Herrera's parking lot has a half dozen cars in it," I said. "Anybody could be there."

"Go back to your office," the operator said. She sounded angry. "Go to the front. Park there. Lock the car door. Do not get out of the car."

I laid the phone down again. I had to turn around somewhere, so I drove into Herrera's lot.

Herrera's is Warner Pier's nicest restaurant, the one Aunt Nettie had selected to entertain the Pier-O-Ettes at lunch. Because it's a white-tablecloth place, its dinner crowd comes in late-ish. At the moment, just before six o'clock, the parking lot was just beginning to fill up. None of the cars looked unusual. None had a bumper sticker that read MOLESTERS UNITE or anything else that singled it out as likely to belong to the person who had tried to waylay me.

As I drove I noticed something. My van was becoming very hard to steer. And it was leaning to the left.

Did I have a flat?

I toyed with the idea of parking at Herrera's and running inside, but I decided against it. Flat or no flat, I wasn't stopping. I was getting back to the shop to meet the cops.

I drove out of the parking lot slowly—still searching the sidewalks and alleys—and I went back to the shop. I had to fight the steering wheel every foot of the way, but I managed. I turned into a parking place at the curb, and I threw on the brakes.

As the van came to a halt, I heard a chugging sound. It was a motorcycle, or maybe a motor scooter. And it wasn't far away.

"He's on a motor scooter or something!" I yelled the words at the 9-1-1 operator.

The idea of a motor scooter was reassuring. If the guy was armed, he'd have to be an acrobat to fire a gun while riding a motor scooter.

Maybe I could still get a look at him. I was out of my parking space and back on the chase in a flash. Ignoring the van's desire to pull to the left and to tip over, I drove around the corner and poked the nose of the van into the alley—the one behind TenHuis Chocolade. It was dark in there. I flashed my headlights to high, and I saw movement at the other end of the block.

It was beyond the reach of my headlights, but it was movement. I headed down the alley as fast as I dared. If I had to buy new tires, okay. I wasn't going to give up my try at getting a look at this guy.

Of course, going down a narrow alley, dodging Dumpsters and piles of boxes and the other stuff people tend to stack in alleys, made me feel as if I was speeding madly. In reality, I was probably going thirty miles an hour, bouncing along with the right side of my van higher than the left.

I hadn't had a clear view of the motor scooter, but I had an impression that it had turned left. When I came out at the other end of the block, I spun the wheel and went in that direction. This brought me back to Fifth Street. And Fifth had streetlights—the type that shed pools of light every thirty feet or so up and down the block. I should be able to see the fleeing motor scooter.

But no. The street was completely empty. Not a pedestrian, a car, a truck, a bicycle, a rickshaw, or a motor scooter in sight. I lowered my side window a few inches and listened. No noise. No motor scooter. No nothing.

I growled into the cell phone. "He must have gone toward Dock Street."

"I don't care where he went. You go back to your shop. Now!"

I decided it was time for me to obey.

"Yes, ma'am." I tried to sound meek. I went to the front of the shop, and I parked. This time I was directly under a streetlight, just two doors down from the corner of Peach Street.

I turned off the motor. This, of course, unlocked my doors, so I hit the magic button and relocked them.

I sat there, listening. There was no sound of a motor scooter. There was no sound of a siren. I was completely alone. I debated getting out of the van to look at my flat, but I decided it was pointless. I couldn't tell what caused it in the dim light. I'd probably picked up a nail in my travels through Warner Pier's alleys. Getting out of the car wasn't a good idea.

I'd wait for the cops.

As soon as that decision had been made, I heard a noise.

It was a footstep. Normally, that's not a very frightening noise, but it made my heart leap into my throat.

I stared frantically around, trying to tell the direction the sound had come from.

The first footstep was followed by more, but still no one was in sight. I picked up the phone, still connected to the 9-1-1 operator, and started to tell her someone was approaching. I assured myself that I was safe from unknown pedestrians; after all, I was locked in my van.

Then, startlingly fast, a man in a ski mask ran around the corner and headed straight toward me.

I screamed. I hit the horn. And I turned the key in the ignition.

I'm locked in, I told myself. I'm locked in.

The man ran up to the van and reached out his hand. I saw he was wearing gloves.

And in his gloved hand was a key.

He used it to unlock the door of my van.

Chapter 14

I daily thank heaven for three things.

First, I had the car window down a few inches.

Second, the person who unlocked my door had on a ski mask, which has eyeholes, rather than a motorcycle helmet of the type that covers the whole head.

Third, one of the useful items on my "no-harm charm" chain was—ta-da!—pepper spray.

I yanked the chain out of its pocket, found the pepper spray, flipped its top open, and made a direct hit on the left eyehole of the guy's mask just as the door lock clicked open.

He grabbed at his left eye, and I aimed for the right one.

I've never known if I hit it or not. The van's motor had caught, and I took off. I might be tipped sideways and traveling on the rim of my left front tire, but I was getting out of there.

As soon as I had a free hand, I began honking madly. The door the guy had unlocked automatically re-locked, and I closed the window. I headed toward Herrera's. There were people there. I should have stayed there in the first place.

As far as I could tell, nobody was following me. I thumped into Herrera's parking lot, pulled into a handicapped parking place—it was closest to the front door—and jumped out clutching my keys in one hand and my phone and "no-harm charms" in the other.

The van was no longer my sanctuary, my fort on wheels. I ran up the front steps of the restaurant and banged in through the front door.

Now I realized that the 9-1-1 operator was talking on my phone. "What's going on? Mrs. Woodyard!"

"I'm okay! I'm inside Herrera's. He didn't follow me."

I leaned against the wall and panted. Then I realized that my old friend Lindy Herrera, night manager of the restaurant, was standing near the door. She looked scared to death. "Lee! What's wrong!"

I shushed her. She listened while I told the operator what had happened. "I'm waiting here," I said. "What's taking the cars so long?"

Her reply sounded petulant. "I told you it would be ten minutes."

Ten minutes? It seemed as if I'd been chasing around Warner Pier's downtown streets and alleys for an hour. But when I looked at my watch, I realized it had been just over five minutes.

Lindy brought me a chair and a glass of water, and I sat down. And I sat. And sat. Since I was safe, finally, the Warner Pier patrolman and the state police car checked out every crack in the pavement in downtown Warner Pier before they came to check on me. It was a third car that arrived at Herrera's. A woman officer in a state police uniform came in to interview me.

Just after she came in I heard steps running up to the front door, and Joe rushed in.

We fell in each other's arms with lots of "How did you know what happened?" and "Why didn't you call me?" remarks. Lindy took us into a private dining room that wasn't in use, and Joe and the state police officer listened to my story.

I didn't get a whole lot of sympathy.

When I came to the part where I cracked the back door so I could look out into the alley, Joe gave a loud, "What!" And when I told about running back out to try to get a look at the guy who'd been in the van, he got up and stomped all around the room, shaking his head, before finally sitting back down. After that he didn't look at me.

When I'd finished talking, I looked at him. "I don't know what's wrong with the tires, Joe."

He got to his feet. "Neither do I, Lee, but it sounds as if the guy you were chasing slashed them."

"Slashed them?"

"Yes." Joe's voice was angry. "He was trying to keep you from chasing him. But what he got was something even better. He was able to trap you out in the open, with no one to help you. You are damn lucky to be alive."

I glanced at the state police officer. She didn't say anything, but she didn't tell me I'd been brave either. It was obvious she agreed with Joe.

Joe headed for the door. But before he left the room, he stopped and turned around to glare at me. "You can sure be stupid, Lee."

He left. I was surprised that he didn't slam the door.

And I lost it. My temper, that is.

Oh, I didn't yell and scream and throw things. But Joe had pricked my ego in a way that . . . Well, right at that moment I believe I could have killed him.

I sat back in my chair and folded my arms. An un-known person had been hiding in my van, lying in wait for me. And I'd not only discovered he was there, by exercising a habit of caution, but I'd also had the presence of mind to pretend I hadn't seen him and to call the police. Then, when he'd tried to get away, I'd chased him, trying to get a look at him.

I wasn't trying to capture him or even to confront him. I just wanted to get a look at him. To know if he was small or tall.

I suppose it's a good thing that I was too mad to cry. The release tears can bring would have felt good at that moment, but I'd been so scared—well, if I had let down, I would have fallen apart completely. And that's not okay. Not for me. I can't lose control completely and keep my good opinion of myself.

Yes, I'm quoting my therapist. When I left my first husband—Rich the rich guy—my whole family and all my friends thought I was crazy. I couldn't figure out how to explain to them that I felt as if Rich thought he had bought me. I was just another toy, a trophy to show his status. If I complained, he bought me a piece of jewelry or a new Lexus. He expected me to think those things were as good as respect and love.

Anyway, I began to think my family and friends might be right. Maybe I *was* crazy. So I went to a coun-selor.

Luckily, I found one who thought Rich was crazy, not me. But the counselor helped me make a list of qualities I valued and wanted to have.

First on the list was intelligence.

Oh, I know. Brains aren't as important as kindness, as concern for others, as love. After all, Rich the rich guy was smart, even though he was a jerk. But the counselor helped me realize that I'm a reasonably intelligent person and that it's important to me for that to be recognized.

I'm sure it's the result of years of being told I was pretty, then having people act surprised to learn that I made good grades. And years of saying the wrong word—hello, Mrs. Malaprop—and having people laugh at me.

I dropped out of counseling before I analyzed the reasons completely. All I know is that if someone says I'm dumb, stupid, unintelligent, that "the light's on, but nobody's home"—it cuts me to the quick.

And Joe had just said it.

The fact that in this particular case he might be right was immaterial. He could say I was impulsive or that I hadn't used good judgment, and I could shrug it off. But saying I was stupid was unforgivable.

Joe knew that.

I folded my arms and sat back in my chair. I waited. I kept my mouth shut.

I was still sitting there, immobile and steaming, when Joe came back in and said we could go home.

"The wrecker is going to tow the van into Holland," he said. "I hope—Ms. Financial Manager—you have a few bucks put aside for new tires and maybe wheels, because you're the one who cut us back to the thousand-dollar-deductible car insurance."

Well. No need to wonder if Joe was still mad. He was. So was I. But I wasn't going to display my anger.

So I smiled sweetly. "That's what the savings account is for, Joe. Emergencies. I think I left my purse in the van. I'll get it."

I stood up and went outside, still steaming. And my cell phone rang.

It was in the pocket of my jacket. I pulled it out and

saw Aunt Nettie's number displayed on its tiny screen. I assumed she'd heard about the man hiding in the van and chasing me. She probably wanted reassurance.

I punched the TALK button. "I'm fine," I said.

"Well, I'm glad to hear that, Lee. Why wouldn't you be?"

So Aunt Nettie hadn't heard about the chase. I took a deep breath and decided not to tell her right that moment. "No reason. What can I do for you?"

"The question is, what can I do for you? I'm returning your call."

"Oh." Then I remembered that I'd called her, ready to make a report on what I'd found out about the Pier-O-Ettes' activities during the football game. That had been hours earlier.

"I wondered if you were ready for a report on that research project you gave me," I said.

She thought that over before she answered. "Have you told Joe what you found out?"

"I haven't had a chance, but he knows what I was doing."

"Why don't the two of you come over for dinner?"

Joe had joined me on the sidewalk outside Herrera's, so I turned to him. "Aunt Nettie wants to know what I found out about the Pier-O-Ettes and the football game. She's invited the two of us for dinner."

Joe's face was still stony. "I'll drop you off."

He walked over to his truck.

I felt madder than ever. But I managed to use a calm tone of voice as I told Aunt Nettie I'd be there in a few minutes. I was tempted to tell Joe I'd walk to her house—it was five or six blocks away—but I didn't really want to do that, and he was so mad he might have let me. So I got my purse and climbed into the truck without a word.

We had to wait while the wrecker from Holland drove off with my van. Then Joe drove me to Aunt Nettie's. Neither of us said anything on the way. I would have gotten out of the truck without a word, but Joe reached over and caught my arm.

"Please do not go off on any more wild chases, Lee."

"I imagine Aunt Nettie will keep my time occupied."

Joe didn't reply directly. All he said was, "I'll be back for you in an hour."

"Thank you. I'd appreciate a ride home."

I got out and went to the house. Joe sat there watching until I was inside.

All the Pier-O-Ettes were apparently feeling festive, or at least talkative. The noise level was not low. And dinner was ready. Aunt Nettie had made lasagna, with salad and garlic bread. I'm sure it was delicious to someone who had an appetite.

My appearance threw the table off-balance, of course, and I got some questioning looks from some of the "girls." But Aunt Nettie didn't explain my presence until after everyone had finished their main course.

Then she had to wait while Ruby finished a slightly ribald story about her third wedding. As soon as the laughter died, Aunt Nettie grabbed the floor.

"Now, girls, I'm sure you're all wondering why I asked Lee to join us this evening."

They chorused assurances that I was a delightful addition to the party, but Aunt Nettie ignored that.

"The truth is," she said, "Lee is my right-hand helper in nearly everything I do. And I gave her a project this afternoon."

She paused for effect, then went on. "I'm afraid some of you have forgotten what a small town Warner Pier is—even some of us who live here. I'm afraid not all of us were strictly factual with what we told Lieutenant Jackson about our activities at the football game last night."

Nervous laughter.

"So I asked Lee to check things out."

The first objection came from Margo Street. "You checked our stories?" I wasn't surprised to hear how irate she sounded.

"I asked Lee to do that." Aunt Nettie was perfectly calm. "I wanted each of you to see just how easy it is to find things out in a town like Warner Pier."

"I didn't lie," Margo said.

Aunt Nettie looked at me. I produced the notes I'd made and began. "I'm afraid you omitted some information, Ms. Street. Our chief Warner Pier gossip is a man named Greg Glossop. Greg happens to be part of the volunteer ambulance team, and they were at the football game last night. He overheard you making two phone calls. And he claims you agreed to step outside the game and meet someone."

Margo Street turned purple. "That was perfectly innocent!"

"I'm sure it was," I said. "But it apparently isn't what you told Lieutenant Jackson. Don't feel too bad. You weren't the only one who had a few discrepancies in her story."

I outlined the rest of the things I'd found out. Julie Hensley had also slipped out of the stadium. Hazel had gone to the restroom and stayed inside longer than she had indicated. Ruby had come out of the stands and talked to people. Then she seemed to disappear.

"As far as I can tell," I said, "Kathy Street was the only person who didn't disappear for a while. She was sitting on a bench near the entrance gate. And Aunt Nettie claims that she stayed in the bleachers and says she has witnesses to prove it. I haven't checked that out yet."

"You'd even check on Nettie?" Margo sounded horrified.

"I asked her to." Aunt Nettie was calm. She sounded as if she was explaining something factual, like why TenHuis chocolates did not contain preservatives. "Lee and I are not planning to follow up on this information in any way. I'm sure each of you had a logical—and innocent—reason for the things you did. But I do plan to call Lieutenant Jackson and set up another round of statements. And I think it would be very wise for all of you to come clean."

"Come clean!" "But I didn't do anything!" These and similar remarks rang out all around the table. The only person who didn't say anything was Kathy Street. She looked around the table, seeming rather excited. I wondered if she understood what was going on.

Aunt Nettie quelled the little rebellion with a gesture. "Lee's inquiries have shown you how easily the authorities will be able to find out if your statements to Jackson weren't exactly true. It won't matter if you amend them yourselves. But if he finds out you fibbed, you could be in trouble."

She stood up. "You think about it while I get the dessert. Lee, will you help me clear?"

The two of us gathered up dirty dishes and left the table. The others sat in silence. But when we got into the kitchen I heard the voices begin to buzz. When I went back for more plates and salad bowls, they were hard at it. I ignored a few angry looks and kept on playing waitress.

We had served everyone with chocolate mousse and were just pouring the coffee when the doorbell rang.

"That's probably Joe," I said. "My van's out of commission, so he was going to pick me up."

Aunt Nettie went herself to let him in. He declined

dinner but accepted an invitation to join the Pier-O-Ettes for dessert. Everyone scooted around to make room for another place, and I introduced him to the people he hadn't met earlier.

Finally we were seated for dessert, and the Pier-O-Ettes pulled that little stunt that I've noticed before. Even successful, confident women do this. They all looked at Joe, deferring to the man among them, waiting for him to start the conversation.

Joe didn't let them down. He addressed the table at large. "Did Lee tell you someone tried to kill her tonight?"

Chapter 15

The Pier-O-Ettes gave a mass gasp.

Then the talk began. All of them demanded to know what Joe was talking about. What had happened? Who had tried to kill me? Joe had to be mistaken.

Joe shrugged, and I had to tell it.

I tried to make it—well, funny. More like an adventure than an exercise in terror. I thought I was doing pretty well until I saw that Aunt Nettie had pulled a tissue from her pocket and was wiping her eyes. Of course, then I had to stop talking and find my own tissues.

I glared at Joe, who had been calmly eating his chocolate mousse while I talked. My voice came out as a croak. "I didn't tell them, Joe, because I didn't want to frighten Aunt Nettie. Or anyone."

He raised his eyebrows. "Just me?"

I ignored that remark. Yes, Joe was still angry with me. And I was still angry with him. It was going to be a long time before I could forgive the word "stupid."

Anyway, I gulped a few times and was able to finish telling about the man in the back of the car and the chases—my chasing him, then his chasing me.

Joe might not have given me the kind of sympathy I wanted, but the Pier-O-Ettes did. They all cooed at me. "How frightening!" "What an experience!" Even "You were so brave, Lee!"

I began to feel guilty. "Don't get too sympathetic," I said. "Joe's mad at me because he thinks I shouldn't have tried to get a look at the guy. And he's probably right."

Ruby spoke up then. "Honestly! To think of a sex maniac in little old Warner Pier. I can't imagine such a thing."

"Neither can I," Joe said. "That's one thing that makes me think it wasn't just a random attack of some sort."

That seemed to shock Ruby more than the attack had. "What do you mean, Joe? What else could it be?"

"I just find it weird that Lee spent an afternoon asking questions—questions about what you ladies were doing Friday night when you claimed you were innocently sitting at the football game—and before dinnertime someone tried to kill her."

If I'd thought the Pier-O-Ettes had given a mass gasp earlier—well, this time they sucked all the air out of the room. Then Kathy Street began to weep, Margo Street began to bluster, and Ruby cackled out a strange laugh, the kind that's caused by nerves, not amusement. Hazel frowned so hard she looked like a gargoyle, and Julie Hensley's eyes grew as big as the chrome hubcaps on her beautiful white limo. Aunt Nettie even made her most extreme comment: "Oh dear!"

I don't know what I did, but I was as astonished as they were. Or was I?

Looking back, I think I was astonished that Joe had made that comment. But his conclusion didn't surprise me. I think that suspicion had been circling the airport in my mind all along.

After a minute or two of exclamations, the Pier-O-Ettes quieted down. All of us were staring at Joe. He pushed his empty mousse dish back and picked up his coffee cup.

I finally spoke. "Okay, Joe, I guess I see where you're coming from. We had a real, genuine, authenticated killing—Verna Rice—twenty-four hours ago. Right here, as Ruby says, in quiet, dull, little old Warner Pier. I spend an afternoon trying to find out more about six of the people who knew the victim. And after that someone tries to kill me."

He nodded. "It seems awfully coincidental."

"But, Joe, nobody knew I was asking about the Pier-O-Ettes."

"Greg Glossop knew."

"Oh. I guess that means that anybody in town could know."

Margo glared at Joe. "You can't possibly think that one of us killed Verna Rice."

Joe sipped his coffee before he answered. "Actually, Ms. Street, I don't see any of you as a likely killer. But Lee has a certain reputation in Warner Pier."

"Ha!" I said. "For nosiness."

"Curiosity. If word got around that she was asking questions, then someone might have decided to cut off her investigations."

I was horrified. "Joe, I wasn't investigating! That isn't what Aunt Nettie asked me to do."

"Then what were you doing, Lee?" Margo Street's voice was icy.

"Aunt Nettie thought several of you had fibbed

about just what happened Friday night. She thought you didn't grasp small-town gossip, that you wouldn't understand that the state police would almost certainly hear about the discrepancies. And she was afraid that would make them question you again. All she asked me to do was demonstrate how easy it is to find out what's going on in a town the size of Warner Pier."

I made a big gesture. "I don't care what any of you were doing! I just wanted you to see how easy it is for the detectives to find out if you had . . . well . . . shaded the truth."

Margo didn't look mollified, and Hazel was still glaring.

But Julie Hensley laughed. "Okay, everyone, I'll confess!"

We all stared at her.

"Oh, not to murder," she said. "But Lee's right. I did leave the football game. It had nothing to do with Verna. Heaven knows, if I'd known someone was going to kill her around that time, I'd have stayed put.

"My son was laid off from his job last year. He and his wife are close to losing their home. I met him out at the Shell station and gave him a check so he can pay his arrears and keep his head above water a little longer."

There were tears in her eyes. "Kyle finds this deeply humiliating, so I'll ask all of you not to say anything about it outside the group. If I slipped away without telling anyone, it was just to save his pride. A year ago he was a car salesman who earned the highest commissions of any salesman in Kalamazoo. This year the dealership changed hands and he's out on the street. He and his wife have a new baby and a seven-year-old daughter. I'm just so glad I have the money to help them out. I'd give him a job myself if I could, but I've had to cut back hours on all my regular drivers. He'd know I had to fire someone."

Murmurs of approval came from Ruby and Aunt Nettie, but Margo and Hazel still looked angry.

It was Hazel who spoke next. "Well. As Nettie can testify after working with me for forty years, I have an intestinal problem. I know where nearly every ladies' room in Warner Pier is located, and last night I had to locate the one in the stadium in a hurry. I settled down in there for a lengthy stay."

She screwed her face into the gargoyle mask again. "Unfortunately, I guess, I have no evidence."

Joe tactfully nodded without looking at her. Aunt Nettie and I ignored her, too. We were both aware of this health problem and of how it embarrassed Hazel.

After a moment of silence, Ruby gave a fruity giggle. "Oh, I might as well confess, too. I slipped off like a kid—to see my boyfriend."

I wasn't too surprised to hear that particular confession. In fact, nobody looked surprised.

Ruby rolled her eyes roguishly. "I guess it's no secret that I like men. I'm single. And I'm certainly over twenty-one! And I'm sure the people who still live in Warner Pier know that I've been seeing Dr. George Gibson."

She turned to Margo and Kathy. "George is a newcomer to Warner Pier. He moved here eighteen months ago, when he retired from his orthopedic practice in St. Louis. But he's still a licensed physician. So he volunteers as team doctor for the football team. He was in a sort of lair under the stands, and I ran down to see him." She smiled. "I'm sure he'll back me up."

"That's not my concern," Joe said. "As Lee explained, we're not interested in proving or disproving anyone's story. We just want all of you to understand how easily the most innocent fib is uncovered in a town the size of Warner Pier."

It was at this point that Kathy Street burst into tears. She opened her mouth and cried just like a baby. "Wah!"

What brought this on? I stared at her, surprised. But none of the Pier-O-Ettes seemed upset by the outburst.

Even the impatient Hazel remained patient. "I'll get her some water," she said. She jumped up, grabbed Kathy's empty water glass, and headed for the kitchen. Julie, Aunt Nettie, and Ruby made soothing noises. And Margo put an arm around her and patted her shoulder as if Kathy were a baby.

I saw that Joe was looking panicky. I didn't know how to reassure him. Men find emotional outbursts terrifying. I made a little gesture I hoped would say, "Stay cool," but I don't really know a signal for "This woman's nuts, but she calms down in a moment." The two of us sat quietly, not participating in the exciting moment Kathy had created.

After two or three minutes of petting, Kathy began to gulp out words: "It's all my fault! I did it!" and other phrases indicating that she blamed herself for something.

Hmmm. Hazel, Ruby, and Julie had "confessed." Margo and Kathy had not. Now Kathy was taking her turn, but none of us could tell what Kathy was confessing to.

When Hazel came back, she brought water and a box of tissues. Kathy blew her nose and began to talk in understandable words.

"It was me, not Margo!"

Every face around the table was blank. Nobody even asked what she was talking about.

"It wasn't Margo who left the stadium to make those

calls—it was me! This gossipy man got the two of us mixed up."

She clutched Margo's hand. "It happens all the time! We're twins, you know! People can't tell us apart."

Joe and I exchanged a glance. Margo and Kathy did resemble each other, but they were not identical. It was easy to tell them apart.

But to someone who didn't know their names, to someone who'd never spoken to them and didn't realize how different their personalities were—well, in that case they might be confusing.

"Anyway, Margo didn't do anything wrong! If anything happened, it was my fault!"

Ye gods. Poor Kathy was confessing, and she hadn't even been accused. If I hadn't had an untouched dish of chocolate mousse in front of me, I believe I would have banged my forehead on the table.

Margo was standing up. "Come on, Kathy. Let's go wash your face. Then you'll feel better. You're all upset over nothing."

"But, Margo—"

"It's all right, Kathy. Come with me. We'll help you into your comfy housecoat."

I was again astonished by how gentle and kind Margo was with Kathy. The stronger sister could be impatient and snappy with other people, but with her needy sister—well, it was a bit inspiring to see how sweet Margo was to her.

They went toward the hall, and I watched them go, almost ready to shed a tear over the scene. But just as they reached the doorway, Kathy turned her head and peeked at us over her shoulder.

And the look was sly.

Kathy was checking to see how we'd taken her confession. Had we believed it? Had we been foolish enough to believe it?

I looked around the table and realized Aunt Nettie was talking and everyone but me was concentrating on her. I was the only one who had seen Kathy's sly look.

I tried to force myself to listen to Aunt Nettie. I realized she was asking Joe about how the guy in my van could have had a key that opened it.

"Lee says he walked right up to the car and opened the door," she said. "How could that happen?"

"I'm sure the state police are checking on that," Joe said. "You'd have to ask a locksmith. But I'm sure car thieves have all sorts of tricks they use to get keys."

She turned to me. "You haven't lost your key?"

"No. I keep it attached to that ring on the outside of my purse. The state police probably think I just left the door unlocked. But I'm sure I didn't."

Joe cleared his throat. "To abruptly introduce an old subject, ladies, I suggest that you contact Lieutenant Jackson and expand your statements. But I don't think there's any serious danger that any of you will be suspected in the death of Verna Rice." He chuckled. "For one thing, I'm sure you were all here together when the phantom motorcyclist chased Lee around downtown Warner Pier between five and six o'clock."

There was a moment of silence. Then all four of the Pier-O-Ettes still at the table burst into laughter.

Ruby finally spoke. "I told you that scavenger hunt was a bad idea!"

Chapter 16

Joe and I were mystified. Ruby explained.

The high school vocal music coach had given them quite a workout, she said. After two hours of practice, everyone was tired. They all went back to Aunt Nettie's house and put their feet up. The conversation continued, and it turned to high school entertainments. "Things we used to do."

Scavenger hunts were mentioned. And how Warner Pier had changed, and how many of the places of their youth had disappeared.

"First thing we knew," Ruby said, "we were putting places on a list. Then we each volunteered to find one of the places. We were each to take a photo to prove we'd been there."

They were dying to show Joe and me the photos. Julie had been assigned to locate the old Root Beer Barrel. Joe and I knew exactly where that had been—in fact, he'd once owned the property. The barrel itself was now gone, blown down by a windstorm, and the scrap lumber had been carried away and sold. Julie had found the site of its demise.

Hazel was to document the spot that was once a lovers' lane. "It was known as the Three Trees," she said, "because a tree with three trunks grew there." The spot was still identifiable, although houses had been built nearby.

"Nobody would want to park there now," Hazel said. "It's too crowded. But one of the tree trunks is still there."

Margo and Kathy—ever a pair—were to report on what had become of the Riverside Chapel, once the site of outdoor religious services at which the Pier-O-Ettes sang. It was now a picnic pavilion, I knew.

Ruby, who still lived in Warner Pier, was sent to get a picture of the building that had once housed Berkowitz's Department Store. "You could buy anything from shoestrings to a hammer at Berkowitz's," she said. "I bought my first bra there."

Joe nodded. "I think my mom's office is in part of that building," he said.

"You're right," Ruby said. "The downtown has changed so much, I had to go to the library to look at an old city directory to make sure I had the right address. Your mom's insurance office and that antique store next door now occupy the building. You'd think I'd have known that, since I've lived here right along. But it looks completely different, and I wasn't sure I was remembering right."

Aunt Nettie said she'd track down the dressing rooms at Warner Pier Beach. The old wooden buildings had been moved years ago, when updated ones were built.

"They were moved to some camp," she said. "But I never could locate them. Anyway, I guess they're now on private property. Or torn down."

Because the group hadn't started on this project until it was late in the afternoon, it was after dark before
any of them got back to Aunt Nettie's.

They'd all enjoyed the scavenger hunt thoroughly.

But the upshot was that a few fuzzy photos were the
only evidence of where the members of the group had
been during the time I chased and was chased by the
phantom motor-scooter rider.

Nobody had an alibi. Not that they needed one. I
felt sure the person I'd chased had been a man.

I told Joe as much on the way home.

"Why are you so sure?" he said.

"Just the way he moved, I guess."

"You told Jackson that you couldn't guess at his
height or weight."

"No, he had on a loose jacket. And that ski mask."

"A loose jacket could hide a woman as well as a
man."

I didn't reply. I couldn't absolutely swear the person
had been a man; I just thought so. I guess when you
find some jerk hiding in your backseat, you expect it to
be a man. I could have been working on that assump-
tion.

I rode the rest of the way home without saying anything. Conversation between Joe and me didn't have its
usual free and easy quality. I was still angry with him.

And Joe still seemed to be angry with me. He
thought I'd taken a foolish risk, and he was upset about
it. I could understand that, but he hadn't had to use the
S word. "Stupid" was still hanging in the atmosphere,
poisoning the air.

I got ready for bed, almost in silence. Joe settled
down in the living room, flipped on the television set,
and watched some old movie. I went to bed and read.

I didn't go out to the living room and ask when he was coming to bed.

It was two a.m. when I fell asleep, and my final waking thought was that Margo had never admitted that she left the football stadium the night before. Was she hiding something? Or had Kathy's outburst simply distracted her?

When I dropped off to sleep, Joe was still in the living room. When I woke up at six—briefly—he was in bed. He had apparently taken care not to wake me when he crawled between the covers.

Things were definitely still not right between us. It was hard to believe we hadn't had a quarrel. But when I looked back at the events of the evening, I realized we hadn't. We'd just gotten mad.

Were we both sulking? I hoped not. Nothing is more childish—yes, more stupid—than sulking. But I was angry, and I didn't want to pretend that I wasn't. It wasn't going to be easy for me to get over it. I didn't want to yell and scream about it, and I was trying to act pleasant and normal. But I didn't feel normal. At all.

That made the next morning, Sunday, hard to face. But it arrived anyway.

And along with breakfast, I thought about a question that still puzzled me. Exactly why had Kathy asked Julie for forgiveness? Hazel had made it clear it was something to do with a guy. But who? And just what had happened? I was as nosy as Greg Glossop.

Joe made French toast, without asking me if it sounded good, and we ate it silently. Then Joe told me he was planning to spend the day at the boat shop.

"Fine," I said. "I need to go to the office and try to get caught up."

At least Joe left without lecturing me about not doing anything else stupid. He didn't kiss me good-bye either.

I took my time getting dressed. The first thing I did when I got to the office was call Aunt Nettie and tell her I needed to talk to her. The girls, she said, were going to the Dutch Reformed Church with Hazel, but she'd try to come by on the way. I saw her sedan pull up in front just after ten o'clock.

I opened the shop's door for her. "I need to be at the church by ten thirty," she said.

"I have just one question, and the length of the answer is up to you. Why did Kathy apologize to Julie?"

Aunt Nettie's eyes dodged away from mine. "Did she apologize?"

"Yes. When Julie arrived Friday, everyone ran to the front door to greet her. There was screaming and hugs and all sorts of excitement from four of you. But not from Kathy. Kathy hung back and waited for Julie to make the first move. And after everyone else had given Julie a major greeting, Julie walked over and gave Kathy a hug. And Kathy said, 'Please forgive me, Julie.'"

Aunt Nettie was staring at her hands.

"Oh, Lee, it all happened so many years ago."

"That's obvious. But it's also obvious that Kathy still felt guilty about something. What?"

"It was one of those high school romance things."

"What? They had a fight over a boy, and Kathy's still guilt ridden about it? That seems pretty extreme, even for Kathy."

"It turned out all right. I guess. Julie got wise and dropped the guy. Not because of Kathy! She dropped him earlier."

"Was Julie engaged to this fellow?"

"Yes. I mean, no." Aunt Nettie gave an impatient

sigh. "Julie was engaged to a fellow who worked at the Castle. She broke up with him. Somehow Kathy . . . made a play for him. Phin—that was the guy's name, Phin Vandercamp—later joined the army. He was killed in Vietnam."

"How sad!"

"Yes, it was tragic." Aunt Nettie leaned forward and dropped her voice. "But I never had much use for Phin, especially after the Kathy episode. I thought he—well, he definitely lacked moral fiber. I'm sorry he was killed, but I never thought he was good enough for Julie. Or Kathy."

Aunt Nettie left then, and I went back to my computer. But before I started on my accounts receivable, I yielded to curiosity one more time. I called up Google and typed in "Phineas Vandercamp."

At least the assistant manager's name hadn't been John Smith. It took only a few seconds for a reference to come up.

"Warner County War Memorial."

I clicked on the page. It was a part of the Web page of the Veterans of Foreign Wars group from Dorinda, our county seat.

"The Dorinda VFW is a primary sponsor of the Warner County War Memorial," it read. "The Memorial was established after World War I, and new panels have been added for each American armed conflict. Over the years, approximately fifty young men and one young woman from Warner County have given their lives for their country. Their names are listed on the memorial.

"In addition, a listing of young men killed in the Civil War may be found at the Dorinda Cemetery."

In larger letters it added, "Their Nation Honors Their Sacrifice."

I now remembered seeing the memorial. It was in the northeast corner of the courthouse square. A life-sized statue of a World War I soldier was in the middle, and panels inscribed with names stood on either side.

The Web page continued with a listing of names, sorted by "armed conflict." Among the Vietnam listings I found Phineas Vandercamp.

How sad. And how odd that neither the Pier-O-Ettes nor the Castle's two bouncers had mentioned him as they talked about the old days. Or was it? If the whole group knew that he'd dallied with Kathy despite his link to Julie, they might not have thought it tactful to bring him up.

I closed the VFW site and went to the *Warner Pier Gazette*'s site. I knew that all the obituaries it had run for the past seventy-five years were accessible online. I called up Phineas Vandercamp.

Phineas had been killed eighteen months after Dan Rice was found shot to death at the Castle Ballroom. He had been twenty-three years old. Details in that first report were a bit sketchy, though knowing exactly where and how he was killed wouldn't have told me much. I was more interested in the account of his life, and I found them in a more formal obituary in the next issue.

Specialist Vandercamp was born in Warner Pier and was a Warner Pier High School graduate, the obituary said. He had attended college for two years. He had worked as assistant manager of the Castle Ballroom. I subtracted his birth date from the date of Dan Rice's death and realized he had been barely past his twenty-first birthday when he worked at the Castle. I wondered what his duties had been.

After the Castle closed, Phin Vandercamp had apparently abandoned or postponed his plans for college and had enlisted in the army instead. He reported for duty with the U.S. Army the next fall. He had been sent to Vietnam about a year later, just two months before he was killed.

"Tragic," I said aloud.

The list of survivors included his parents and a brother, Victor Vandercamp.

Again I thought it was sad that Phin Vandercamp's name hadn't come up in the reminiscences at Aunt Nettie's house. He must be a painful memory.

Maybe these thoughts inspired the rather odd thing I did next. Or maybe it wasn't odd. After all, it's well-known that I'm the nosiest person in Warner Pier—and there's quite a lot of competition for that title. But that morning I surpassed myself.

I called Shep Stone's cell phone number.

He answered quickly.

"Shep? This is Lee Woodyard. I have a question for you. Is this a good time?"

"Actually, no. I'll call you back." Click.

No excuses, no reasons. Just click. Hmmm.

I got started on my own work, but about a half hour later Shep knocked at the front door. I let him in.

"I guess I need chocolate," he said.

"What flavor?"

He picked a mocha pyramid ("milky chocolate interior in a dark chocolate pyramid") and I added one of the souvenir items—a dark chocolate pastille in the shape of a mortarboard. I had made a small pot of coffee when I arrived, so I got him a cup before I asked what had brought on his craving for chocolate.

"I just spent an hour with the Michigan State Police," he said. "They asked me not to leave town. It seems they think I might be some guy who chased you last night."

"Oh." I thought about that. "I hadn't considered you for the role."

"That's a mercy!" He bit his mocha pyramid. "I was alone in a motel room, so I don't have an alibi. But they didn't explain exactly what happened to you."

"If you don't mind, I'd rather not discuss it." I suddenly had a vivid memory of the guy in the ski mask walking up to the door of the van—with a key in his hand—and I shuddered. No. I didn't want to talk about it.

Shep immediately looked contrite. "I'm sorry, Lee. I shouldn't have come here and bugged you."

"No! It's all right. I called you, remember."

"Here I am. You said you had a question. Ask away."

"I just learned from Aunt Nettie that Julie Hensley was engaged to the assistant manager of the Castle."

Shep's only answer was an uneasy nod.

I nodded. "But in all the reminiscences at Aunt Nettie's house, nobody ever mentioned him."

Now Shep frowned. Or maybe he glared. Anyway, his expression looked angry.

"It's best not to bring Phin up," he said. "Julie dropped him, so she probably doesn't want to talk about him."

"He was killed in Vietnam."

"I didn't know that."

"I just thought it was interesting that nobody even mentioned his existence. I'd like to know more about him."

"I didn't know him all that well."

"Your opinion will do."

Shep frowned and looked off into space. I wondered

why he didn't want to tell me what he remembered about Phin Vandercamp. I tried to urge him, tactfully. But my twisted tongue tangled me up.

"I'd just like to hear your frank opinion," I said. "Your idea of the undressed—I mean, unadorned! The unadorned truth."

Shep gasped. Then he turned as red as one of Ten-Huis Chocolade's festive Christmas boxes.

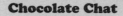

Chocolate Chat

Chocolate Places: Las Vegas

Las Vegas is a city devoted to fun and to indulging the senses. So it should be no surprise that chocolate is part of its attraction.

Ethel M Chocolates is the fine-chocolate arm of the Mars Company, producer of mass-market chocolates such as M&M'S, Mars bars, and Milky Ways. One Ethel M chocolate factory is in Henderson, Nevada, just a short drive from the Las Vegas Strip.

The Ethel M Chocolate Factory and Botanical Cactus Gardens draw around seven hundred thousand people a year. The visitors get to see chocolate made, then relax and nibble samples in an Ethel's Chocolate Lounge. They can visit acres of cacti in the adjoining botanical gardens. Ethel M has eight retail outlets in Las Vegas, so there's no excuse for missing your chocolate fix.

Another Las Vegas chocolate feature is at the Bellagio Hotel, where the world's tallest chocolate fountain is located.

The twenty-seven-foot fountain is in the Jean-Philippe Patisserie down a hall off the Bellagio's main lobby. It continuously cascades two tons of dark, milk, and white chocolate through a fountain designed by artist Michel Mailhot.

After you've checked out the fountain, naturally you can buy chocolate at the Patisserie.

Chapter 17

I'll never understand why "undressed" came out instead of "unadorned." But my slip of the tongue seemed to force Shep into a decision.

With his face still flaming red, he jumped to his feet. "The whole thing was a prank that got out of hand," he said. "As you can imagine, it's not a happy memory. Let's not drag it up now."

"What are you talking about?"

"The same thing you're talking about. The 'undressed' truth."

"Shep, I don't know anything about anything. The word 'undressed' was just another of the slips of the tongue I'm famous for."

"If you don't already know about it, you don't need to. I'm not going to volunteer to add to anyone's humiliation."

At that he marched out of the shop, leaving his chocolate mortarboard and half a cup of coffee on the edge of my desk.

I almost let him go without protesting. He seemed

so angry and embarrassed that anything I did would probably make the situation worse.

But Shep was a friend of Aunt Nettie's. I wanted to get along with him. I hadn't embarrassed him on purpose, and I wanted him to understand that.

So I picked up his chocolate and coffee and followed him out onto the sidewalk.

"Shep, I don't know what you're talking about. Aunt Nettie is my only source, and she's never talked about any of the events at the Castle Ballroom. She never even mentioned the Pier-O-Ettes until Ruby brought them up early in the summer."

"That's hard to believe." Shep glared at me, but he took the coffee and the chocolate.

"It's true. My question about Phin Vandercamp didn't have any hidden meanings. I am simply curious about how you, Charlie, and the six Pier-O-Ettes could talk all morning—discussing Dan and Verna Rice, the janitor, and everybody else who worked there—and never mention Phin Vandercamp. His name never came up. Why not?"

"All he did was sit in the office and work on the books."

"He was the bookkeeper?"

"Yes. He paid the bills, ordered the food, called the liquor supplier."

"What I do."

"At this shop?" Shep shrugged. "Somebody's got to take care of the details. And it sure wasn't going to be Dan Rice."

"Was Phin good-looking?"

"I didn't think so. I guess he appealed to Julie. And she was a knockout in those days."

"I've seen a picture of her, and it's hard to think she

wouldn't have had her pick of the guys in Warner Pier. Phin must have had something going for him."

"I never saw what it was," Shep said. "But at least two girls went for him big-time."

I nodded. "Aunt Nettie told me that Kathy made a play for him."

"She sure did. And she lived to regret it. Dan Rice saw to that."

"What happened?"

Shep sipped his coffee and looked at his feet. "You're sure Nettie didn't tell you all this?"

"Positive. I can't dig any details out of her. I've tried."

His eyes narrowed. "Next time you try, ask her about how they found Dan Rice."

"What do you mean, 'how they found him'? The night patrolman found the light on and the door un-locked. He went into the Castle office, and there he was."

"That's not what I mean. I mean the condition of the body."

"Why would I ask her about that?"

He leaned closer. "Ask her what he was wearing."

"What was he wearing?"

"Nothing, Lee. Not a stitch."

"Huh?"

"Yeah. That's right. The guy was in his office, lying beside his chair, stark naked."

"Is this the 'prank' you mentioned? The one that got out of hand?"

Shep turned and walked away. "They kept it out of the papers. But it's true. Ask the Pier-O-Ettes why."

This time I let Shep go. Then I thought about what he'd said.

Dan Rice had been found naked? In his office?

Getting naked is no crime. It's not even a sin. But ordinarily people get naked in their homes, not their offices. That would be—well, unusual.

In fact, it was so odd it was unbelievable. Shep had sounded as if he was certain, but suddenly I didn't believe a word he had said.

How could I check it? Who would know?

Joe said he had seen Hogan's private copy of the report on the investigation into Dan Rice's death. He would probably let me see it—but with things as uneasy between us as they were, I didn't want to ask. He'd just lecture me about staying out of a murder investigation.

Probably Verna Rice's lawyer had a copy of the report. He would have needed it for the insurance claims.

Insurance claims. Hmmm. That made me wonder. Had Joe's mom handled any of the insurance work? Would she have seen a copy of the police report?

More important, would she give me a detail or two? Such as what Dan Rice had been wearing when he died.

I resolutely stepped off the curb and jaywalked across Fifth Street to Joe's mom's office, the only insurance office in Warner Pier. Mercy Woodyard was often there on Sundays, since her husband, Mayor Mike Herrera—as a restaurant owner—usually had to work all weekend. Mercy had called our house the previous night, so she knew all the details of the big chase through Warner Pier, although I didn't think she knew Joe and I were feuding over it.

I knocked on the glass in the outer door of the agency, and in about thirty seconds Mercy appeared from her inner office. She let me in.

We exchanged a hug before I spoke. "I know you

wouldn't be here if you weren't busy. I'll try not to take too much of your time."

Mercy smiled. "I always have time to talk to a client."

"You've already got all my insurance business. I'm just here for gossip."

"What about?"

"Did you ever have anything to do with the controversy over Dan Rice's insurance?"

"Not a thing. His insurance was handled by an agency in Holland. Besides, I was in junior high when he committed suicide—or was killed in a shooting accident, as the case may be. I didn't work here until ten years later."

"Okay. Never mind, then." I started to get up.

"Wait a minute! Actually, if you want to know something about Dan Rice, the fact that I don't have any direct knowledge might be good thing. I couldn't tell you anything about a client, but I can sure gossip about a fellow Warner Pier citizen. And the schoolkids gossiped about the Rices a lot."

"Mrs. Rice taught at the high school, didn't she?"

"Right. And you know how kids are. She was an unpopular teacher, so we loved to hear stuff about her. Then we embellished it and passed it along. We were rotten! What did you want to know?"

I laughed. "It's funny that everybody's so ready to talk about Dan Rice since his wife was killed. But I've lived here three and a half years and I'd never even heard of either of them until this happened."

"I guess after he supposedly shot himself everybody felt sorry for Mrs. Rice. Probably a lot of us felt guilty because we hadn't treated her very well, and people with more delicate feelings—like your aunt— wouldn't gossip about her or about her husband. But believe me, when Dan was alive there was plenty of talk about him."

"What kind of talk?"

"He was supposed to be a chaser."

"Oh? I'm surprised Aunt Nettie's parents let her work there."

"I think some of the Pier-O-Ette parents hung around, at least when the girls first worked there. Later, I guess they felt the situation was under control."

"Well, the thing I heard was—that when they found Dan Rice dead . . ."

I paused, and Mercy finished my sentence.

"He was naked."

"Yes! Was it true?"

"I didn't see the body, Lee. So I can't swear it's true. But that was the story that went around town."

"Golly! That sure would cause talk in Warner Pier!"

"I think it would cause talk anyplace. After all, if he'd died at home, nobody would have thought much about what he was wearing. There's nothing particularly scandalous about sleeping in the nude, or even walking around the house in the nude. But at the office?"

I laughed. "Even if the place was closed up."

"Yes, it's a decidedly odd place to take all your clothes off. But there was more to the story."

"Do tell. What else could there be?"

"His clothes were missing."

"Missing!"

Mercy nodded. "And I got that on pretty good authority. One of the sheriff's deputies told my dad, and he repeated it to my mom, and I eavesdropped. Dan Rice was not only naked, but there were no clothes in his office. No clothes in the whole place. Nothing but an apron."

"An apron?"

"Yes, two of those big white food-service aprons were lying on the floor."

Mercy and I shook our heads over that. What on earth had happened to Dan's clothes? What did aprons have to do with anything? No explanations jumped to mind. But Mercy felt sure her information was correct.

I told her that Shep had said the whole thing was a prank that got out of hand. Neither of us could figure that out either.

After ten minutes, I got up. "I've got to go back to work," I said. "Shep said the Pier-O-Ettes knew something. I'll have to twist Aunt Nettie's arm until she tells all."

"Well, you tried this bouncer, Shep. How about the second one?"

"Oh! Good-Time Charlie."

"Maybe he'd tell you something."

"He talks all the time, but he rarely says anything."

I went back to my office. I tried to work. But Mercy's idea of Charlie as a source of information was lurking in my mind.

Finally, I gave up and got out the Holland phone book. Good-Time Charlie probably had an unlisted number.

There were only a dozen McCoys listed. None of them was Charles or Charlie, but two had an initial C: A. C. McCoy and Damon C. McCoy. I dialed the number for A.C. and the happy voice of Good-Time Charlie answered on the third ring. I identified myself.

"Hi, Lee," he said. "I hear that boomerangs are coming back."

"Groan," I said. "That's awful."

"Pretty bad, I admit. What can I do for you?"

"I just heard that the body of Dan Rice was nude when it was found. Do you know why?"

There was a long silence. "Why are you asking me?"

"Because Shep told me it was something about a 'prank gone wrong.' But he refused to say more."

"I'm the jokester, so you thought I must have been involved."

"Actually, I just thought you were the second bouncer, so you should have known what was going on behind the scenes at the Castle, I hadn't applied it to your affinity for jokes."

"The thought of ol' Dan in his birthday suit has a certain element of humor, but I didn't have anything to do with him stripping down."

"Do you know what happened to his clothes?"

"Well, yes. I do know the answer to that one. The police found them a couple of days after Dan died. They were wrapped around a steam iron, stuffed in a garbage bag, and dropped off the deck."

"Off the deck? What deck?"

"The deck of the Castle. The area along the river where boats could tie up. Someone had put the clothes in a sack, weighed them down with the steam iron from the dressing room, and thrown them into the river."

"Huh?" I thought about it. "I guess it was some sort of a prank, then."

"I doubt that Dan thought it was very funny."

"I doubt he thought it was funny at all. Somebody must have been extremely mad at him. Do you have any idea who that could have been?"

Charlie gave a low, mean chuckle. "You could ask some of the Pier-O-Ettes. Maybe Margo."

He hung up, and I didn't call him back.

But I was grateful for one thing. He didn't ask me about the big chase the night before. I felt sure no one had told him about that or he would have mentioned it. Charlie wasn't shy, and he certainly wasn't sensitive about bringing up touchy subjects.

But why had he thought Margo would know why somebody had been mad enough to play a naughty trick on Dan Rice?

Did I have the nerve to ask her?

Before I could answer that question, Lieutenant Jackson rattled the door of the shop. I let him in, and he walked into my office and threw himself into my visitor's chair.

"Are you sure that guy who chased you last night was on a motor scooter?"

Chapter 18

I stared. "Yes, I'm sure."

Jackson looked doubtful.

"Listen," I said, "I'm not positive it wasn't some sort of small motorcycle, but it was definitely a two-wheeled motor vehicle without any kind of cab."

Now the detective nodded. But he looked discouraged and unconvinced.

"Why are you questioning this?" I said.

"Because nobody else heard or saw a motor scooter in the Warner Pier business district last night."

"I was probably the only person there to hear it."

"We've asked everyone who lives down here."

"Which isn't many people."

"There are a dozen upstairs apartments occupied."

"The only one occupied in our block is Dolly Jolly's place, and she's out of town."

He ignored that. "Besides, no one saw a motor scooter leaving town."

"I didn't make it up."

Jackson nodded. "But we can't figure out where that motor scooter went."

"A motor scooter is quick. It could be out of town in no time. And it's small. It would be pretty easy to hide, compared to a car or a truck. You could stash it behind a bush, in a Dumpster, up a tree. Well, maybe not up a tree. But it wouldn't be hard to find a place to hide it."

"True." Jackson paused, then spoke again. "But all the vehicles we've identified as being parked on the streets last night belong there. None are unaccounted for. No strangers seem to have been around."

"There were cars in Herrera's lot. What about them?"

"That's where we started. And we matched every car with a Herrera's customer."

I stared out the window. "I can't explain what happened to the motor scooter. But I assure you that I didn't make the whole thing up. Somebody did hide in the back of my van. Somebody did run down the alley. I actually did hear and see a motor scooter. Somebody slashed my tires, or punched them with an ice pick, or something. And somebody in a ski mask walked up to my van and unlocked the door."

I shuddered. "And that episode bothers me more than the rest of it put together. The guy has a key to my van. How could that be?"

"That's not too hard to understand. If the guy's a car thief."

"They have master keys?"

"Lots of them just break a window, or jimmy the lock, but others—yes, he could have something like a master key."

"But he wasn't trying to steal the van."

"No, Lee. If it all happened the way you say, it was a targeted attack."

"With me as the target." I jumped to my feet. "I think I need chocolate. Bad. How about you?"

I got myself an Amaretto truffle ("a milk chocolate interior coated in white chocolate") and Jackson took a double-fudge bonbon ("layers of milk and dark chocolate fudge in a dark chocolate coating"). He declined coffee, and I didn't bother with it either. We both sat silently on either side of my desk while we ate our goodies.

Then I looked directly at Jackson. "Listen. I did not make this whole thing up."

"I admit that if it were anyone else, I might think you had. It's a crazy story." I started to speak, but he stopped me with a gesture. "But guys who've worked with you before say you've always been a solid witness. And your uncle called and vouched for you."

"Hogan?" I was touched.

"I'm sure you're telling the story as accurately as you can. But it's nutty. Some of the guys . . ."

He shrugged and stood up. "If you think of anything else, give me a ring." He gave me a business card with his private number in the lower right-hand corner; then he left.

And he left me upset. What a mess. My husband was mad at me over the way I'd handled the whole thing, and the cops thought I'd made it up.

But I was the victim. The victim. The one who had been threatened. How could I convince them of that?

I wondered if a good cry would help matters. But just then Joe called and said my van was ready to pick up. He'd had it towed to a place with Sunday service. Whenever I could get free, he'd drive me into Holland to get it. I decided that right that moment was as good a time as any, since I was so thoroughly distracted that I might as well quit trying to pretend I was working.

It takes half an hour to drive from Warner Pier to Holland, and that driving time was as quiet as any thirty minutes I've ever spent. Not a word was said by either Joe or me.

There's nothing wrong with silence between two people who like each other. A companionable silence often falls between Joe and me. We can spend a whole evening together without saying much. Reading, listening to music—we both love jazz—even balancing the checkbook or doing some other chore. But that wasn't the kind of silence we faced that day.

We were simply so unhappy with each other that we couldn't even fight about it.

Joe finally spoke on the outskirts of Holland. "Do you want to get lunch at Russ's?"

"They're closed on Sunday," I said.

"I forgot it was Sunday," Joe said. "We'll have to fight the after-church crowd everyplace."

We went to some fast-food place and ate silently. Joe ordered onion rings, and I didn't even ask him for a couple. I love onion rings, but I can't eat a whole order.

It was a relief to pick up my car with its two new tires and head home by myself.

On the trip I still felt like crying, but instead I resolutely analyzed my problems.

First, the state police thought my story of being chased—and chasing the chaser—was so unlikely that there were apparently people on the force who thought I made the whole thing up.

Second, my husband was so angry because I had chased the sex fiend or whoever had hidden in the backseat of my van that he had used the word "stupid."

Third, Lieutenant Jackson's arrival had completely sidetracked my effort to find out about the mysterious Phin Vandercamp.

By the time I hit the north edge of Warner Pier I had decided what to do. I couldn't do anything about changing Jackson's mind. And I was still too unhappy with Joe to tell him how deeply he had hurt me. But I could go by Aunt Nettie's and quiz her about Phin Vandercamp.

Luckily, my route to Aunt Nettie's took me by the high school, and I spotted Julie's white limo parked in a visitor's spot. I checked the time and realized that the Pier-O-Ettes were there for their daily session with the high school vocal coach. I wheeled the van into the spot next to the limo.

I was afraid that the school would be locked up, but the front door was open, and I walked on down to the vocal music room. When I peeked in, I realized a few current students were listening to the practice, too. I slid into a seat in the back row.

Then I spent a delightful half hour listening to old songs. Aunt Nettie and her pals were practicing a medley of sixties hits—"(I Love You) More Today than Yesterday," "The Loco-Motion," and "Itsy Bitsy Teenie Weenie Yellow Polkadot Bikini." I knew they were also singing some songs from the thirties and forties, their parents' music, but apparently they were concentrating on the things from their own youth for that practice session.

In each number Kathy Street was the lead singer. It was amazing how such a shy person could belt it out when she sang. The high school students and I all applauded when the Pier-O-Ettes ended up with a spirited version of "Harper Valley P.T.A."

They all did their signature pirouettes and took bows. Then each gave a deep sigh and the comments began. "We made it!" "Why did we say we'd do this?" But they all looked happy.

After they left the stage, Aunt Nettie walked back to greet me, giving me a hug and whispering in my ear, "I hope you're all right, Lee."

"I'm fine, and I've got the van back. I need to talk to you."

"Can we talk in the ladies' room? That's where I'm headed."

I followed her down the hall. Since school was not in session, the restroom was empty. I waited until Aunt Nettie was washing her hands.

"What did you want to talk about, Lee?"

"Phin Vandercamp."

Aunt Nettie stared at me. "Why on earth do you want to know about him?"

"Because he was not only engaged to Julie; he was also assistant manager at the Castle. You hadn't told me that. Yet the six of you gals, plus Shep and Charlie, talked about the old days at the Castle for hours, and his name never came up."

"Why should it?"

"Because I've finally deduced that there was some sort of brouhaha on the day before Dan Rice shot himself—or didn't shoot himself—and Phin was involved."

"Lee, that's all dead and buried! It should be forgotten."

"But Mrs. Rice never forgot. For forty years she kept telling people her husband had been killed in an accident. She fought the cops. She fought the insurance company. She called Joe and told him she had new evidence. She even told me that the Pier-O-Ettes knew something. And now she's been killed! Murdered! What if all that long-ago stuff had something to do with her death?"

"It didn't! I'm sure it didn't! It was just unhappy events that we'd all like to forget!"

We stared at each other. It was as major a confrontation as Aunt Nettie and I had ever had.

Oh gee! First I'd had a major fight with my husband. Now I was having one with my aunt, an aunt who was closer to me than my mother.

The silence between us grew. Then Aunt Nettie took a deep breath. I thought she was going to speak.

But before any words came out, an unexpected sound made us both whirl.

A toilet flushed.

Then the door to the farthest stall swung open, and Kathy Street came walking out.

"It's all right, Nettie," she said. "I can tell Lee about my affair with Phin. It's the only affair Margo ever let me have."

Chapter 19

Aunt Nettie gave a deep sigh. "Check the other stalls first," she said. "Heaven knows who else is in here."

While Kathy washed her hands, massaging them as if the high school's liquid soap had come from some exclusive salon, I tried the door to each stall, then looked inside. "No one there."

Kathy patted her hands dry, looking at them with deep concentration. The high school's rough paper towels might have been made of the finest linen. I noticed she wore an antique ring. Her slacks and shirt, as usual, were the same color of blue as the outfit Margo had on, but her shirt was trimmed with ruffles, and Margo's had been strictly tailored.

Once her hands were dry enough to suit her, Kathy smiled at me. "Margo said I shouldn't talk about this, but all the Pier-O-Ettes knew I was in love with Phin. He was always nice to me. He never made fun of me. He didn't have too much to say, you know. He was quiet. Shy. He didn't do wild things like so many of the Warner Pier boys did. He did his work. He didn't cut up or drink. I always knew he liked me. But he was engaged to Julie."

She smiled a beautiful, sweet smile. "Then they broke up. It happened the night Mr. Rice died. Julie told all of us about it backstage the night of the contest. She said she didn't want to talk about why, but it had been her idea. She was angry with Phin. And after the show was over, I thought—well, I thought that if Phin wasn't going to marry Julie, maybe he would be interested in me.

"And he was! I went into the office, where he was always working late at night. And he was so discouraged. I just felt terrible for him. I sat down by his desk and told him so. I told him that Julie had treated him badly, and that I was sorry. I told him I loved him, even if she didn't."

Kathy beamed. "And it turned out he had really loved me all along! I was the reason for his breakup with Julie!"

"Oh, Kathy!" Aunt Nettie's voice was dismayed. "I didn't know he told you that."

"Yes, Phin said he'd always cared about me, but he had been all mixed up with Julie. She bossed him something awful, you know. But now he was free to love me. Me! Anyway, he kissed me. It was lovely."

Tears arose in Aunt Nettie's eyes. She took Kathy's hand.

But Kathy turned to me. "Phin and I became lovers, you know. Right there! We just couldn't wait."

I gulped back a few tears, too. I nodded. Poor Kathy! Phin had seen his chance, the jerk, and had taken advantage of her innocence.

Then Kathy's face crumbled. "But that awful Mr. Rice came in! He ruined everything."

At that point Kathy, Aunt Nettie, and I were all three

tearing up. "Mr. Rice l-l-laughed at us," Kathy said. "He made fun of us. He was terrible!

"And the worst part was, he wouldn't let me put my clothes on!"

"What!" I yelped out the word.

Kathy nodded. "He said I was skinny and ugly. But he still wanted to look at me. He wouldn't let me get dressed."

I was horrified. But Aunt Nettie didn't look surprised. I realized she must have heard this part of the story long ago.

"He made me cry. And he took pictures of me! And then he laughed."

"What about Phin?" I said.

"Oh, Phin tried to act like it was all a joke. But I didn't think it was funny."

"I guess not," I said.

"Anyway, finally Mr. Rice went away, and Phin left, and I got dressed, and I went home. And Margo found out what happened. I tried not to tell her, but she made me. I was afraid she'd be angry or that she'd tell Mama. And she was mad. But she wasn't mad at me. She was mad at Phin. And at Mr. Rice. She said she was going to get even with him."

"With him?"

"With both of them. With Mr. Rice and Phin. Because they laughed at me."

Margo had said she was going to get even with Mr. Rice.

The words chilled me, of course. Dan Rice had died that same night, and no one had ever figured out if he'd killed himself or if someone had killed him or if he had died in some sort of accident. What had Margo done to get even with him? I hesitated to ask Kathy that question.

Just then the door to the hall opened, and Margo came in. "Kathy? What's going on?"

Kathy looked scared, and Aunt Nettie patted her hand again. "We were just talking," she said. "Are you two coming back over to the house now?"

"I'll stop at the Superette and buy some wine," Margo said. "If that would go with dinner."

"Tonight is strictly informal. We're going to have brats and beans."

"A back-to-Michigan menu! I'll get some beer, then. And a bottle of red wine."

"That would be nice, Margo."

Margo left, motioning for Kathy to follow her. Kathy obeyed.

I turned to Aunt Nettie, but she shook her head. "This isn't a good place to discuss anything. Can you drive me home? We can talk on the way."

"Sure." We said no more until we were in the van. Then I burst out angrily. "If I had that Phin guy here, there would be another murder. I just don't think Kathy is capable of consenting to sex."

"It wouldn't be rape in a court of law, Lee. She was eighteen. She certainly didn't understand the implications of a sexual relationship, but Phin didn't use coercion. Luckily, they didn't actually have sex."

"They didn't?"

"Apparently Dan Rice interrupted them before the actual act. Kathy was so innocent—and so ignorant—that she didn't have a chance against Phin."

"You called Phin a manipulator. He must have been an expert."

"Oh, yes. He manipulated Julie all through high school. He was one of these 'poor me, I'm going to go eat worms' people. Always felt sorry for himself. Al-

ways made other people feel that they'd done something mean to him."

"But to use that technique on poor Kathy—that was
despicable."

"You don't have to convince me."

"Did all the Pier-O-Ettes know about this?"

Aunt Nettie nodded. "Margo got us together about
midnight that night and told us what had happened."

"Why did she do that?"

"Because she was serious about getting even with
Phin and Dan Rice, and she needed our help."

"Oh gee! What did Margo come up with?"

A rather sly smile crept over Aunt Nettie's face. "We
all helped her. All but Kathy. Even Julie came along."

"What happened?"

"Margo snitched a pistol from her grandfather."

"A pistol! She shot Rice?"

"No, Lee. She did not. She just got hold of a pistol.
And I got one from my father."

"Aunt Nettie!"

"Lots of people who live in the country or in small
towns have a pistol. You know that. Ruby got one that
was her dad's. Hazel had her brother's twenty-two. Julie was in charge of the camera."

"Camera! You took pictures?"

"We certainly did. Dan Rice took pictures. We went
to Mr. Rice's office when he and Phin were there, about
two o'clock, after the place closed. We held them at
gunpoint. And we made them strip off their clothes."

"But, Aunt Nettie—frankly, I'd think Dan Rice
might have enjoyed that."

"He didn't enjoy the part where Margo fired a bullet
to show she wasn't kidding."

"Fired a bullet!"

"Yes, she fired a bullet. After that Phin and Dan Rice both believed we meant business. Which was a lucky thing." Aunt Nettie laughed. "Because it was the only bullet we brought along."

"All those guns were unloaded?"

"Certainly. We weren't going to take the chance of actually hurting anybody."

"So you threatened them with unloaded guns, made the two of them take off their clothes, then took pictures of them." I considered it all. "Frankly, Aunt Nettie, that sounds pretty tame by today's standards, with stupid teenagers sending sexy pictures of themselves to one another's phones."

"This was forty-five years ago, Lee. In those days girls at slumber parties still had big discussions about whether you should take your nightgown off on your wedding night. Doctors were just beginning to be willing to talk to brides about birth control *before* the honeymoon. Besides, Warner Pier was no larger then than it is now."

"You mean you threatened to show the pictures around town?"

"Worse than that! We threatened to show them to Mrs. Rice. And to tell her why we took them."

"Ouch! So were you all responsible for dumping the clothes over the side of the deck?"

"We certainly were." Aunt Nettie's chin was firm. "We were all so furious at what Phin and Mr. Rice had done to Kathy—well, they were lucky that we didn't have live ammunition in those pistols we lifted from home."

"Have I got this straight? Kathy fell for Phin, and the two of them were doing some heavy petting in the office . . ."

"The green room."

"The green room of the Castle. Mr. Rice caught them, and he deliberately humiliated Kathy by taking pictures of her and by not allowing her to put her clothes on. Phin also laughed at her."

Aunt Nettie nodded, and I went on.

"Margo vowed revenge on both men, particularly Mr. Rice. So all of you armed yourselves—"

"With unloaded guns."

"Then you forced the two of them to disrobe, and you took pictures, threatening to show them to Mrs. Rice. Their clothes were bundled into a garbage bag, weighed down with a steam iron, and thrown off the deck into the Warner River."

"Yes. That's what happened." Aunt Nettie giggled. "We could have gotten into a whole lot of trouble, but we thought Mr. Rice wouldn't dare report the whole thing."

"But he committed suicide that same night. Or somebody shot him."

"Lee, I've never been able to see any connection between what we did and his death."

I sighed. "I certainly understand why you did it."

"What else could we do? We simply couldn't let him bully and humiliate Kathy like that—and get away with it! If we'd waited as long as morning, one of those awful guys would have told the story. It would have been all over Warner Pier in a minute. Kathy would have been ruined forever."

"I guess you could have reported Dan Rice to the police."

"Not in a town the size of Warner Pier! The whole point was to conceal Kathy's humiliation. If we'd reported—well, Phin would have been embarrassed, but he would have made everybody think he was a victim. Mr. Rice might have gotten in some trouble, but

Kathy's mom wouldn't have pressed charges against him. Probably the police of those days would have thought it was funny."

I considered that as I turned the corner into Aunt Nettie's street. It had been an odd situation. And she was right; Kathy and Margo's mom would probably have been most interested in avoiding gossip, not sending Dan Rice to court.

"I guess vigilante action was your only recourse," I said.

"I've never regretted doing it."

"I understand. My only problem is that for all these years you've added to the mystery of what really happened to Mr. Rice. Mrs. Rice had all those lawsuits and everything. Knowing this background might have helped the authorities figure out how he was killed."

"What we did had nothing to do with his death. To tell the truth, I've always thought Mrs. Rice shot him herself."

Chapter 20

I was so surprised that I ran my right front tire up onto Aunt Nettie's curb.

"Rats!" I said. "If I ruin one of my new tires, Joe and I really will go to fist city."

"Oh dear, Lee! Are you and Joe having problems?"

"No! I'm joking. He wasn't very happy about me chasing that guy last night. But we'll work it out without coming to blows. I'm more concerned about the news you just announced. Let's go over that again. You think that Verna Rice killed her husband?"

"I don't know what happened to him, but I've always thought it was likely. She was mean enough."

"Okay. That's a given. And if she found him nude, with his clothes over the side of the deck, she was probably mad enough. It doesn't sound as if that situation would have appealed to her sense of humor. But do you have any actual evidence against her?"

"No."

"Do you know whose gun shot Dan Rice?"

"No. But it wasn't one of our guns. We took them all away with us."

"Are you sure?"

"Yes. Margo made us show them before we left."

"Margo should have been a general. But she left a bullet from her own gun."

Aunt Nettie laughed. "Lee, she fired it into a pail of sand."

"A pail of sand. Where did she get a pail of sand?"

"It was for the smokers. Everybody smoked back then. There were ashtrays on every table in every restaurant, for example. Businesses with outdoor areas, like the Castle's deck, had big pails of sand sitting around for people to put their cigarettes out in. Margo brought one of the pails into the office so she'd have it handy for target practice. When she wanted to make a believer out of Mr. Rice, she fired her pistol into it. Then she put the pail outside again."

"Did she sift the sand to get the bullet out?"

Aunt Nettie laughed. "Not to my knowledge. Who was going to look for it?"

"After Dan Rice was shot . . ."

"Lee, they had the bullet—and the gun—that killed him. No officer was going to sift a bucket of sand full of cigarette butts on the off chance that he'd find a stray bullet. They thought Dan Rice shot himself, after all. They didn't search too hard."

"True. But this whole thing adds up to the craziest story I ever heard in my life."

"Maybe so. However, it's the truth." Aunt Nettie got out of the van. "But you see why we didn't want to tell the police about all this."

"Yes, I certainly see that!"

"Anyway, thanks for the ride. I'd better get the

house open and some crackers and cheese out before everyone gets here."

"Aunt Nettie! We can't just leave things like this."

"Like what, Lee?"

"You've told me all this. I feel—well, shouldn't we do something about it?"

"What?"

"I'm not sure."

"Lee, you kept probing around until Kathy told you the beginning of the story, so I felt that I had to tell the rest, the part she doesn't know. Kathy is too innocent to think about you passing the story on. But I would never have told you my part if I hadn't felt I could trust you not to repeat this. Even to Joe."

"But—"

"I've never told Hogan." Aunt Nettie's voice was firm. That statement put an end to the whole thing as far as she was concerned.

She slammed the van's door and leaned toward the open window. "I'll see you later, Lee. Bye for now. And you be real nice to Joe. Make things up with him."

"Wait just a dadgum minute, Aunt Nettie. What did you do with the film?"

"The pictures we took? Margo destroyed that film years ago."

"What about the film of Kathy?"

"Oh. Margo destroyed that, too."

I must have looked worried, because Aunt Nettie used her most reassuring voice. "Now, Lee, it's been forty-five years since all that happened. So I think we can forget about it. Now, you run on home."

She walked away, leaving me sitting in my van feeling as blank as I've ever felt in my life. That was the craziest story I'd ever heard. I banged my head against the steering wheel.

But Aunt Nettie was calling back to me. "Now, Lee, you go home, and be really nice to Joe."

I should be nice to him? He was the one who'd used the word "stupid." I thought that, but I didn't say anything. I needed to absorb what Aunt Nettie had said. I couldn't worry about Joe right that moment.

Aunt Nettie went away, leaving me feeling as if the world had turned upside down.

Aunt Nettie forcing two men to strip off their clothes? Holding them at gunpoint? Aunt Nettie did that? My dear, kind aunt Nettie?

It was as if the sky had fallen. As if the whole natural order of things had gone kerflop.

But what could I do about it? Aunt Nettie was right about one thing. It had all happened forty-five years earlier. There was very little chance it had even a remote connection with the present-day problem, the killing of Mrs. Rice. So I couldn't feel that I was concealing evidence in any current crime investigation.

I started the van's motor, carefully backed off the curb, and drove to the office. Maybe if I did routine things—like my job—I could move the earth back into its normal orbit.

But no. That wasn't going to happen. When I parked in front of the shop, I saw Charlie McCoy's flashy white Corvette sitting at the curb.

What did Good-Time Charlie want? Somehow I doubted that he'd simply come by for a pound of crème de menthe bonbons, especially since we weren't open that afternoon.

I parked beside the Vette, and he got out of the low-slung car quite gracefully considering what a tubby guy he was. His only concession to cool was sunglasses.

I greeted him warily, waiting for a bad joke, but for once his mood seemed to be serious.

"Lee! I just heard about your awful experience last night."

"I seem to be recovering."

"I'm glad to hear it. You're a brave young woman. But that must have been terribly frightening."

"I'm only sorry I didn't get a good look at the guy."

"From what I hear, you tried."

"Not very effectively." It was time to change the subject. "What are you up to today?"

"Shep called and told me about your adventure. I was coming down to Warner Pier this afternoon anyway, so I thought I'd drop by."

"You've been around Warner Pier a lot lately. Is this a regular thing for you?"

"No. When the Castle closed—back in the dim days of my youth—I moved to Holland, and a few months later I opened my first car lot. I've never been here again, even though it was so close. Horning in on the Pier-O-Ette reunion enticed me back. Saturday was the first time I'd been in town in forty-five years."

"I guess the town has changed a lot."

"Wooee, hasn't it! But the whole country has changed a lot. Forty-five years ago there was a drug dealer on every corner."

"In Warner Pier?"

"Everywhere. Grand Rapids, Detroit, Chicago—you could buy stuff anywhere."

"Joe says the Warner Pier City Council of that day tried to crack down."

"He's right. They did. But there was always a guy wearing a psychedelic shirt sitting over there by the drugstore with a ready supply."

"Right on Peach Street?"

"Yes, sirree. And there was another guy who worked at Warner Pier Beach."

"Were drugs a problem at the Castle?"

Charlie sounded suspicious. "What do you mean?"

"A problem for the bouncers. You and Shep said the Rices tried to keep the hippie element out, and the two of you were supposed to be keeping order."

"Oh. The Castle didn't appeal to the drug crowd. That's why it was losing money, I guess. That and Mrs. Rice."

"Was she involved in managing the Castle?"

"No." Charlie laughed. "She was too good to work in a dance hall. Or that was what she handed out. If she had been involved, she and Dan probably would have made money. At least they would have kept it. She was the type who never lets go of a penny. But she stayed away from the operations of the place, except to make sure Dan wasn't chasing the help."

"Then how could she have had anything to do with the Castle's downward financial slide?"

"She insisted that Dan hire musicians who were old-fashioned. She encouraged him to go with the 'family-fun' theme. But families had stopped going to places like the Castle. She needed to cater to young people."

"Sex, drugs, and rock 'n' roll? The way you described the era at lunch yesterday?"

Charlie laughed. "If she and Dan had turned the Castle into a disco—well, it sounds old-fashioned now, but at the time . . ."

"It might have saved the day?"

"Some people made big money then." Charlie moved toward his car. "I didn't mean to chew your ear off talking about the bad old days. I was just going to say I'm sorry you had that scary experience."

"How did you know I'd be here?"

"Your home phone is in the directory. No one was there, so I tried Joe's shop. He said you were working down here this afternoon."

I assured Charlie I appreciated his dropping by, then watched as he climbed into his beautiful Corvette, gunned the engine loudly, and drove off with a roar.

I spoke aloud. "And what," I said, "was that all about?"

Yes, I wondered, why had Charlie McCoy come by? He said he came to express sympathy for my scary experience, but there was no reason that he needed to do that. I barely knew him. If Aunt Nettie or Joe's mom or my best friend, Lindy, called to check or came by with a shoulder for me to cry on, it would be because they loved me and really cared. But Charlie McCoy was practically a stranger to me. I certainly wasn't about to confide in him, and he obviously hadn't expected me to pour out my heart.

In fact, he hadn't even asked any questions. And that was odd, too. If something like a man hiding in the backseat of your car happens, and strangers talk about it, it usually means they want more details than they're entitled to know.

And speaking of details, I suddenly had a question for Aunt Nettie. As soon as I was in my office, I picked up the phone and punched in her number. It was answered on the first ring, but the person on the line wasn't Aunt Nettie. It was Margo Street.

Aunt Nettie, she said, wasn't available.

"Oh," I said. "I'll call back."

Margo sounded exasperated. "I suppose Nettie told you we all have to meet with that Lieutenant Jackson again tomorrow morning."

My question answered. "I forgot to ask her. But I was wondering if you all had worked that out."

Again I wondered whom Margo had called from the stadium, and why she'd left during the game. But I didn't have the courage to ask her.

She was speaking once more. "I suppose we have to talk to him, but I still don't see how our harmless little omissions could impede a murder investigation."

"Joe thinks—"

"Oh, I know what Joe thinks, but I assure you there were plenty of reasons that someone might have wanted to kill Mrs. Rice—and for her own sins, behavior that had nothing to do with her husband's death."

"I know she was irritating."

"Irritating! People can stand irritating. She was crooked!"

"Crooked? I hadn't heard that."

"I'm not making it up. The old bat tried to blackmail me!"

Chocolate Chat

Chocolate Places: Santa Fe

The official state vegetables of New Mexico are the chile pepper and the frijole, but chocolate grabs plenty of attention, too.

In Santa Fe, the oldest capital city in what is now the United States, four chocolate companies have banded together to create the "Santa Fe Chocolate Trail." C. G. Higgins Confections, The ChocolateSmith, Kakawa Chocolate House, and Todos Santos Chocolates all have received national attention for the high quality of their products. All offer chocolates that draw on the history and traditions of "the city different."

This seems suitable. After all, the Spanish discovered chocolate when they came to the New World. They took it back to Spain, where it was almost a state secret for centuries before a Spanish princess took it to France as part of her dowry. Somehow, it just feels right for chocolate to have an important presence in a city declared the capital of its region by conquistador Pedro de Peralta in 1610.

Viva the Santa Fe Trail! And viva its cousin, the Santa Fe Chocolate Trail!

Chapter 21

Blackmail? Mrs. Rice had tried to blackmail Margo? I admit that the first thing that went through my mind was that Mrs. Rice had had more nerve than I had. I wouldn't have blackmailed Margo if I'd found her standing over a murder victim with a smoking gun and she'd been begging me to take the hush money.

Luckily, I didn't blurt that out. But I did blurt out the second thing that popped into my mind.

"You didn't pay her!"

"Certainly not! As somebody or other said, I told her to publish and be damned!"

"Good for you!"

I blurted that out, too, but apparently it was the right thing to say. Anyway, Margo replied smugly. "It's the only way to deal with people like that."

"If you have the nerve."

"And if you don't have too much to lose. Aren't you going to ask me what she tried to blackmail me about?"

"I suppose you'll tell me if you want me to know."

"You already know. Nettie said she told you the whole story."

"About how the Pier-O-Ettes got even with Dan Rice?"

"Yes."

"How did Mrs. Rice find out what had happened?"

"I have no idea. Maybe that creep Phin told her before he left town."

"Dan Rice deserved what you gals gave him. My only qualm is—can you be sure it didn't have anything to do with his death?"

"Not unless Mrs. Rice found out that night and got so mad over the whole thing that she shot him. And if she did, I'm not going to feel guilty. If she was going to shoot him, she would have found a different excuse another time."

I approached the next question cautiously, using my least confrontational voice.

"If Mrs. Rice killed her husband, then who killed her?"

"I don't know! And I don't really care."

"Joe thinks the same person must be . . . involved."

"I know, I know. But forty-five years separated the two crimes—if Dan Rice's death was a crime. I think they are two unconnected events."

I didn't reply, but I had to admit her opinion sounded logical. Of course, Joe's sounded logical, too.

While Margo was in a confiding mood, I decided to try one more question.

"Ms. Street," I said, "why did the mere sight of the Pier-O-Ettes' trophy upset your sister?"

"I can't answer that," she said. And she hung up.

She hadn't said she didn't know. She had said she couldn't tell me. The question I'd just asked Margo— why did the trophy upset Kathy?—was the one I'd started with two days earlier. And I still had no answer.

There were a lot of questions I couldn't answer.

Who invited Shep to the reunion? And why?

Who was the guy on the motor scooter?

Was he the killer of Mrs. Rice?

Where did he go?

Had I really—as Joe thought—uncovered something about him, something that made me a threat? Something that would make him want to kill me?

But I didn't know anything! It seemed to me I'd asked a million questions, and I knew nothing.

I decided to go home. I wasn't accomplishing anything at the office, so I might as well stop occupying space. I got out my purse and car keys in a mood I admit was pretty close to a huff.

But Margo's comments had turned my thoughts in a different direction. Before I headed for the door, I considered Mrs. Rice.

Where did she come from? How did she meet Dan Rice? Why had she spent forty-plus years devoted to his memory, although people who had known them as a couple said they had been quarrelsome and contemptuous of each other?

Why had Mrs. Rice become a teacher, when her former students had universally said she was unhappy and miserable in the role? And if she had resigned as a teacher after Dan's death, what had she lived on during the many years since his demise? No one had mentioned her holding a job.

Hmmm. It was easy to check a few of these things. Joe's mom had known her when Joe was growing up, known her well enough that she made Joe mow her lawn. Mercy must know something about her. Still sitting with my purse in my lap and my car keys in one hand, I picked up my phone and punched the speed-dial button for Mercy's office. Luckily she was still there.

"Just a quick question," I said. "All these years that

Mrs. Rice spent fighting for her insurance settlement—how did she live? I mean, if she didn't get the insurance money, how did she support herself?"

"I don't know for sure, Lee, but apparently she inherited quite of bit of money from her parents."

"Who were her parents?"

"I don't know that either. She was from over around Alma."

"So she wasn't a Warner Pier native?"

"No, I'm sure she came here when she married Dan Rice. And if there was any possibility of an inheritance from him, she squandered it on legal battles. Of course, she made money renting out her house."

"She used her house as a summer rental?"

"Oh, yes. That's why she wanted Joe to mow her lawn. In fact, it was a sort of odd situation."

"How odd?"

"Extremely odd. For several years back then, every spring she would come over and tell me she needed Joe to mow her lawn. She said she was going away to stay with relatives and renting the house out for the summer. And the house was really a problem to the neighborhood. Lots of wild parties."

"In *your* neighborhood?"

"Her renters seemed to be single guys. And they didn't come for the beach or the boating. It was party time several nights a week. One year there was even nude sunbathing in the backyard."

"Was a Warner Pier Realtor handling the house?"

"None of them ever admitted it. And one year it got so bad I tried to find out."

"Did you complain to Mrs. Rice?"

"Yes, but the situation didn't change. She just said that the renter had a lease, and she couldn't control his behavior."

"Seems as if the lease would have some provision that would have given her some control."

"It should have. The whole situation was really odd. Mrs. Rice was so very prim and proper, yet she rented her house to these—well, unprim and improper people."

"Did she ever tell you who the mysterious renter was?"

"She may have said he was a car dealer. Anyway, he was using the house to entertain clients." Mercy paused. "But that's not very illuminating. You know what a summer rental costs in Warner Pier. Only well-to-do people can afford one."

Mrs. Rice said that her renter was a car dealer? Of course I thought of Good-Time Charlie. But Americans usually use "car dealer" to refer to a person who owns a new-car franchise. Charlie might own a big, successful operation, but I'd still call him a used-car salesman.

Mercy was speaking again. "Why did you want to know all this?"

"I just got curious. I guess you'd say Mrs. Rice is an interesting character. For example, everybody agrees she was a terrible teacher who didn't like her students. So why did she become a teacher at all?"

"In her day it was considered a good job for a woman. It was that or secretarial school. I went for secretarial school."

"You're a lot younger than she was, Mercy!"

"Yeah, but my parents had her generation's attitude. I was just lucky I landed with my own business. Whoops! Mike's on the other line."

Mercy hung up, and I stared at my desk. Yes, I thought, Mercy had been lucky. But she'd also been smart. She'd been in her mid-twenties when she was left a widow with a five-year-old son. Joe's dad was killed in a work-related accident, so she received an insurance settlement. She was smart enough to invest that money. Then, with babysitting help from her parents, she'd gone to work as a secretary at the local insurance agency. She learned the insurance business from the ground up, passed the required exams, and when the agent retired ten years later, she was able to use the money from her investments to buy him out. Joe had told me she'd been able to save much of the Social Security survivors payments she received for his support as a college nest egg for him. I had great admiration for my mother-in-law's financial and professional acumen.

Two widows—Mercy Woodyard and Verna Rice. It was interesting to contrast the way each of them had handled their lives financially.

Did their actions reflect the states of their marriages? Joe's dad had been less than thirty when he died. A crewman on a Great Lakes freighter, he drowned when the ship sank in a storm. Joe's parents had been married only six or seven years, and, as a freighter crewman, his dad had spent long periods of time working away from home. But one of Joe's few memories of him was how happy his parents had always been to see each other when his dad came home.

How old had Verna Rice been when Dan Rice died? Since she had been well over eighty when she died, she must have been around forty. The Rices had never had the long separations that Joe's parents had had, but the descriptions Charlie and Shep provided didn't make their marriage sound happy.

Once again I wondered why Verna Rice had spent forty-plus years of her life trying to prove her husband hadn't committed suicide. Was it just the money? Then why did she refuse a settlement when the insurance company finally offered one? Why didn't she move on with her life?

I'd done all that musing, and I was still at the office when I wanted to be home. I stood up to leave, but the phone rang. The caller ID told me it was Joe.

I was still so mad at him that I almost didn't answer. I let three rings go by before I picked up.

"Lee, the weirdest thing just happened!" Joe's voice sounded eager. "You remember the note that Shep Stone claimed he got? The invitation Nettie says she didn't send."

"Sure."

"Shep found it."

"Where was it?"

"In the motel wastebasket. I guess the trash never got dumped over the weekend. And it was still in the envelope."

"What does the handwriting look like?"

"Nothing like Nettie's. Shep still thinks Mrs. Rice sent it. Jackson is now trying to find something Mrs. Rice wrote so he can compare."

"That's interesting, Joe, but—"

"Jackson's calling me," he said. "I wanted you to know that Nettie definitely didn't write it. Now, if we can just convince Jackson you didn't slash your own tires, both the TenHuis women will be in the clear. Talk to you later."

He hung up, leaving me with my jaw dropped clear to my bosom.

"In the clear?" He was trying to get Aunt Nettie and me in the clear?

I punched the OFF button of my phone viciously. Honestly! The idea that either of us had done those things—written the note to Shep or fabricated that chase story—was totally idiotic. It was simply impossible that Lieutenant Jackson could be thinking that of either of us.

Was Joe losing his mind? Or was Lieutenant Jackson losing his?

It was the stupidest thing I'd ever heard of.

Darn. There was that word again. Stupid. I hadn't forgiven Joe for using it to refer to me, and I'd better not use it either.

I tried to push the fight with Joe out of my mind. So Shep Stone actually had received a letter purporting to be from Aunt Nettie. I could hardly blame the investigating officers for questioning this. Earlier that afternoon he said he'd been closely quizzed about Mrs. Rice's death. He could be darn lucky the motel maids hadn't gotten around to dumping his trash.

And Shep still suspected that Mrs. Rice had sent him the letter. But why? Why had she wanted Shep to come to Warner Pier? Did Shep know?

I could ask him.

I considered that for maybe thirty seconds, then shrugged and reached for my phone. After all, I was already known as the nosiest person in Warner Pier. I might as well call Shep and quiz him.

I still had his cell number in my little notebook, and he picked up on the first ring.

"I hear you found the invitation that claimed to come from Aunt Nettie," I said.

"Yeah. I gave it to the cops."

"Would you mind telling me exactly what it said?"

"It was kind of silly. I guess I should have known it didn't come from Nettie. She was always—sweet, you know. And fun. But not silly."

"But people change over the years, so you wouldn't have known. What did it say?"

"Well, it said the Pier-O-Ettes were having a reunion with members of their high school class. And even though I hadn't gone to high school here, she thought

I would enjoy the reunion, and she wanted to ask me to come."

He paused, and I gave him a nudge. "Did she say who else was coming?"

"No. She just said she had always remembered working with me at the old Castle. Some dumb remark about I'd always been a real Southern gentleman and it would be good to see me again. Then she added a PS saying to be sure to bring any pictures I had from those days. I thought that was kind of odd."

"Why? After all, you're a professional photographer."

Shep didn't answer, and in a moment I spoke again.

"Shep, I can understand why you came. It was a nice note and perfectly plausible."

"I did wonder about why she didn't send her phone number."

"Obviously, whoever really sent it wouldn't want you to call."

"I tried to find the number. But the note was just signed 'Nettie Vanderheide Jones.' And even in Warner Pier, I'm not going to call every Jones number to see if it's the right one."

"Actually, Hogan and Aunt Nettie have an unlisted number because of his being chief of police. But if you'd called any Jones in Warner Pier, they might have told you."

"So whoever wrote it was taking a risk. But it was somebody who knew I'd been sweet on Nettie."

"Oh, really?"

"Sure. She was as pretty as a picture and as nice as a cotton hat. Just like she is today."

"She's sure been nice to me. Do you still think the note came from Mrs. Rice?"

"Either her or—well, there's one other person. Of

course, there's another question; how did the letter writer find me?"

"It's pretty easy to find people today thanks to the Internet. Google 'em. Or use AnyWho."

AnyWho. Suddenly I remembered my first glimpse of Mrs. Rice. She'd been at the Warner Pier Public Library, using the computer. I was so taken aback that I didn't hear what Shep said and had to ask him to repeat his comment.

He sighed. "I said, but Nettie doesn't seem to use the Internet."

"True. Hogan and I have talked her into carrying a cell phone, but she still stays away from e-mail."

When Shep spoke again, he moved to a completely different subject.

"Hey, your husband's a lawyer, right?"

"Yes."

"I may need one. I'm not sure how much I should tell these Michigan cops."

"Joe's not in private practice."

"What does that mean?"

"It means he works for an agency that provides legal services for people who can't afford to pay for them."

Shep gave a short, barking laugh. "That sounds like most of us."

"He mostly helps with custody cases, appeals. Not much criminal work. Maybe he could recommend somebody."

That idea seemed to appeal to Shep, so I offered to have Joe call him. Joe could make up his own mind about how much advice he was willing to give Shep.

I hung up more curious than ever. Then I called Joe to pass on Shep's request.

He answered shortly, and he didn't sound happy to hear what I had to say. I found his attitude annoying, but right at that moment I was still finding everything Joe did annoying.

I knew Joe usually turned requests like Shep's over to a lawyer buddy. So I volunteered to pass him on. "Shall I tell Shep to call Webb?"

Joe sighed. "No. If Shep knows something, he needs an answer today, and Webb's out of town. I'll talk to him."

He took Shep's number.

I got up, again headed for home. I needed to get away from the office and quit thinking. I didn't want to think about guys hiding in the backseats of cars, or naked men found dead in ballroom offices, or obnoxious old women running their cars into trees, or teenaged girl singers who grew up to be middle-aged women who got hysterical at the sight of trophies. Or about retired photographers who were antsy about talking to the police. Thirty minutes of mindless entertainment— that's what I needed. I could barely wait to get home, prop my feet up, and turn on HGTV. A half hour of home décor sounded great.

And the telephone rang again.

"Now what!" I glared at the receiver on my desk. Then I sighed and answered it.

"Lee!" It was Aunt Nettie. "Is there a map of Warner Pier at the office?"

"I think there's one in my filing cabinet. Why do you need it? I'd think you know every alley in Warner Pier."

Aunt Nettie laughed. "I do, but some of these girls have forgotten."

"What are the Pier-O-Ettes up to now?"

"We're going on a bike hike!"

Chapter 22

"Where did you get that many bikes?"

"We're getting them from Bob the Bike Man."

Bob the Bike Man rents bikes to Warner Pier tourists from Memorial Day until Labor Day. "Oh," I said, "I thought he'd packed everything away for the winter."

"He said he could get six out easily."

"Does everybody remember how to ride?"

Aunt Nettie laughed. "None of us do! We're renting the three-wheelers. Bob assures us we can manage. They have comfortable seats, and they don't fall over."

"Where are you going?"

"Each of us wants to visit her old neighborhood—except Ruby. She lived too far in the country to ride out there. But when we did the scavenger hunt yesterday, a couple of people got turned around. So they wanted a map."

"Not a bad idea. Just which neighborhoods are you going to ride through? Not that you have that many choices in a town this size."

"Bob's going to deliver the bikes at Julie's house—I mean, the house where Julie lived when she was a kid. It's farthest up on the hill. Then we'll wind down toward the river until we pass all the houses."

"So you'll be going downhill for the whole ride?"

"Basically. Bob assures us the bikes have good brakes, and I hope he's right! When we come down that hill on Fifth Street, we could fly right into the river!"

I agreed to bring the map by Aunt Nettie's house, and we said good-bye. Aunt Nettie was still giggling, ready for the next adventure.

After I hung up I decided it was smarter to get the "girls" new maps, so they'd be up-to-date and each could have her own. I drove to the chamber of commerce office, went to the outside box they maintain for tourists, and picked up eight copies of the newest edition: one for each Pier-O-Ette, plus new ones for me and Joe.

Then, as soon as I'd dropped them off at Aunt Nettie's, I drove home and figured out who had killed Verna Rice and might have killed her husband.

I didn't intend to do that, of course. It was just the way my thought processes followed a series of ideas inspired by things people told me. Solving the mystery was purely accidental.

The first inspiration came when I saw the Garretts' Cadillac parked in their drive.

The Garrett driveway is directly across Lake Shore Drive from our little sandy lane, and Dick and Garnet—yes, her name is Garnet Garrett—are friends of ours. They spend most of their time in Grand Rapids, where they lived full-time until Dick retired.

I had checked out their drive Friday night when Joe and I walked down to the scene of Mrs. Rice's accident, and at that time a dark-colored truck had been parked in it. I had flashed my flashlight on it, wondering whether Dick and Garnet had come down unexpectedly, but then I ignored the truck, thinking that someone had pulled in there so they could walk down Lake Shore Drive and gawk at the accident. I'd noticed the license tag, which was 7214, just because I'm a number person and I notice numbers. The truck had been gone when Joe and I walked home, and I had pushed the episode out of my mind.

Now, seeing the Garretts' car in the same spot made me remember the small truck. But again, I didn't pay much attention. I was hoping for half an hour of mindless television watching. As soon as I got into the house—and I was nervous enough that I locked the doors once I was inside—I got a Diet Coke from the refrigerator, turned on the television, sat on the couch, and propped my feet up.

But somehow I couldn't think about TV. That new map I'd picked up began to haunt me. I kept thinking about what it might show. I got up and retrieved my copy from my purse. Spreading it out on the coffee table, I looked at the downtown area.

That didn't take long. Warner Pier's downtown is five blocks long and two and a half blocks wide. I had been wondering how the guy on the motor scooter had managed to disappear so quickly, but after all, he hadn't had far to go.

The last time I'd seen him, he'd been on foot right in front of TenHuis Chocolade, on Fifth Street, not far from Peach Street. (Nearly all Warner Pier streets are named for fruits; this is orchard country.)

I'd sprayed him with pepper spray through my partly open window. Then I'd driven off on my rims, tearing up two tires in the process. I'd gone two blocks to Herrera's parking lot, located at the end of the business district. The Warner Pier PD and the Michigan State Police had arrived two or three minutes after that and started looking for the guy on the motor scooter. But no sign of him had been found.

The state police, judging from what both Lieutenant Jackson and Joe had said, were assuming that he might not exist.

But I knew he existed. He must have gotten out of the downtown area quickly. But why hadn't I heard the sound of his engine? Actually, earlier the motor scooter had been surprisingly quiet, so maybe I had simply been too excited to listen for it. But I believed I would have heard something if he had ridden off.

A motor scooter would be fairly easy to hide. I hadn't measured it, but it looked to be about five feet long and three feet high. The rider could have stashed it behind a large bush until the search for it was over.

However, there are no large bushes in downtown Warner Pier. We have ornamental trees planted in holes in the sidewalk, but we do not have bushes large enough to hide even a small motor scooter.

What did our downtown have that *could* hide a motor scooter?

A Dumpster? I was sure the law officers had searched behind every Dumpster in the downtown area. They'd probably searched inside every Dumpster, too, but it would be hard to lift a motor scooter into one. I didn't think that was a practical plan.

Trucks or other vehicles? In movies they hide small cars inside trucks, but semis or even large panel trucks are not commonly found in downtown Warner Pier at night. The only one I could think of was the furniture store's delivery vehicle, and after the store closes, it's usually locked in the store's garage.

Garage!

What a simple idea. And it would work. The rider could simply have ridden, or even pushed, his motor scooter into a garage. Then he'd lock the door and stay there until the coast was clear.

But there weren't all that many garages in downtown Warner Pier. Which meant I knew where nearly all of them were.

I pored over the map. Where was the garage nearest to TenHuis Chocolade?

In ten seconds I was laughing.

The nearest garage was right behind our shop.

It was the garage and storeroom that TenHuis Chocolade had rented for twenty-five years and which Dolly Jolly had used for her Jeep until the owner of the building wanted it back.

The garage was right across the alley from where my van had been parked when its tires were slashed. And that garage was empty and nearly cleared out. Dolly and I, with Joe's help, had seen to that the previous Friday.

We would turn the garage and the adjoining storeroom back to the landlord as soon as Joe and I took the final load of junk to the dump. And since it held nothing valuable, I'd left it unlocked.

But it sure seemed to be a far-fetched hiding place. It simply was too crazy. I was amused by the idea, but I didn't believe it.

I toyed with the idea of going back downtown and looking in the garage, just to see if there was any evidence that a motor scooter had been hidden there.

Immediately I heard Joe's voice—just as loudly as if he'd been in the room. And the voice was saying, "Stupid. Stupid, Lee. Don't do anything stupid."

In fact, it was saying, "Don't do anything *else* stupid."

No, it wouldn't be smart for me to go down a lonely alley, late on a fall afternoon, with the sun beginning to go down and the light getting dim. Not only would it be stupid; I simply didn't want to do that.

So I sat there, staring at the television, not seeing what was on the screen, and wondering if I should call Joe—or the Warner Pier PD or the Michigan State Police or somebody—and tell them about my latest brainstorm.

But it seemed so far-fetched.

I probably wouldn't have done anything about it if Joe hadn't called me.

He called to say he had an appointment with Shep at five o'clock, so he would be late coming home.

"Okay," I said. "Joe . . . there was one thing I might mention to you."

When I told him about the garage idea, he sounded more exasperated than interested. But he listened. And he didn't say it was stupid. I think he'd figured out that he'd better not.

What he did say was "We need to check on that storeroom anyway. I'll run by and see if there's any sign that somebody's been fooling around in there."

"I guess it's a far-fetched idea."

"It won't hurt to check. But even if the guy hid the scooter there last night, he's probably gotten it out by now."

"When could he do that?"

"Oh, probably around six this morning. The Warner Pier business district isn't exactly thronged with people at any hour this time of the year, but it's definitely deserted then."

Relieved to have shifted the responsibility for my idea, I settled back to watch the TV. And another thought began to nudge my imagination.

I began to think about the Garretts' Cadillac sedan, now parked on their driveway, near their cottage. I idly wondered about the strange vehicle I had seen there Friday night. Had the driver of the truck simply been someone who stopped to gawk at Mrs. Rice's accident? The van's license tag figures—7214—still lingered in my number-oriented brain.

I had ignored the letters on the license plate, but the numbers were easy for me to remember.

That strange vehicle kept bugging me. It reminded me of something. But what? The only thing I'd even noticed about it was the dark color and the tag number.

I don't notice every car tag number I pass on the street. The only other one I'd noticed lately was the tag on Good-Time Charlie's antique Corvette. That one was 7321.

So?

Both numbers began with seven. Again, so what? A license tag number has to begin with something.

But—

I sat up straight on the couch. Both numbers followed the same pattern. They began with seven, and if the seven was multiplied by the second number, you got the final two numbers.

Charlie had told Joe and me that he deliberately sought out tag numbers that were sevens and multiples of seven.

It could be.

All Michigan vehicle owners are encouraged to buy tags by computer, so most Michigan license plates were issued at random. But it is possible to go to a secretary of state office and get a tag. Considering how much business a car dealer like Charlie might do at such an office, he could well be able to get a small favor—such as a special number request—from the clerk behind the counter.

In small-town Texas, where I grew up, it would have been a snap. Local officials like to keep their constituents sweet. I was willing to bet it wouldn't be too hard in Michigan either.

Of course, Michigan auto owners can order special tags—vanity tags. But I didn't think these had been vanity tags. Those usually had words on them. And these had followed the standard Michigan pattern of a three-letter prefix followed by numbers.

But the two tags had followed the same pattern, and this coincidence could be checked. If the SUV was registered to Good-Time Charlie, the state of Michigan would know. I called the Warner Pier PD and asked for Jerry Cherry. He wasn't there, but the secretary-dispatcher said she'd have him call me. I felt confident that Jerry would check the license numbers if I asked him to. Of course, since I didn't know the letters, it might take a while. Quite a while.

And again, so what? If I proved that both license tags were for cars registered to Charlie McCoy, would it matter?

Yes, I decided. Because Charlie had told the state police that he hadn't been in Warner Pier Friday night. He had told me that until Saturday he hadn't been to Warner Pier for forty-five years. But that small panel truck sure had been there. In fact, it had been about a block from where Mrs. Rice was killed. A shudder ran down my back. I hadn't considered Charlie—joking Charlie with all the puns—as a killer.

But when I did consider him as a killer, I came up with another factor that was interesting. Charlie owned a whole car lot full of vehicles. Charlie could easily have access to a motor scooter and a small commercial van, as well as a flashy Corvette.

But wouldn't they have dealers' tags? Not, I decided, if Charlie was planning to use them for some nefarious purpose. Dealers' tags would be much more noticeable. Charlie could borrow a truck from his lot if he needed one, then switch one of his own tags to it.

And that small panel truck I'd seen—the one with the numbers 7214 on its tag—was big enough to haul a motor scooter away. It had solid side panels. And it might even have a mechanical lift, making it easy to get an object like a motor scooter in through the back doors.

I assured myself that I was letting my imagination run away with me. Then I settled back on my couch, took a drink of my Diet Coke, and checked the television.

But I couldn't pay attention to it. I clicked the set off and considered Charlie as a killer. What motive would he have for killing Mrs. Rice?

I had no answer. He had known her for nearly fifty years. He had worked for her husband.

But what motive could he have? Charlie had told me he had never come back to Warner Pier.

When Joe's mom had told me Mrs. Rice told her— talk about hearsay—that she rented her house to a Holland car dealer, the name of Good-Time Charlie had immediately popped into my mind. I had, however, rejected that idea because I would have called Charlie a used-car salesman, not a car dealer. I would reserve that term for someone who had a manufacturer's franchise. A Chevy dealer, a Cadillac dealer.

But what if Charlie *had* been the person who rented the house? The person who allowed "unprim and improper" people to use it?

Why would Mrs. Rice agree to that?

Because she was forced to?

Bingo! Blackmail!

If Good-Time Charlie had something on Mrs. Rice, he might want money to keep it quiet. But Mrs. Rice had only a limited amount of money to begin with. And this rental deal happened around twenty years after Dan Rice died. By then Mrs. Rice might have had no more money to pay a blackmailer. So Charlie might have forced her to let him use her house.

Margo said Mrs. Rice had tried to blackmail her. Maybe she got the idea from Charlie.

I wondered if an audit of finances for Charlie's original car lot would show Mrs. Rice as an investor.

But why would Charlie stop demanding money and kill Mrs. Rice?

Because something had happened to change their relationship. Charlie had been exploiting Mrs. Rice. And she was willing to pay up. But after forty-five years of submitting to blackmail, she found "new evidence" and rebelled.

I was sure this was right. After all, the last person Mrs. Rice had spoken to was Joe. And she had told him she had "new evidence" in her husband's death. How could Mrs. Rice have found "new evidence" at nine o'clock on a Friday night? What had happened on that Friday that might have produced new evidence about an event that happened forty-five years earlier?

It had been a busy day. Dolly and I had cleaned out the garage. The Pier-O-Ettes' reunion had begun. And Shep had showed up in town.

Well, I knew Dolly and I hadn't found evidence in the garage. I was almost positive that none of the Pier-O-Ettes had talked to Mrs. Rice. That left Shep.

Shep had to know something he had never told about the death of Dan Rice. Maybe even something he didn't realize was important. Something that changed the whole relationship of Charlie and Mrs. Rice and forced Charlie to kill her.

I stood up and walked around the living room, telling myself to calm down. This was more speculation than deduction. I forced myself to sit down again.

After all, Mrs. Rice seemed to encourage people to dislike her. I'd met her for less than ten minutes, and I'd been ready to yell at her. But dislike and hatred are two different things. I might have bawled her out, but I wouldn't have killed her.

Then I remembered something Hogan Jones had told me once. Motive doesn't matter.

A professional law officer, he had said, wants to know who committed a particular crime. If knowing the motive helps, that's a good thing. But knowing who did it and how they did it counts more than knowing why.

"We can figure out why after the arrest," he had said.

So the first question was: Was it physically possible for Charlie to be the killer?

First, I thought the killer had hidden his motor scooter in the garage off our alley. Did Charlie even know that garage existed?

Yes, he did. I had told him myself on Saturday. I had mentioned that I found the Pier-O-Ette memorabilia while cleaning out a garage, and I described where it was.

Second, could he have made a copy of the key to my car?

Yes, if he had the skill to make one—a skill Sergeant Hugh Jackson said many used-car dealers would have—he'd gotten a good look at my keys that same morning. They hung on the outside of my purse.

I was concentrating so hard on Good-Time Charlie

and on what Hogan had said that when the phone rang I nearly fell off the couch. Then I nearly dropped the phone when I picked it up.

"Lee? Miz Woodyard?"

"Shep?"

"Yes. I'm sorry to bother you at home. Is Joe there?"

"No. He said he was going to call you."

"Yes. We agreed to meet here at the Sidewalk Café half an hour ago, but he hasn't shown up. I wondered if I had the place mixed up. Or the time. Or something."

"It's not like Joe not to keep an appointment. Or at least call."

"He did call to say he'd be a few minutes late. He said he had to make a stop first. Is something wrong with his car? He said he wanted to check with the garage."

Chapter 23

I had to swallow a yelp. "Garage" was a significant word for me right at that moment.

Joe had told me he'd make a check on the TenHuis garage and storage room. But he'd indicated it would be a quick check of a location less than a block away from the Sidewalk Café. A routine check shouldn't have taken as long as half an hour.

I felt sure he'd run into trouble, but I didn't tell Shep that. I promised Shep that I'd try to reach Joe; then I hung up rudely. Shep was still talking.

I immediately called Joe's cell, but after four rings I got the voice mail.

I tried not to panic. Joe might have left his phone in the truck. Or he could be walking into the Sidewalk Café at that moment. But I didn't believe it. I was afraid that Joe had gone to check out that garage and had met up with Good-Time Charlie. Or whoever had been riding the motor scooter.

I'd called the garage to Joe's attention before I began to suspect that Charlie was the person who had been involved with the big motor-scooter chase and tire-slashing episode. If Joe ran into Charlie, he wouldn't see him as a threat. He would just see him as a buffoon.

I stood there in the kitchen with the phone in one hand and the fingers of my other hand hovering over 9-1-1.

But if I called the police, what could I tell them? That I was afraid we'd had an intruder in an almost empty garage? Warner Pier had only one patrolman on duty at a time. He wouldn't give a call like that high priority.

Could I ask some neighboring businessman to go and check on the garage? No, I couldn't do that without endangering someone who had nothing to do with all this.

I put the phone away and picked up my purse and car keys. I had to go downtown and look at that garage in person.

All the way I told myself I was being truly dumb. Stupid, just the way Joe had said. I vowed that if everything was all right, I'd never let Joe, or anyone else, know that I'd gone there looking for him. But I still felt compelled to go.

I drove across the Warner River Bridge looking closely at every truck that came toward me. None of them were Joe's. He wasn't headed home. I turned onto Fifth Street and drove slowly down it. And there, at the curb half a block from the Sidewalk Café, I saw Joe's truck.

"Whew!" I gave a loud sigh of relief. I pulled in beside the truck, jumped out of my van, and ran inside the Sidewalk. Shep was sitting at the bar.

"Lee?" He looked surprised.

"Where's Joe?"

"I don't know, Lee. I'm still waitin', just like you said to do."

"His truck's outside."

"Then he's got to be someplace close by."

I didn't say another word. I just turned around and went back out the door. I ran to the corner, cut across the street to the alley, and headed for that garage.

It wasn't dark yet, but sunset was near. There was sunlight on the street, but shadows made the alley dark. As soon as I was inside it, I began to walk carefully. It was an alley, after all, used for stuff like old boxes and trash. I wasn't eager to fall over a tin can or slip on a banana peel. I watched where I was putting my feet, stepping gingerly.

Our garage was almost halfway down the block, on the left. Because I was watching my footing, not looking straight ahead, I was well into the alley when I saw a dark panel truck outside the garage.

If I'd been scared before, that truck sent me into absolute terror.

I yanked out my cell phone, and for the second time in ten minutes, my fingers hovered over 9-1-1. But I didn't punch the numbers.

My certainty that a dark truck was involved in Mrs. Rice's death was not based on any proof that would be accepted by investigators. It was just a wild guess on my part. I could be wrong. And if I involved the police, even the Warner Pier police, and I was wrong—well, the state police already thought I was some sort of nut. That would confirm their impression.

So what? If it kept Joe safe, did I care what the state police thought of me?

Not really. But I cared what Joe thought of me. If he was at the garage for some logical reason, if he didn't

want the police involved, if he wasn't there at all—
well, we were not on the best of terms anyway. I'd better not embarrass him.

So I clutched that phone in my hand, and I hugged
the wall, and I walked toward the truck and the garage
as quietly as I could. I almost stepped on a bottle as I
passed the wine shop's Dumpster. I picked it up and
kept tiptoeing along.

As I got closer I heard the murmur of voices, and I
realized the garage door was open. Not the ordinary
door. That was the one that went into the storage side of
the big room. It was the overhead door that was open.
But its light wasn't on. It took me a moment to remember that the bulb had been burned out.

I felt for my "no-harm charm" chain. The tiny flashlight on it might prove to be valuable. And I kept walking as silently as possible, headed for that door.

Then I heard a voice speaking clearly. And it wasn't
Joe.

"Okay, Woodyard," it said. "I'm sorry you got involved in this, but you and that pretty wife of yours—
well, you're just too damn curious. Now, you close the
door, and then we can turn on the light."

I recognized the voice. It was Charlie. Good-Time
Charlie. My wild guess had been right.

Charlie wasn't making any jokes this time. And neither was Joe. I could tell by his voice. He was deadly
serious.

"We could turn on the overhead light right now,
Charlie. Nobody will see it. Not back in this alley."

"Close that door!" Charlie's voice sounded as if he
were talking to a junior salesman who had let an easy
sale escape. "Now!"

When I heard Charlie talking I had stopped walking, and now I discovered I was standing in front of the

single door. I leaned back against it, and it moved slightly. The door wasn't closed tightly.

The overhead door rattled and began to move downward slowly.

I was certain Charlie had killed Mrs. Rice. If the garage door was closed, Charlie could fire a gun and the noise would be muffled. That must be the reason he wanted it shut. If Joe was closed up in that garage with Charlie, I was sure Charlie would kill him.

I reached into my purse, yanked out the garage door opener that had been there since the previous Friday, and punched the button.

The overhead door wavered. Then it stopped going down and started to go back up.

"What the hell?" Charlie's voice was angry. "Why'd you do that?"

"I didn't." Joe sounded surprised, too. "I just punched the button once."

"Punch it again."

The door clattered and groaned. Again it started down. I let it get about two feet down, then punched my opener. It quivered to a stop and went back up.

It wasn't completely dark inside the garage. There was some sort of light in there, and I figured out that it was coming from the makeshift light over the little workbench at the back of the garage. I was familiar with that light. It wasn't a real lamp; it was a mechanic's work light clamped onto a hook on the wall. It cast a glaring light on the workbench, but it left the rest of the big room pitch dark. The wall-mounted garage door opener was over the bench.

If Charlie and Joe tried to look out into the garage, they couldn't see anything. I decided I could push the small door open a few inches without getting caught.

Luck was with me. When I peeked into the garage,

there was no reaction from either Charlie or Joe. I opened the door wide enough that I could slip inside, and I pushed the door almost shut behind me. The three big filing cabinets were between me and Good-Time Charlie. Plus, he was turned away from me.

I heard Charlie growl. "There's something screwy going on. You must have the opener."

"Not me." I could see Joe holding his hands under the work light.

I could see Charlie's hands, too, and I had been right. A silver pistol was in one of them.

"To hell with it," Charlie said. "I'm not waiting any longer."

The words chilled me. Fooling around with the garage door opener wasn't going to save Joe. I had to do something fast.

So I swung back the bottle in my hand, and I threw it as hard as I could. It smashed into the back wall.

"Run!" I yelled it with full lung power. "Run, Joe!"

I turned and ran myself, yanking the small door open and plunging out into the alley. I made a hard right and ran toward the cross street.

"Help! Murder!" I shrieked all the way up the alley. And I zigzagged. I knew Charlie still had that gun, and I didn't want to be an easy target.

I heard feet pounding behind me. I hoped it was Joe, but I didn't turn around to see. I just kept running and screaming.

I came to the end of the alley and rushed out into Peach Street.

And I was surrounded by a throng of bicycles.

The sun was just setting, and there was plenty of light. "Lee! Lee!" People were yelling at me. Bicycles and women were all around me, going every which way. The scene was mass confusion.

I had run into Aunt Nettie and the Pier-O-Ettes. All six of them—and each on a three-wheeled bicycle. They were circling around, teetering this way and that, yelling, stopping, riding—any action that can be done on a bike was being performed.

I skidded to a halt. I wanted to run, but I was surrounded. I didn't know which way to jump.

I whirled around toward the alley, and I realized that I needed to move some way. I'd better not stand still.

Charlie had just come dashing out of the alley, close on my heels. I needed to keep running away from him.

But I couldn't.. I was surrounded by those darn women on three-wheelers. If I ran right, if I ran left, I was going to smash into one of them. And if I did, one of us was going to go kerflop, right into the gutter, or up the curb, or onto the roof of a car—someplace we didn't want to be.

But Charlie was in the same predicament. He couldn't move either. He stood there, waving a pistol, and turning round and round.

He looked like a madman. His face was frantic.

More footsteps pounded, and Joe ran out of the alley. Charlie apparently heard him, and he swung around, pointing that pistol toward him.

"No!" That was me, screaming.

"No!" That was Aunt Nettie, screaming.

"No!" That was Joe. Growling. He ran straight toward Charlie.

Charlie pointed his pistol directly at Joe.

If Charlie was any kind of a shot at all, Joe was dead.

Then Aunt Nettie rode in from the left, hit Charlie full-on with her three-wheeler, knocked him flat, and ran over him.

The pistol went off and shattered the upstairs window of the souvenir shop on the corner.

And Joe jumped on top of Charlie and wrestled him to the mat—I mean, the pavement—just the way he had pinned his opponent in the high school wrestling finals fifteen years earlier.

After grabbing Charlie, Joe ended up with the older man in some sort of scissors hold. This meant Joe was almost lying on his back on the street, with Charlie tied in a knot on top of him. Ruby ran over and sat on Charlie's legs.

The silver pistol went flying. It landed at the feet of Kathy Street. Kathy got off her bike, picked it up, and stood looking at it seriously.

"Oh," she said. "This is the first time I've held a gun since the night I shot Mr. Rice."

It's strange to remember, but I hardly noticed Kathy's remark. I was so mad at Joe Woodyard that it went right over my head.

I knelt on Charlie's left arm, joining the tangle of limbs, and I managed to look Joe in the eye.

"Joe! That was the dumbest thing I ever saw! How could an intelligent person do anything so stupid?"

Then I yelled at Aunt Nettie. "And you! You could have been killed!"

She stood there beside her bike. "Well, I didn't think about that," she said calmly. "I just didn't want Charlie to shoot anyone. But neither Joe nor I is hurt."

"Not for lack of trying!"

I shifted my irate gaze to Joe. "You ran right at a man who was pointing a loaded gun at you!"

Joe tightened his grip on Charlie. "Was that any stupider than trying to chase down a guy on a motor scooter when your van had two flat tires?" he said.

He had me there.

Shep ran up and reported that the police were on

the way. Then he produced a camera from that black bag he always carried. And he snapped a few pictures.

Finally, he dropped to one knee beside Joe. "Do you need help from an old photog?"

"Hang around," Joe said. "It depends on how long it takes the guys with the handcuffs to get here."

Shep grabbed another arm that was flailing around, shoved it to the ground, and leaned on it with both hands and his whole weight. Charlie stopped struggling.

We all waited, with Charlie pinned head and foot, until the cops got there. That's when things got really confusing. The cops didn't know what to do with Charlie.

I immediately told them he had killed Verna Rice, but my unsubstantiated opinion didn't seem to give them a good reason to arrest him.

Then Joe and I said we were willing to charge Charlie with assault, since he'd threatened both of us with a pistol.

Charlie countered by saying he was going to charge me with assault because I'd thrown a bottle at him.

I said I hadn't thrown it at him. I had thrown it into another part of the garage, and the shattered glass would be there to prove it.

Besides, Joe said, the missing motor scooter was at that moment in the back of Charlie's panel truck, so the cops could hold Charlie on evidence that he'd been the one who chased me and slashed my tires twenty-four hours earlier.

Plus, I figured out why Charlie came by to see me that afternoon, carrying on an almost pointless conversation. He must have been showing me his eyes were all right, trying to allay any suspicions I might have had that he was the guy I hit with pepper spray.

And all the Pier-O-Ettes, plus Shep, plus the bartender from the Sidewalk, who had seen the whole thing through the restaurant's window—all of them said they were willing to testify that Charlie had run out of the alley with a pistol in his hand, pointing it as if he were going to fire at someone.

So the police finally collected enough on Charlie to justify taking him to the hoosegow. But as they loaded him in the patrol car, he was saying he would ask his lawyer to meet them at the jail.

And that brought it clearly home—at least to Joe-the-lawyer and to me—that at that point there was no real evidence that Charlie had killed Mrs. Rice. As for the license number of the panel truck, the clue that had tipped me off, that would simply be my word against his, since I hadn't told anyone about seeing the panel truck parked in the Garretts' driveway until after I'd seen the panel truck again in our alley. And even if I had seen it, being in the area where a crime had been committed didn't mean Charlie had done the slightest thing wrong.

I could see that Joe was concerned about the whole thing. Charlie could easily walk free, unless some sort of forensic evidence linking him to Mrs. Rice's death turned up in that panel truck that was now in the alley.

As soon as Charlie had been taken away, Aunt Nettie invited everyone—all the Pier-O-Ettes, plus Shep, Joe, and me—over to her house. No one said no.

Bob the Bike Man showed up to collect his tricycles. He was loading them in his truck when Margo Street took Joe aside. "Joe, I think Kathy is going to need a lawyer. Can you represent her?"

"I can refer you to someone, Ms. Street."

"I'd appreciate that." The light was dim, but I

thought I saw a tear in the corner of Margo Street's eye. "I guess I knew all this would come out someday."

She turned to me. "I suppose you told Joe about the revenge of the Pier-O-Ettes."

"No. Aunt Nettie said I shouldn't."

"You'd better tell him now." So I took Joe aside and told him the tale of Kathy being forced to stand naked before Daniel Rice and how her friends got even with him and tried to enforce his silence.

Joe obviously couldn't figure out if he was supposed to laugh or cry. He settled for shaking his head. "Aunt Nettie did this? Ruby I could believe. Even Margo Street. But Aunt Nettie?"

"She did it, Joe, and she says she'd do it again." I punched him on the arm for emphasis. "And I'd help her."

Joe put his arms around me. "And I'd hold your coats," he said. "Let's be friends again, Lee." Then he kissed me.

My mouth was too busy to form words, but I nodded.

Chapter 24

An hour later we were gathered at Aunt Nettie's. The brats were ready to go on the grill, and we had opened a couple of bottles of red wine and poured some beer. The initial excitement of the chase and capture of Good-Time Charlie was wearing off when Margo cleared her throat and silence automatically fell.

Gosh! What I wouldn't give to have the authoritative personality of that woman. Or would it be a good thing? I don't know.

"Joe is going to help Kathy and me get a local lawyer," Margo said. "But tomorrow we'll tell the police the whole story of what happened the night Dan Rice died. I doubt that any of you will have any trouble about it. Not after all this time."

There were murmurs from all the Pier-O-Ettes, assuring Margo that she must do what was best for Kathy. "We're all ready to face the music," Julie said.

Kathy touched her eyes with a handkerchief. "It's all my fault! Margo said I should never tell what happened, but tonight I just forgot."

All the Pier-O-Ettes murmured again, and Margo patted Kathy's hand. "It's all right. I'm sure the police will understand it was all an accident." She sounded confident, but she looked worried as she went on.

"I guess Joe and Shep now know about how the Pier-O-Ettes went to Daniel Rice's office and made him take his clothes off."

Aunt Nettie giggled. "At gunpoint. It's one of the best memories of my life."

"The subsequent happenings weren't so funny," Margo said. She sipped her wine and seemed to steel herself to continue. "When I got home, Kathy had slipped out. Our mother, of course, had no idea what had happened earlier in the evening. She was frantically worried about Kathy. She said Kathy had been talking wildly about returning the trophy our sextet had won. And Kathy had taken the trophy with her." Margo paused. "So I ran back to the Castle, hoping I could head Kathy off. When I got there, she was in Dan Rice's office."

Kathy giggled. "He was wearing an apron. Two aprons. One in front, and one in back."

We all snickered at the thought. Hmmm, I thought. One mystery solved. Now we knew why aprons were found in Dan's office.

"I guess Dan got them from the kitchen," Margo said. "I know he couldn't swim, so he wouldn't have been able to dive for his clothes, even if he figured out where we sank them." She shook her head. "He was the maddest man I ever saw.

"Kathy was holding the trophy, and she told him the Pier-O-Ettes didn't want it. She said, 'We don't want anything from you, Mr. Rice. Not ever again.' I was proud of her. She was very dignified.

"But Rice was incoherent. He reached in his desk drawer, and he pulled out a pistol."

The whole group gasped.

Margo went on. "I had no idea he kept a pistol there. If I had, I would have put it over the side of the deck with his clothes. But he turned toward me, which put his side toward Kathy. He pointed the pistol at me, and he said, 'I should kill you for what you've done.' And Kathy, bless her brave little heart, swung the trophy like a club and hit his arm."

"Yea!" We all applauded.

Kathy wiped away another tear. "If that's all I did, it would have been fine. But the gun fell out of his hand. And it landed on the desk, right in front of me. And I picked it up."

Margo slid an arm around Kathy's shoulders. "She was my brave sister," she said. "Unfortunately, the pistol went off."

I felt tears welling. The picture of the two sisters—just eighteen years old—confronting a half-naked, furious man was dramatic enough. To picture them suddenly faced with that man lying there, shot—well, it was shocking.

We all sat silent. Finally Aunt Nettie spoke. "Was he dead, Margo?"

"Oh no! It seems anticlimactic, but he didn't even seem to be hurt—at least not badly. He ducked down behind his desk. I thought he was going to crawl under it. And I yelled at him, 'Are you hurt?' And he yelled back, 'I'm all right. Just get out of here, both of you!' And we did!"

"We ran like bunnies!" Kathy said. "We were clear home before I realized I had picked the trophy up again. I wanted to throw it away, but Margo was afraid someone would find it. So we gave it to Nettie."

"But none of us wanted it anymore," Aunt Nettie said. "I hid it in a closet, and years later I did throw it out. I guess Phil found it and thought I'd be sorry that I hadn't kept it. He must have locked it in the filing cabinet."

"Anyway," Margo said, "when Kathy and I left the Castle, we thought Dan Rice was all right. I was appalled when we heard that he'd been shot to death."

I spoke. "But if the shooting wasn't deliberate . . ."

"Yes, it might have been smarter to go to the police. And, of course, we would have done that if anyone had ever been accused of the crime. But with the police thinking it was suicide . . ."

"But Mrs. Rice fought for her insurance settlement," I said. "She claimed it was an accident."

"We didn't know that," Margo said. "Our mom had already sold our house, and we moved to Los Angeles just two weeks later. I went to UCLA, and Kathy took classes there in L.A. I didn't hear anything about Mrs. Rice's fight with the insurance company until we came back this weekend."

Joe and I looked at each other. The story of Dan Rice's shooting could leave Kathy in a world of hurt. There would be no way to prove the shot was fired accidently. It was hard to believe the gentle and innocent Kathy could have deliberately shot someone, but on the other hand, she didn't seem to be real responsible, mentally.

One thing was certain. Kathy and Margo definitely needed a good lawyer. Luckily, Margo could afford to hire one.

Margo was speaking again. "Anyway, when Mrs. Rice tried to blackmail me—"

Joe yelped at that. "Blackmail!"

Margo nodded. "Yes. But all she had on me was the episode when the five of us made Daniel strip. I don't know how she found out about it. And she didn't have any proof. I told her she could tell everyone about that. I felt pretty confident that she wouldn't blab about it. And I was right."

"When was this?" Joe said.

"About ten years ago. Right after my investment strategy was written up in *Business Week*. Why?"

"I was wondering if you were the only one she tried to blackmail."

He looked around the room. No one jumped up and confessed that they'd been blackmailed. Aunt Nettie spoke. "Actually, Joe, there's no point in blackmailing someone unless they have money. Margo is the only one of the old crowd who has been really successful financially."

Shep growled, "Margo and Charlie."

Joe nodded. "Actually, although I feel sure Charlie killed Mrs. Rice, I don't know why. And blackmail makes such a good motive."

"Joe," I said, "I think it was the other way around. I think Charlie had been blackmailing Mrs. Rice."

Joe frowned, and I outlined the reasons I had come up with earlier—ending with her allowing her house to be used for wild parties and nude sunbathing.

"I don't know what Charlie knew," I concluded, "but Mrs. Rice by all accounts was a woman who cared a lot about respectability and her position in the community. A person like that, frankly, is easy to blackmail."

Joe didn't look convinced. "But what would he have been blackmailing her about?"

"Drugs," Shep said. "Charlie was selling drugs, back in the old days. He could have convinced Mrs. Rice that Dan was in on the deal."

"Drugs!" all the Pier-O-Ettes burst out. "Drugs!"

But I didn't say anything. I was remembering how

Charlie had several times described—almost proudly—the Warner Pier drug scene of forty-five years earlier.

"Oh, he kept it quiet," Shep said. "I worked with Charlie two summers before I figured it out. But he and his buddy Phin were selling pot and pills, right there on the deck of the Castle Ballroom."

Every eye swung toward Julie. She nodded. "I'm afraid that's right. When I figured it out, I broke up with Phin. But I didn't tell anyone why."

"Charlie bragged about how he was able to start his business the year he left the Castle," I said.

Shep spoke again. "I sure wasn't able to save that much money working there. Charlie always had more money than his salary and the few tips we got. When I figured out what was going on with the drugs, I should have gone to the cops, but—the truth is, I was scared to. I was afraid they were in on it. Back then the sheriff had a bad reputation."

I leaned forward. "Shep, did you see Mrs. Rice the night she died?"

He stared at me. "What makes you think that?"

"You said she'd been a good-looking woman forty-five years ago. Then you referred to her as 'looking like a witch and acting like a bitch.' So I thought you had seen her recently."

"I wanted to talk to a lawyer before I said anything," Shep said.

Joe nodded. "That might be a good idea, Shep. Even in an informal gathering like this one."

But Shep shook his head. "It's not as if I did anything to her. She contacted me."

"With that letter?"

"That first. But she came to the motel . . ." He paused. "I guess I'd better begin with my take on what happened the night Dan was shot."

There were murmurs of assent.

"I didn't know anything about Kathy and Phin or anything else," Shep said. "After we closed up, at midnight that last night at the Castle, Dan sent Charlie and me home. He'd been trying to cut our hours to save money. He said he could finish up the few things that still needed to be done.

"So I was getting ready for bed a little after one a.m., and the phone rang. It was Dan, and he was—well, like Margo says, he was the maddest man I ever talked to. And he says, 'Can you swim?' Of course, I don't have any idea what he's talking about, and he doesn't explain. He tells me to come back to the Castle."

Joe frowned. "He didn't make you dive into that river water, did he?"

"That may have been what he had in mind. He wasn't making a lot of sense. Anyway, when I get to the Castle around one a.m., it's like Kathy and Margo say—Dan was wearing nothing but two aprons."

Margo broke in. "Was he hurt?"

"Not that I could see," Shep said. "Like I said, he was furious. But he wasn't bleeding or anything."

"Thank God." Margo barely breathed the words.

Shep went on. "Dan hands me his camera, and he tells me to keep it. 'Don't let anybody have it,' he says. Then he says his clothes are over the side of the deck, and he needs something else to wear. 'I wasn't thinking straight, or I would have told you to bring me your tux,' he says. 'I can wear it home and make Verna think it's mine.'

"Of course, I wanted to know what the heck had happened. He told me he got some nude pictures of Kathy, and that all the Pier-O-Ettes came and took some of him to get even. Then he laughs. 'I fooled them. I gave them the wrong film. But don't lose the roll in that camera. There are some other pictures on it that are worth a lot of money.'"

Shep turned to Margo. "He said a shot had been fired. Then he laughed. 'It went out the window, of all the dumb luck.'"

Shep took a swig of beer. "So I went home to get my tux for Dan, and when I got back Charlie was coming out of the office. He grabs me, turns me around, pushes me back to my car. He whispers in my ear, 'Dan's dead! He's committed suicide!'

"I told him we had to call the cops. But he says, 'Listen, there's no reason for you and me to get involved.'"

Shep sighed deeply. "I'm ashamed of this. But I let him talk me into it. We both went back to our rooms—we roomed in the same place—and we waited until we heard the sirens. Then we walked back."

Joe frowned. "Did you think that Dan had committed suicide, Shep?"

Shep considered Joe's question seriously. "It didn't seem impossible. He'd been completely frantic when I had left him in the office. Charlie told me some big story about how Dan had been involved in the drug business, and how he'd been afraid of his drug supplier. Charlie claimed he'd been there when Dan pulled out a pistol and shot himself in the heart."

Joe's voice was carefully neutral. "Did you believe his story?"

"I convinced myself it was true. And it did have a certain logic to it. Except for one thing."

We were all hanging on his words. Three of us spoke. "What? What made his story illogical?"

"The gun. When I left to get Dan my tux, his pistol had been lying on the desk. Charlie said Dan had opened his right-hand desk drawer and pulled it out to shoot himself."

We all took that in. Margo spoke. "It was lying on the desk when Kathy and I left."

"I guess I was a coward about the whole thing. First, I hadn't had any connection with Dan's death, and I didn't want to get involved with the law over it. Or some drug dealer."

He stared at his feet. "Second, I had that film of Kathy. I didn't—well, I'm not the biggest gentleman in the world, but I didn't want that crummy sheriff to get it!"

I remembered stories about the man who had been sheriff in those days. No, I wouldn't have wanted him to get hold of that film either.

"The next day I took the film out of the camera, and I got a new roll. I took half a roll of pictures—you know, lake and beach shots. The kind Dan always took. Then I returned the camera to Mrs. Rice. I just didn't say anything about the first roll that had been in it.

"But now—well, ever since I got back to Warner Pier, Charlie's been hanging around hinting that he'd like to see any 'old pictures' from those days."

Joe's voice was eager. "What was on the roll, Shep?"

"I've never developed it."

Kathy gave a little gasp.

"Would the pictures still be good?" Joe said.

Shep shrugged. "I don't know why not. I kept the film cool."

"What do you think they might show?"

"I told you Dan was experimenting with available light. Now that all this has come to a head, I wonder if he didn't get some pictures of Charlie that would prove he'd been selling drugs. I wouldn't want to guess what he planned to do with them. Give them to the cops? Or make Charlie cut him in? It's hard to guess."

Shep pulled a roll of 35-millimeter film from his pocket. "I guess I'll have to share 'em with the cops. They'll probably want to develop them themselves."

After the film was developed, Shep handed half the roll over to Margo, and she burned it. The other pictures did show Charlie with a man who was identified from later mug shots as a drug distributor from forty-five years ago. Of course, all that was so long ago that Charlie's past as a drug dealer seemed to be of little importance, at least next to the case against him for killing Mrs. Rice.

And somehow a flashlight with blood on it turned up in the dark panel truck. So I didn't have to go on the witness stand to explain my convoluted reasoning about license plates.

Eventually, on the advice of a very sharp lawyer, Charlie told Lieutenant Jackson he had been sitting beside Mrs. Rice when she infuriated him so much he hit her. He claimed he hadn't intended to kill her.

In the van, the state police also found a little gadget, a sort of clipper. A person who knows how can use it to make a duplicate car key. It's especially easy, the police technician told me, with older cars. He said people who make car loans—such as big used-car lots—and might want to repossess one learn to use them.

Charlie admitted Mrs. Rice had known her husband suspected him of dealing drugs. He had kept her quiet by threatening to tell the cops Dan was in on the deal. He denied blackmailing Mrs. Rice, of course, but I didn't believe him.

One big letdown for Margo was that for all these years she thought that she had destroyed the film with the naked pictures of Kathy. And all the time Shep had had it.

Mrs. Rice had apparently believed that Shep had the film all along, or at least since about the time he left Warner Pier. But she didn't know how to find him. I'll always believe that she mastered the library's computers so she could track him down.

It turned out not to be a smart action, since finding Shep indirectly led to her death.

One small mystery was cleared up by Kathy. She got that sly look again, and she took me aside and whispered in my ear, "Margo has a boyfriend."

"That's nice," I said.

"Yes. That's why she snuck out of the football game," Kathy said. "She wanted to talk to him without anybody hearing. I tell her it would be all right if he moved in with us. I like him fine. But he never has."

One more romance seemed to bud, just slightly, after that week. Shep decided not to go back to Kentucky right away. He paid a long visit to Grand Rapids, and Julie entertained him.

Joe and I saw our romance bud, too. Maybe it flowered completely. But he's never used the word "stupid" around me again. And if he ever does—well, I just won't hear it.

The reunion went off fine. The old classmates had a great time at the picnic, the boat excursion, and the banquet. The weather was perfect. The foliage was beautiful.

And the Pier-O-Ettes were fabulous.

Author's Note

Authors are often asked to speak about writing, and my favorite topic is research. I call my research speech "Just Ask Somebody."

I learned to research as a newspaper reporter. For nearly every story, a reporter needs a "source." This is a person who can explain the topic simply enough for an ordinary reader to understand it and can provide colorful quotes while doing it.

As a fiction writer I rely on two kinds of sources: people I already know and people I have to find.

For this book, the people I knew were Jeff Smith, my insurance agent; the late Don Fisher, a collector of puns; Jim Avance, retired lawman; Jeff Dixon, photographer; Elizabeth Garber, chocolatier; and Dr. Ralph Alexander, professor of psychology.

The people I had to go out and find were Clarence and Ginny Weber, of Jeff's Keys, and Tommie Ledford, operations manager for the local Yamaha dealer. In each case, I just walked into their place of business and started asking questions. All three of them cheerfully helped me.

Many writers seem to be afraid to ask questions, especially of strangers. They shouldn't be. Everyone is an expert on something, and they are happy to tell the world what they know.

And if something in the book is wrong—I did it. All of these people gave me accurate information.

It all began when I accidently ran into Sissy Smith at the South Haven supermarket—twice.

Luckily, no one was injured either time.

I had never met Sissy before that day. Our contact began as I was standing in the laundry supply aisle, trying to remember which brand of fabric softener made my husband, Joe, break out in a rash around the elastic of his boxer briefs. A threatening voice rumbled from the next aisle over and aroused me from my musings.

"Sissy," it said, "I'm going to win, so why don't you just give up? Fighting the inevitable won't get you any more money."

A feminine voice answered. "Money is the root of all evil. Let me by, please."

That exchange got my attention fast. It was much more interesting than fabric softener.

The man's voice became deeper. "I have the resources, Sissy."

"Actually, the quote is, 'The love of money is the

root of all evil.' It's First Timothy, but I forget the verse. Let me by, Ace."

"You're penniless. You don't even have a job."

"Yeah, I guess I should have picked my grandparents better, so I wouldn't need a job. Let. Me. By."

"I'm not going to let my grandson be raised in a hovel."

"Sticks and stones. Let me by."

"I don't intend to break your bones, but it's not safe to oppose me, Sissy."

The guy wasn't shouting. He didn't even sound particularly angry. That made his words even more frightening.

"I'm going to get him, Sissy. And if you get hurt, I've warned you. I can crush you. And I'm willing to do it."

The woman quit making her snappy replies. She just kept requesting that the man let her by.

She didn't sound scared. In fact, she sounded slightly amused. After several more exchanges she said, "What's eating you, Ace? Have the boys in the locker room been teasing you again?"

I won't repeat what the masculine voice replied to that, but it began with, "You little—!"

Scoffing at the size of this guy's anatomy had apparently touched a nerve. The masculine voice went on and on. But all the insults and the threats were spoken in this quiet, deadly monotone.

The cold-blooded way the man was insulting and threatening the woman was impossible for me to ignore. And he obviously had boxed her in and was preventing her from moving away from him. I was beginning to be afraid things might get rough.

What should I do? I considered calling a security guard, but I wasn't sure the store had one. And I considered hauling the store manager into the situation, but I wasn't sure just what he could do. I thought about calling 9-1-1 on my cell phone, but I'd heard no threat of immediate violence.

I decided my next step was to get a look at the people one aisle over.

Moving rapidly, I shoved my cart down to the end of the fabric softener display and did a U-turn to the left, into the aisle where the ugly talking was going on.

A slender man jumped aside, and I crashed head-on into Sissy's cart. At least, I assumed it was Sissy's cart. There were only two people in the aisle.

I yanked my cart back, pretending to be contrite. "Oh! I do oppose. I mean, apologize!" Darn! My tongue has a habit of getting twisted. Once again it had embarrassed me.

"It's all right. These carts are tough, and so am I." Sissy's voice was still controlled, but it was determined. She was a tiny thing—five-one or two, small boned, and delicate. Eyes of an unusual sea green looked at me boldly, and a sheet of glossy black hair swung out as she turned her head. I was facing a very striking young woman.

She pulled her cart back a few inches and moved it to her right. Then she went around me, ignoring the man she'd been arguing with. At the end of the aisle she turned left, walking rapidly toward the canned goods section.

I pushed my cart so that it blocked most of the aisle. I hoped this would keep the man from following her, and it worked. I was standing amidst racks of paper towels and toilet paper, alone with the man who had talked so ugly.

I turned toward him, ready to face a monster. But instead I saw a handsome man, probably around sixty, sleek and smiling suavely. He was casually dressed—

khakis, a knit shirt in a soft blue, and Top-Siders—and his outfit was high-end.

He smiled and spoke. "We need collision insurance to navigate this place, don't we?" Then he spun his cart toward the other end of the aisle and walked away, graciousness personified.

He was definitely a summer person.

I don't shop in South Haven all that often. My usual hangout is Warner Pier, twenty miles away and one-third the size of South Haven. But I'd been delivering chocolate to that particular supermarket, so I'd decided to do my shopping there as part of the trip. After all, if the South Haven supermarket was buying our chocolates, I could buy their fabric softener. Not many supermarkets carry our line of luxury European-style bonbons, truffles, and molded chocolates. They're mainly found in high-end gift and specialty shops.

South Haven and Warner Pier are both Lake Michigan resorts, and both draw wealthy "summer people"—such as the guy with the ugly mouth and the nice clothes—who own vacation homes in our communities. So both towns have supermarkets that aren't typical of small towns. Yes, it takes a special small-town market to stock prime beef, thirty kinds of imported cheese, and out-of-season fruits. And now the South Haven market had decided to add a selection of fancy chocolates. Naturally—ahem—they'd asked TenHuis Chocolade to supply a dozen flavors of bonbons and truffles, plus an assortment of our special molded items. This summer's special items were Michigan animals. Aunt Nettie and her genius crew were producing beautiful chocolate deer, moose, otters, raccoons, and foxes.

Our part of west Michigan has some of the most beautiful beaches in the world, and it's been a resort area for well over a hundred years. In summer, the dozens of towns along the shore of Lake Michigan are packed, and the people packed into them can be classified into three distinct categories—tourists, summer people, and locals.

Tourists come for short periods of time: a day or a week or two weeks. They rent rooms from motels or bed-and-breakfast inns. They come in tour buses or private cars. They tend to wear shorts and T-shirts that advertise other resorts they've visited, such as Lake Placid, Indiana Dunes, and St. Louis Arch. Sometimes the shirts even say PARIS or LOCAL JUNIOR COLLEGE. They clog our streets, wandering up and down and buying souvenirs.

We love 'em. They bring money to town and leave it behind.

Summer people own or lease cottages and stay the whole summer. Or at least they come for weekends. They are often members of wealthy families—property on Lake Michigan doesn't come cheap—and some of them have visited this area for generations. They dress out of the L.L. Bean catalog. If their T-shirts say anything, it's HARVARD or at least UNIVERSITY OF MICHIGAN. Of course, not all of them are wealthy, but they all pay property taxes.

We love them, too. They bring even more money than the tourists do.

Then there are us locals. We live here year-round, and most of us make our livings from tourists and summer people. We mow their lawns, put up their shutters, repair their air conditioners, roof their houses. We sell them food, clothing, gasoline, wine, hedge clippers, and—in my case—fancy chocolates. We wear shorts and tees, too, but ours tend to say things such as HERITAGE BOAT RESTORATION or TENHUIS CHOCOLADE.

I went back an aisle to get my fabric softener; then I moved into the grocery department. I kept an eye out for Sissy. My brief look at her had titillated my curiosity. For one thing, she seemed familiar, though I couldn't figure out just why.

Sissy had been—well, "vivid" may be the best word. That glossy black hair was gorgeous, and her green eyes were riveting. She had been wearing khaki shorts, like three-quarters of the other shoppers, but her off-white tunic was trimmed in colorful embroidery I was willing to bet had been hand done. Her sandals had a handmade look.

I wanted to figure out where I'd seen her before, so I tried to get another look at her. But I caught only one more glimpse, and that was clear down an aisle. She was buying a big box of Cheerios, and she disappeared into another aisle while I was looking at shredded wheat.

I didn't see her again until I backed into her in the parking lot.

Great. First I whanged into her grocery cart; then I dented her car.

My excuse for the accident is modern automobile design. I have trouble seeing out the back of my van, no matter how I twist my neck. I try to park where I can exit by pulling forward, but during the summer tourist season that's not always possible in that particular lot, even on Monday, so I had to back out of my parking spot, and I backed into the right front fender of a light blue Volkswagen that seemed to come from nowhere.

We didn't hit hard, luckily. We both stopped, got out of our vehicles, and went back to survey the damage. I had a dented bumper, and Sissy had a ding in her fender. The blue Volkswagen was vintage—probably forty years old—but it had been in good shape before I hit it.

Sissy looked dismayed as she surveyed the damage. Our fender bender seemed to have upset her even more than the run-in with the summer guy with the foul mouth.

"I know it's best not to admit fault," I said, "but I will say I have trouble seeing what's behind this darn van. Luckily, I have really good insurance."

"I was upset," Sissy said. "I may not have looked as carefully as I should have. Do we have to call the cops?"

"I doubt the cops want to fool with a minor accident like this, especially on private property. I think we can exchange information and go."

Anyway, Sissy and I got out our information, and I found a notebook so we could write it all down. Sissy wrote my information down first, then tore out the page and handed the notebook back with her license and insurance card.

I started copying, beginning with her license.

The name at the top wasn't "Sissy," which wasn't too surprising. Her legal name was "Forsythia"—Forsythia Smith.

It was impossible not to comment on a name that unusual. "Forsythia!" I said. "My favorite spring flower."

Belatedly I remembered who Forsythia Smith was. Darn. I'd put my foot in it.

Sissy scowled. "My mom and dad were given to flights of fancy."

"At least no one will ever forget it."

She laughed harshly. "That's true. No one will ever forget Forsythia Smith. The southwest Michigan murderess."

That was a conversation stopper.

I don't know if I gasped or grinned. But I do know I didn't say anything aloud. I kept copying off the information on Sissy's driver's license and insurance card, gluing my eyes on the bits of paper.

When I finished writing and looked at Sissy, she had dropped her head and was staring vacantly at the parking lot's asphalt surface. She looked desperately unhappy.

She raised her head when I handed her cards back. I tried to smile. And I spoke, but why I said what I said—well, I still don't understand it.

"Hang in there," I said. "You don't snare me. I mean, you don't scare me!"

Sissy raised her head. "You're the exception," she said. Her expression didn't change.

"I'll be in touch about your bumper. If you could go on and get an estimate, it might help."

She nodded, and we each went our own way.

I guided the van out of the parking lot, cursing myself because I'd twisted my tongue again. I do that when I'm nervous, but I reminded myself that Sissy couldn't know that. She'd just think I was an idiot—if she thought about it at all.

I drove across South Haven and negotiated the crazy entrance to I-196. As I headed home, I kept thinking about Sissy and her life.

I had remembered who Forsythia Smith was, of course.

A few miles up the interstate, I pulled into a rest area and parked. I sat a few minutes, still thinking. Then I took out my cell phone and called my aunt.

Aunt Nettie answered the telephone herself. "Ten-Huis Chocolade."

"Hi," I said. "How would you and Hogan like to come over for dinner tonight?"

"That sounds wonderful. We've had a really busy day here, and it would be delightful not to cook. And I sure don't want to go out to dinner. In June. In Warner Pier. Not during what I'm happy to say is a successful tourist season."

"Great! Come at six thirty. Or seven. Whenever you can make it."

I restarted the van and headed on toward Warner Pier. My curiosity bump was still itching, longing to know more about Forsythia Smith, but I had taken steps that would lead to scratching it.

Now, I want to make one thing perfectly clear. That afternoon, I had no intention of getting involved in Sissy Smith's life. I just wanted to know who the guy bawling her out had been, and I wanted to know why Sissy called herself a murderess.

I'm a nosy person, and that was all I had in mind. I swear.

JoAnna Carl
The Chocoholic Mystery Series

**EACH BOOK INCLUDES YUMMY
CHOCOLATE TRIVIA!**

Looking for a fresh start, divorcée Lee McKinney
moves back to Michigan to work for her aunt's
chocolate business—and finds that her new job
offers plenty of murderous treats.

The Chocolate Cat Caper
The Chocolate Bear Burglary
The Chocolate Frog Frame-Up
The Chocolate Puppy Puzzle
The Chocolate Mouse Trap
The Chocolate Jewel Case
The Chocolate Snowman Murders
The Chocolate Cupid Killings
The Chocolate Pirate Plot
The Chocolate Castle Clue
The Chocolate Moose Motive

Available wherever books are sold or at
penguin.com

facebook.com/TheCrimeSceneBooks